MW01153766

The Awakening of Lord Ambrose

The Lost Lords
Book Six

Chasity Bowlin

Copyright © 2019 by Chasity Bowlin
Print Edition

Published by Dragonblade Publishing, an imprint of Kathryn Le Veque Novels, Inc

All rights reserved. No part of this book may be used or reproduced in any manner
whatsoever without written permission, except in the case of brief quotations
embodied in critical articles or reviews.

Books from Dragonblade Publishing

Dangerous Lords Series by Maggi Andersen
The Baron's Betrothal
Seducing the Earl
The Viscount's Widowed Lady
Governess to the Duke's Heir

Also from Maggi Andersen
The Marquess Meets His Match

Knights of Honor Series by Alexa Aston
Word of Honor
Marked by Honor
Code of Honor
Journey to Honor
Heart of Honor
Bold in Honor
Love and Honor
Gift of Honor
Path to Honor
Return to Honor

The King's Cousins Series by Alexa Aston
The Pawn

Beastly Lords Series by Sydney Jane Baily
Lord Despair
Lord Anguish

Legends of Love Series by Avril Borthiry
The Wishing Well
Isolated Hearts
Sentinel

Highlands Forever Series by Violetta Rand
Unbreakable
Undeniable

Viking's Fury Series by Violetta Rand
Love's Fury
Desire's Fury
Passion's Fury

Also from Violetta Rand
Viking Hearts

The Sins and Scoundrels Series by Scarlett Scott
Duke of Depravity

The Unconventional Ladies Series by Ellie St. Clair
Lady of Mystery

The Sons of Scotland Series by Victoria Vane
Virtue
Valor

Dry Bayou Brides Series by Lynn Winchester
The Shepherd's Daughter
The Seamstress
The Widow

Men of Blood Series by Rosamund Winchester
The Blood & The Bloom

Cornelius Garrett, Lord Ambrose, has withdrawn from society in the wake of scandal in order to focus on finding the numerous illegitimate children that his father sired. Desperate to locate his many siblings and build some semblance of a family for himself, Cornelius is ill-prepared for the many complications that his most recently discovered sibling, Lila, brings with her—namely her older sister, Primrose Collier.

Primrose is the most stunningly beautiful woman he's ever encountered. She's also fiercely proud and protective with a well-founded distrust for the opposite sex. It takes all of his considerable powers of persuasion to sway her to bring her young siblings and move to his estate, Avondale. But no good deed goes unpunished. Cornelius' unscrupulous neighbor, Lord Samford, also has a prior acquaintance with the Collier family. Threatened by their presence and the ugly secrets of his past that they might expose, Samford sets out to eliminate what he views as a complication.

Samford's machinations result in Prim being injured and spending a night, unchaperoned, with Cornelius. In order to preserve Prim's reputation and also to afford her and her siblings more protection, Cornelius proposes marriage. But it isn't all duty and obligation. For the first time in his life, Cornelius must find balance between what honor demands and what he desires.

Determined to stop Samford at any cost, they set out on a journey fraught with danger and with discovery. Primrose has awakened something inside him he did not know existed—something fierce, passionate and impetuous. Could it be love?

Prologue

Blackfield Village, 1823

T HE PISTOL HUNG from his limp fingers and the acrid smell of smoke burned his nose. The tableau before him was certainly an odd one. Lady Ramsleigh lay on the ground, her nightrail covered in mud and a spreading stain of crimson. His half-brother, Dr. Nicholas Warner, crouched over her, clearly distraught. And all of this was taking place in the small cemetery that butted up against the pictur-esque church, backlit in the purple and gold shades of the coming dawn, as a crowd of people stood over the exhumed corpse of the girl buried in Lady Ramsleigh's stead.

The magistrate came forward, wearing a heavy dressing gown over his nightshirt. He had also hastily donned and misbuttoned breeches with boots that appeared to be on the wrong feet.

"You had no choice, Ambrose. We all know it," the magistrate said, reaching to slip the pistol from his lifeless fingers.

He felt strange without it, Garrett realized. In that split second, that weapon had become a part of him and he would likely feel the presence of it there forever. "I was too late. So it doesn't really matter, does it? He's killed her."

"He might have had yet another pistol on him. It's likely he did and would have shot the good doctor, as well. I've no wish to take you into custody, but there must be an inquest, at the very least, as you were both gentlemen of standing. You understand that you cannot leave Blackfield until it is done?"

"I understand," Garrett agreed. An inquest meant records of what he'd done, meant newspaper accounts of the day that he, Cornelius

1

Garrett, Lord Ambrose, became a murderer. Whatever his reasons were, and he did not question that they had been sound and that the choice hadn't been a choice at all, the fact remained he had taken another man's life. It would not be easily forgotten or forgiven. "I will return to Castle Black. You may send word when I am needed for the inquest."

"Good. Good. It'll all be sorted out in no time. You shall see," the magistrate said. It was clear from the man's discomfiture that offering sympathy and reassurance were somewhat alien to him. As a magistrate, he should have been better equipped.

"We shall all see, I daresay." One thing he could be entirely certain of, he'd just cemented his place in the ignoble history of the Ambrose line. There was no coming back from having done murder. He would be painted with the same brush his father had been in his profligate life. All the discretion and grace with which Cornelius had attempted to live his life to that moment would be for naught. He had not salvaged his family's honor in the least, but rather smudged it further. Somehow, it would be worse, because he had been above reproach for so long. How often had it been commented on that he was not at all like his father, not reckless or wild, or given to fits of temper or strong passions. He was a man of a placid and kind nature, of peace and refinement. *And now a murderer.* The further the fall from grace, the more it was bandied about by the gossips. They would whisper his name for years with glee. All for naught. All the self-denial, all the mindfulness of his choices... gone.

Turning, Garrett mounted the same horse that had brought him to that fateful spot and followed the road away from the village and toward the rugged, hulking silhouette of the castle perched on a cliff high above the village. But it was not to the castle he retired. Instead, he took the path around it that led to the rock-strewn beach below. In those dark moments, the sea offered him no solace, but the incessant ebb and flow of the waves did remind him that there was an order to all things.

Even as the tide shifted and those waves became fiercer, the whitecaps frothing and churning as the spray from them dampened his face and clothes, there was still a rhythm and a pattern. He would find his way through the ruin that would unfairly fall upon his head, but only if he could accept what came at him, just as those rocks on the beach sat unmoving in the face of the sea's wrath. They might be dulled by the constant beating of the water against them, their edges rounded and worn away, but they remained. As would he.

Chapter One

Salisbury, October 15th, 1825

"LILA WILL NEED a new dress," Prim said. Their youngest sister, aged eleven, was quite possibly the clumsiest child to ever draw breath. She could actually trip on air. Prim had seen it, time and again.

"We haven't money for a new dress for her," their elder sister protested as she held her hand to her head. "She will simply have to make do. If you are to work for Lady Linden, you cannot do so in rags. Showing up to such a fine house in torn dresses, or worse, dresses so worn that when you bend to wipe down a table the seams split—no. That cannot happen."

"My not-quite-red-anymore cotton is not so bad off as that. And it's long past the days of being considered my good dress. I will not have a new dress and we will use the wool for her. Besides, I will be doing little more than lighting the fires and scrubbing the floors. A new dress would be wasted on me, Hy," Prim protested.

Hyacinth Collier gave her sister a baleful stare. "And it would not be wasted on Lila who attracts dirt like bees to honey?"

"It cannot be helped. She's outgrown one of the two gowns she possesses and the other one is so threadbare I hold my breath and pray any time it must be laundered."

"We will add a ruffle to the bottom of it then and to the sleeves if they are too short."

Prim sighed wearily. "It is not her height that is the problem. That dress was made for her two years ago, Hy. Her figure is altering and becoming that of a young woman. She's not a little girl, now."

Hyacinth looked at her levelly. "Then we will take one of the gowns that Mrs. Dalrymple gave me and cut it down for her."

Mrs. Dalrymple was their benefactress, of sorts, as much of one as they had to be sure. She often sent food items to them from her own larder and had taken to giving any cast-off clothes or furnishings to them for the small cottage that they leased on her property. It was barely large enough for them to turn about in and as the children continued to grow, it was feeling smaller and smaller. "That dress is thirty years out of fashion, Hy."

"So it is. And little enough Lila will care one way or another. She could walk naked into the lane and hardly be bothered to notice." Hyacinth rubbed her forehead and winced.

Prim had no answer for that, as it was entirely true. Lilac Hester Collier was the most distracted child she'd ever encountered in all of her life. Instead, she focused on something else that was just as worrisome. Hyacinth appeared to be having another one of her attacks. Her elder sister was rubbing her forehead, her eyes tightly closed against the light which pained her. "You're having another megrim?"

"I always do when we discuss our lack of funds, all the things we need and can't afford, and—well, I suppose that's all we discuss anymore, isn't it?"

"We'll make do, Hy. We always do," Prim pointed out.

"Will there ever be a time in our lives when making do isn't quite so hard?"

"We shall complete the dress for Lila tonight and Sunday after church we will put together a new dress for me."

"Well enough," Hy agreed. "And if there is enough fabric left over, and I think there should be, we will sew a new coat for Rowan. His has gotten terribly tight over the shoulders… if not, we will simply add a bit of fabric at the seams, though I am afraid that would look quite shabby."

Shabby. It was an apt description of everything about their lives, but it was still a far cry from the hovel she could recall from their time in London. The small room with the leaking roof, smoking hearth, and uneven floor had housed the lot of them. Their mother had a bed behind a curtain where she had *"entertained."* The three of them had slept on a pallet on the floor beneath the drafty window. Poor Lila had only been a baby then, and it was likely she had no memory of it at all. For herself, she'd been close to the age that Lila was now and Hyacinth two years her elder. Rowan had come along just after they moved. In fact, he had, in some ways, been the very reason they could move. His father had been a wealthy man, the son and heir apparent of a titled gentleman. He had claimed to be in love with her, had scandalized her parents with suggestions that he might actually marry a woman who was little better than a doxy.

The man's father had paid them a visit, offered her mother a significant enough sum of money that they'd used to keep body and soul together. As the amount had dwindled, they'd stretched it thinner and thinner until even the very last shred of it was gone. But it was with those funds that they'd fled London in the darkest of hours, just before the dawn had begun to break. They'd sought shelter in the heart of Devonshire, only a few miles from whence Isabelle Collier had been born and bred. It had been a happy place for them, at first. But over time, rumors of their parentage and of their mother's past had slowly caught up to them.

Rowan had been born only a few short months later. Whether he was the son of that gentleman or not, Prim could not hazard to guess. Regardless, they were living a better life for that man's generosity, regardless of his motives.

"And the cottage rent? How far are we from meeting it this month?" Prim asked.

Hy frowned. "Too far. Mrs. Dalrymple did not mind so much, but now that her nephew is here and managing the estate in her stead... I fear that will change. We were late last month and he threatened to tack on a fine if we were late again."

Prim snorted. "And if we could afford to pay his blasted fines we'd not be late with it to begin with! I've heard things about him... he's been taking up with some woman in the village. I think he means to install her right here in this very cottage as his mistress."

"Why would that matter? You'd think he'd be strutting like a peacock for the world to know he had a mistress given how pinched and homely he is," Hyacinth said. It was a rare thing for her sister to have a negative word about anyone.

Prim smiled. "I heard some very unflattering comments about the duration of his visits to his mistress. Apparently he only stays a very, very short time."

"Oh," Hyacinth said and giggled. "I see. So it's not a question of his morals but his prowess."

"So it would seem. Though I daresay, amusing as it is, it's to our detriment that he lacks... stamina."

Hyacinth sighed wearily. "We have no lease, Prim. Mrs. Dalrymple allowed us to stay here but the truth of it is that this cottage was leased to mother and not us. Upon her death, that contract became null and void. There is nothing to protect us from being thrown out or to prevent the rents from being doubled if he chooses to demand more."

And he would, Prim thought. The man was a toad. Or perhaps a weasel as he had the smallest and beadiest eyes she'd ever seen. He always gave the appearance of being furtive, as if looking around for anything he could steal or swindle.

A loud knock upon the door startled her out of her reverie. She looked at Hyacinth who was looking back at her equally nonplussed. "You go into the next room," Hy said. "And so help me, if that is Jeb Turner come one more time to ask you to walk out with him, I've half a mind to take the fire poker to him!"

Jeb Turner was not a bad man, but he was not a man who held any interest for her. No man did. She'd seen enough of her mother's lot in life to know that men brought nothing but ruin and heartbreak. To that end, she followed her sister's instructions and ducked into the small parlor where she promptly concealed herself behind the door. The last thing she wanted was for Jeb to catch a glimpse of her. They'd never get rid of him otherwise.

Of course, if it was Mrs. Dalrymple's rodent-like nephew there to demand the rent from them, she'd have preferred Jeb Turner. And if he were smitten enough with her to allow Hy, Lila, and Rowan to move into his little farmhouse with them, she could do worse than to marry him. That glum thought nearly brought her to tears and Prim prayed for some other possibility beyond the two she'd just imagined.

GARRETT RAPPED ON the door. Beside him, Nicholas glanced at him from the corner of his eye. It was clearly a look of disapproval.

"They'll not answer the door to that," his brother said. "They'll likely think you're the bailiff come to collect something!"

"They might have been upstairs," Garrett insisted. "I don't wish to stand here on their doorstep all day!"

Nicholas rolled his eyes. "It was your idea to come here, wasn't it? The mother was a known prostitute. How can we even be certain that this girl is our sister?"

Garrett sighed. "There has always been a marked resemblance in our family. That certainly held true for us. Why shouldn't it hold true for our younger sister, as well?"

Nicholas shuddered. "If she looks like the pair of us then there's far more stacked against her in this life than simply her status of birth!"

Garrett would have replied, was poised to do so in fact with his mouth hanging open when the door opened to reveal a pretty but not extraordinary woman with reddish-blonde hair and a smattering of freckles across a nose that could only be described as gamine. Indeed, everything about her appeared to be wispy and fragile.

"May I help you?" she inquired softly. Her voice was cordial but also clearly concerned.

"Are you Miss Hyacinth Collier?" Nicholas asked as Garrett attempted to regain his composure.

"I am. But as you are on my doorstep that is clearly not unexpected news, gentlemen. But perhaps a more pertinent question would be who the two of you are and why you are currently on *my* doorstep?"

She might have been small in stature and possess the immediate impression of feminine softness, but it was evident that there was steel in her. Garrett felt a grudging respect. "I am Cornelius Garrett, Lord Ambrose, and this is my half-brother, Dr. Nicholas Warner... and I believe we have a half-sister in common. Lilac?"

The young woman's lips firmed into a thin hard line. "She prefers to be called Lila. And I've no notion what you are doing here, but you may simply turn yourselves about and go back from whence you came. I will not just give Lila into the care of strangers regardless of what relationship they claim."

"Miss Collier, I have not come to take your sister from you. What I have done is come to make some sort of restitution to your family for her care and to provide for her future as our profligate father should have done. Perhaps, if you'd permit us to come inside we could discuss this further? I assure you, we are here with the best of intentions," Garrett insisted.

It was clear that she was conflicted. She stood there for the longest time and then finally, as if it seemed she was about to slam the door in his face, he heard another voice—just as feminine, but certainly not sweet. It was slightly husky and strangely seductive, though he had yet to see the owner of it.

"Let them in, Hy. It certainly can't hurt to hear them out."

The first woman, Hyacinth, stepped back and held the door wide in a somewhat less than gracious invitation. She turned to her right and said to the unseen woman, "Whatever the outcome, it's on your head."

"We're in bedlam," Nicholas whispered. "I could be at home with my wife right now."

Garrett meant to shush him, but as the mystery woman stepped forward from a side room, he forgot everything else. To say that she was beautiful would not have been entirely accurate. Not because it wasn't true, but because she seemed to be so much more than that. Her face was shifting constantly, a myriad of expressions fleeting across it until, finally, she managed to school it into some semblance of neutrality. Her hair was a lustrous shade of brown, slightly deeper than chestnut, but with strands of auburn and perhaps even a dark blonde woven into it. It caught the light and flashed a dozen different colors at him. Wide blue eyes, softly rounded cheeks, a stubborn chin and a perfect cupid's bow of full lips completed the assemblage of delicate features that held him in sway.

"My sister, Primrose Collier," Hyacinth said. "And I see you are struck as dumb as every other man upon meeting her."

"Not every man," Nicholas said. "Lovely as you both are, my beautiful wife is waiting for me at home and, if possible, I'd very much like to get on the road back to her today and certainly tomorrow at the latest. Perhaps we could begin the discussion of my now mute brother's plans for Lila?"

Forcing himself to think, to speak, to not make an utter fool of himself, Ambrose added, "Yes. Forgive my lapse in manners. If we might sit and discuss this... I think that you'll find my offer to be very generous."

"Why don't we adjourn to the sitting room then?" Primrose suggested.

Ambrose would have followed her into hell had she asked it.

Chapter Two

PRIM SEATED HERSELF beside Hyacinth on the small settee and faced the two dark-haired men who'd simply dropped into their lives. It was patently obvious from even a glance that they were, in fact, related to Lila. She had the same dark hair and eyes, the same high cheekbones and there was something else, some indefinable thing about the way they were put together, that also reminded her of her sister. But Lila was a much more fey creature than either of those gentlemen had been or likely ever would be short of taking too many blows to the head. Lila, bless her, could get lost in the middle of the room simply by being taken over by her own thoughts. It was the artist in her, Prim thought. The girl loved to paint, to draw, even to sculpt. They'd find her after a rain making things out of mud in the yard.

"How did you find us? More importantly, how did you find Lila?" Hy asked.

It was a good question. If Prim hadn't been quite so addled by the one gentleman she might have asked it herself. They were both handsome, but it was the more smartly-dressed of the two who had immediately drawn her attention. If she were to be unkind she could have blamed it on the way he gaped at her as if she'd sprouted two heads. But it wasn't that, at all. She had felt a strange breathlessness when she looked at him, a sense of expectation that she could not account for. Perhaps, she tried to convince herself, it was the promise of some sort of relief from the endless stress of their current impover-ishment. But she knew better. It was as if something had awakened inside her. She'd seen the giddy rush of romanticism and passion in her mother every time Isabelle had met a new man who promised her love. In the end, they delivered only disappointment and heartbreak.

"Our father passed away over five years ago. But I have been sifting through ledgers, diaries, papers, letters and other correspondence for almost the entirety of that time in an attempt to locate my half-siblings," the one who'd called himself Lord Ambrose said. He glanced sideways at Prim, their gazes meeting for a heartbeat, locking with a jolt of intimacy that took her breath away, before he once more faced Hyacinth. "There have been a lot of false starts and dead ends in trying to find them all."

"How many?" Prim asked, against her better judgment. She had faint recollections of the former Lord Ambrose. He'd been loud, laughed constantly and had usually brought some sweet or tossed a few coins to her and Hyacinth before dancing away with her mother. But that had been before the squalid little room in the Devil's Acre where they'd wound up.

"I have identified three, thus far. One was transported for thievery, another died of fever, and the third is at my side," Ambrose replied. "I'm certain there are more, but the work is tedious and there are a vast number of dead ends. I would not have known about Lilac at all had I not found an old letter from your mother to my father after she'd moved here. She wrote to him asking for assistance."

"You mean funds," Hy said accusingly.

The man flushed. "Yes, I do."

The deep well of shame that existed inside her suddenly spilled over and Prim had to look away. "Of course, she did."

"You misunderstand, Miss Collier. It was not as if she were extorting him or even begging. She simply stated that her children were in need of clothing and food and she would be grateful for any assistance he could provide. There was nothing in it that should reflect poorly on her," he stated. "There was another letter that followed, where she thanked him for his generosity and apprised him that her eldest children, you and your sister presumably, were both doing well. He had asked after you in his response, I presume. So he must have had some small fondness for you both I think. But in that letter, she also advised him that she had two other children besides. She informed him that Lilac was seven and Rowan was two at that time. Another series of letters followed and, in the last one, she had assured my father that she had no expectations he should acknowledge the girl. Your mother was doing what she must to provide for her children. And my father, who was responsible for the conception of one of those children, was shirking his duty to her and to the woman who bore her. If there is shame to be felt or guilt, it should be his and, derivatively, my own."

Prim looked back at him, moved by the rather impassioned nature of his speech, but more so because it seemed as if he had seen straight into the heart of her. That alone was enough reason to get him far, far from them. Anyone or anything that could evoke such an emotional response in her, who could get past her defenses with such apparent ease, posed a threat to her and to those she loved. "Thank you for your understanding, Lord Ambrose. Let's just get right to the point, shall we? Lila doesn't know you. Nor did she know your father. He had finished with our mother long before she was born and never bothered to look back. And I do not harbor any resentments for him for that. The truth be told, I remember him fondly. He was kind to both Hyacinth and me, which is far more than can be said of any of the other men who drifted through our mother's life. While I appreciate the fact that you wish to provide for her in some way, something that your father felt no need to do other than his occasional charity to our mother, I'm not certain it's in her best interest to know anything about where she came from. She's too young to remember much of our lives in London. She certainly doesn't remember what our mother was forced to endure in order to provide for us. I can't imagine that there could be anything that would induce us to alter that."

His eyebrows rose slightly, but his expression remained neutral while his companion appeared to be quickly losing patience with the lot of them. When Lord Ambrose did finally speak, he sounded slightly amused by her reply. "Miss Collier, while I may have been to the manor born as it were, I'm not so entirely out of touch that I do not recognize the signs of struggle your family is currently displaying. Empty corners and marks on the floor where furnishings once stood. Sold off, no doubt. And as pretty as that flounced hem is on your dress, it doesn't take a great deal of deduction to conclude it serves a greater purpose than mere decoration. I imagine it was made for you when you were much younger, or perhaps it was made for someone else entirely?"

Prim's chin lifted and her shoulders stiffened of their own accord. Her temper, fearsome as it could be, was rising to the forefront and he'd made a terrible error in engaging it. "Have you finished, Lord Ambrose? Or are there yet more humiliating aspects of our impoverished state you'd like to expound upon? If not, I will happily show you to the door."

"It is not humiliating to be poor, Miss Collier," he protested.

"As you are incapable of speaking from experience on that score, my lord, I will respectfully beg to differ." Before Prim could say anything further, the front door suddenly burst open. But it wasn't their younger siblings returning. It was Mrs. Dalrymple's nephew, Lewis Severne. It was not the first time he'd just let himself into their cottage but, of course, he did not view it as theirs. In his mind, they were the interlopers.

"Misses Collier," he said, sparing a dismissive glance at the gentlemen seated opposite them. "I've come for the rent, assuming you have it."

And now, Prim thought, their humiliation was to be complete. All they needed was for Lila to come in covered in dirt and Rowan to toss up the contents of his stomach on the single carpet they possessed. She closed her eyes and uttered a silent prayer for it all to be a bad dream.

Chapter Three

GARRETT KNEW THAT they didn't have the rent, of course. He'd made inquiries in the village and while the Misses Collier and their younger siblings were well liked, it was a known fact that only sheer stubbornness was allowing them to keep body and soul together. Having finally laid eyes on them, it was glaringly apparent to him that the description given time and again by every person they'd inquired with was absolutely true. If he were an intelligent man, that stubbornness he'd been warned of would have made him take her at her word and walk out of their humble cottage never to return. Instead, it only seemed to entrance him more. There was only one word he could think of to adequately describe Miss Primrose Collier. *Dangerous.* She was beautiful, but it wasn't the outer shell of her that compelled him. There was a connection that he felt to her instantly, something that defied logic and explanation.

"Mr. Severne, as you can see, we have guests. Now is not the time. We will bring the funds to your aunt, Mrs. Dalrymple, this afternoon," the eldest sister said calmly.

"My aunt is ill. She's taken to her bed and will likely not recover," Mr. Severne answered. It was apparent that he was not overly concerned for the woman's imminent demise. In fact, he sounded only too pleased by it.

Immediately, the women's expressions changed. He might have had no fondness for his aunt, but it was apparent they did.

"She was fine yesterday. We spoke with her! She had some clothing she wished to gift to us for the children!" Hyacinth proclaimed.

"I cannot believe that Mrs. Dalrymple would refuse to see us regardless of how ill she is! Why, when she fell and broke her leg last year, we went there daily and read to her while she recovered!" Primrose insisted. "I do not think you are reciting Mrs. Dalrymple's wishes at all. I think if she's not being allowed to have visitors that it is a decision you have made, Mr. Severne!"

The man had the nerve to smile but it was a chilled expression and revealed far more of his character than even his rude entrance had. "It is of no consequence what you believe, Miss Primrose. You have no authority with which to question me or how I see to the welfare of any female relative that is in my dominion. Now, I will have the rent or you will be out by nightfall."

"Mr. Severne, we do not have the rent in its entirety but we do have almost all of it," Hyacinth began, only to be cut off abruptly by Severne.

"If you can't pay all the rent then you can't live in all of the house, now can you? Which room shall I let out to someone else, Miss Collier? The kitchen or one of the bedchambers? Well, what's it to be?" he demanded snidely.

"I've half a mind to call you out, sir," Ambrose said mildly.

Severne looked at him. "Who are you?"

"Lord Ambrose," he said. For once, he was grateful that his sullied reputation preceded him. He watched the other man blanch, watched him recoil with fear. *Murderer. Cold-blooded. Worse than his father ever dreamed of.* It appeared that all the things whispered of him had reached Mr. Severne's ears. "And yes, I'm as good with pistols as they say. How do you think you'll fare, Mr. Severne?"

"Now see here, Ambrose, this is no business of yours—"

"If it were not my business then perhaps you should not have aired it in front of me to start," Ambrose said and calmly reached into his pocket for the small purse he carried. "What is the rent, Severne?"

"Two pounds six," Severne replied.

Given the obscenely small space of the cottage and that he could see water spots on the floor, it was robbery. Still perturbed with the man, Ambrose removed the appropriate coins and tossed them to the floor in front of Severne. It was an insult but he didn't care. It was worth it to watch the bastard have to stoop and scrounge for the coins. "You've been paid. Now, you'll leave this cottage and the next time you enter it, you will do so after knocking and being given permission. Do we have an understanding, sir?"

Severne rose, glared at him, but nodded. "We do. I bid you all a good day."

"My lord, I am very appreciative of your assistance, but we cannot accept such charity!"

That had come from Hyacinth. One glance at Primrose told him she was too furious to speak. "It wasn't charity, Miss Collier. The coins were well spent just to see him eat a bit of crow. I detest a bully. The question does remain, however, what will you do when the rents are due next month and again the month after?"

"We will make do, Lord Ambrose, as we have always done," Primrose answered. Her manner was stiff, her shoulders stiffer still, and her chin jutted forward with a mixture of stubborn pride and banked fury. It was an easy thing to read in her eyes.

"And what if you could get by without having to simply *make do*?" he asked.

"We will manage, Lord Ambrose," Primrose snapped. "We have always done so and we do not require your assistance!"

"Misses Collier," Nicholas said, "I apologize for my brother's high-handedness. He means well, but as a person who has never been in the position of struggling to meet financial obligations, he doesn't understand how that feels. Please know that any offer of assistance, for today or for the future, does not come with obligations attached for you."

Garrett blinked in shock. Surely they had not thought he meant to have them be beholden to him in some way. But then, what else would they have thought given their experiences in life with men like his father and like Severne?

"I am only here to offer assistance and to make amends," Garrett stated emphatically. "There is a cottage on my estate near Taunton in Somerset. It's slightly larger than this one though I daresay not by much. But it does at least offer three bedrooms and a roof that doesn't leak. It is yours. You and your siblings may live there free of rent. An annuity would be provided for you that would allow you to live comfortably. I will see to it that a governess is hired for Lila and for your younger brother if that is your wish. When it is time, I will help him get into a school and learn a trade where he might be able to provide for himself and a family of his own. This is a good offer... a fair and reasonable offer. You have but to take it!" he implored. He wanted to know his sister, he wanted to provide for her. But his intention had only ever been to provide them funds, not to take them home with him. And yet, now, with the offer hanging there between them and Nicholas looking at him as if he'd lost his wits, he couldn't regret it.

Primrose was regarding him suspiciously. "You speak only of what you may offer us. But what does that offer provide for you in return, my lord? No man does so much for so little!"

"It affords me a chance to know my sister... to build a relationship with her and to ensure that the sort of fate that befell her mother will never await Lila. It is a chance to right the wrongs of my father, Miss Collier." There was truth in it. But not the entire truth. He didn't know why he'd made the offer or what ultimately it would provide. But he knew he couldn't walk out of there that day and never lay eyes upon her again.

"That is hardly a compelling reason for our part, Dr. Warner," Primrose snapped.

"Misses Collier," Nicholas interrupted her once more. "I'll be the first person to admit that it is often difficult to accept such generosity at face value. But I can assure you that my brother is here with only the best of purest intentions. As much as it pains me to praise him, I've never known a more honorable man in my life. I would stake my life and my reputation as a physician on it. Do not allow pride and cynicism to influence your decision to the exclusion of things that would dramatically improve both your lives and the lives of your younger siblings. At least consider it."

"It isn't your reputation that—"

"We must think on it, Lord Ambrose," Hyacinth interjected, cutting off what was likely to be a scathing retort and an outright refusal from Primrose.

Primrose looked to her sister, her blue eyes flashing with anger, with temper and pride. But it was the most receptive response he'd had to anything he'd said since they arrived on the Colliers' doorstep. It seemed like a good moment for a strategic retreat. He rose. "I will be at the inn in the village until tomorrow. Send word to me if you decide to accept. It will take time, of course, for you to make all the necessary arrangements but I will be happy to send carriages for you whenever you require them."

He turned to leave, Nicholas following behind him. Garrett could feel his half-brother smirking at his back. But he wasn't in the mood for Nicholas' needling. The Collier sisters, or more particularly Primrose Collier, had gotten under his skin in a way that no one else ever had. It was bad enough to have happened, but worse still for it to have been witnessed by someone like Nicholas Warner who would beat that dead horse until they were both exhausted from the topic.

"I wasn't aware that primroses were quite so thorny, Brother. Perhaps it's your sparkling personality that brings out her rather argumentative nature?"

"I had things handled in there," Garrett insisted.

"Oh, please. We both know you were making a muck of it!"

"I was not! They were on the verge of seeing reason."

Nicholas laughed at that. He quite literally threw his head back and guffawed like a drunkard in a tavern. "Of course you did," he said after he recovered his composure. "I'll forgive you delusions, Brother, seeing as how you were struck dumb at the sight of the younger Miss Collier."

"I found her rather shocking is all," Garrett lied.

"Shocking is one word for it. Another is smitten. Infatuated. You,

Brother, took one look at her and went cow-eyed."

Garrett sighed. It had begun. Nicholas would make his life hell. And so would Primrose Collier.

Chapter Four

"WE CANNOT SIMPLY pack the children up and move them to Somerset!" Primrose insisted.

"What choice do we have, Prim?" Hy countered. "We're out of money. Even with your wages from Lady Linden and even if we could manage to double the amount of sewing and washing we take in, we'd still barely be able to pay the rent. And if we do that, neither one of us will have time to sleep. Our budget for food would be nonexistent and if, heaven forbid, something were to happen and either one of us or the children became ill—Prim, we are sinking here. Lord Ambrose's offer is a godsend! We'd be fools not to at least consider it."

Prim wasn't so certain of that. Surely God could have nothing to do with the feelings Lord Ambrose stirred in her. Irritation, anger, resentment, and then, beneath it all, there was still that irresistible pull. His presence played on her worst fear—that somewhere deep inside, she was just like her mother and would fall victim to her own desires and poor judgment in men. "Hyacinth, we can find another way!"

"Yes. I'm certain we could. But at what cost? Should we all continue to exist in poverty? To go to bed with empty bellies and wake up in cold rooms when there is another way?" her sister retorted hotly. "We are failing, Prim. And we can't continue this way. Not without succumbing to the very fate we swore to avoid. I don't want to sell my body and my soul to feed our siblings. But you and I both know, we are quickly approaching the point of no return. If it came down to it, and it was that or seeing them starving or in the streets, what would you do? What would I do?"

To Prim's horror, Hyacinth sank onto the settee again and the iron will she'd come to rely on in her sister simply evaporated. Her dear sister simply shattered before her like the most fragile of glass. Petite and pale, Hy always looked fragile, but rarely did her behavior and her appearance match. Harsh, wracking sobs escaped her and a well of tears that she had denied herself for years fell down her cheeks. Uncertain of what else to do, Prim dropped down beside her, pressed Hyacinth's head to her shoulder and held her older sister as she cried.

After the longest time, when the sobs had subsided to the occasional hiccup and a punctuating sniff, Hy continued, "I cannot watch them suffer for the sake of my own pride, Prim. And I'm begging you not to either!"

"It isn't just pride," Prim insisted. "I'm afraid of him."

Hyacinth rose and looked at her. "I do not think he is a bad man, Prim. Despite his display with Mr. Severne, which I must admit I enjoyed more than a small amount, I felt he was quite well spoken and gave every appearance of being an honorable gentleman!"

"I am not afraid of him in that way, Hy," Prim admitted. "He's not dangerous to you or to the children. But I'm very much afraid that he might be terribly dangerous to me."

Understanding dawned bright and clear and Hyacinth's lips parted on a soft "o." "I see... well, he is very handsome."

"And very titled and very much out of my league. A man like that would—well, he could never have honorable intentions toward a woman like me. Assuming he has any intentions at all. But if I am constantly in his path, if I see him day after day, Hy, what if I do something rash? What if that same base and desperate nature that prompted our mother's demise suddenly takes over in me? I'm not afraid of men, Hyacinth. I know what they are capable of. But I am afraid of loving one and of being broken by him."

Hyacinth shook her head. "That will not happen. I will not let it. Mother was vulnerable because she was alone, because there was no one else to care for her and no one else to see that she did not succumb to the wickedness of the world. We will look after one another, Prim, just as we always have."

The front door opened and they could hear Lila's quiet tones and the excited chatter of Rowan. At just past nine years of age, he had not yet mastered the ability of curbing the natural exuberance of his voice. He was mad for horses and had apparently seen an exquisite matched pair on the lane. Likely Lord Ambrose's, she thought.

"They were gray, P-p-prim," he said, stammering her name as he often did. It was always worse when he was excited or scared. It was clear from the gleam in his eyes that it was the former and not the latter. *If they took him to Somerset he might even learn to ride,* a little voice whispered in her mind. What would she be depriving them of if she succumbed to her fears?

"Yes, Rowan. I heard you say that very loudly as you came in the door," she said. "I'm certain they were grand."

"They were, Prim," he said, his eyes as round as saucers. "And the carriage was all black with gold on it and the curtains inside it were yellow!"

"They were gold," Lila corrected. "They were gold damask, like Lady Linden's but not faded and old."

Prim didn't know why Lila detested Lady Linden but she did. In fact, the girl always had. "Lila, you know you mustn't speak of Lady Linden so. She's been very good to this family."

"And she likes to tell everyone how good she's been to us, as well," Hy muttered under her breath.

Lila nodded at Hyacinth and added, "I heard her in the market saying she'd taken you on as a housemaid. It was her Christian duty to see that you did not fall. Whatever that means."

Prim sighed heavily. She knew what it meant, and so did Hyacinth. It was the very thing they had just discussed. In the decade they'd lived there in the village, their mother posing as a widow of the war with Rowan growing in her belly even then, people had, by turns, pitied and reviled them. But Lady Linden had made them her own personal charity and she never let anyone forget it. Prim gave her elder sister a quelling look. "Go and wash up, please," she said to Lila. "And be certain Rowan does as well. Hands and face must be washed. We could grow turnips in the dirt on your neck, young man! When you're done with that, there's something very important we need to talk with you about."

Lila's expression became instantly anxious. "Is it very bad? Will we have to go to the workhouse?"

"Who on earth said we'd go to the workhouse?"

"You did," Lila countered. "Well, you didn't say it to me. You said it to Hy and I heard it because you were very upset and very loud and I was just outside the kitchen window picking herbs like you'd asked! I can get a job! I could help sew or I could dig for truffles in the woods!"

Guilt washed over Prim. They were struggling and had been for some time. But for Lila to be aware of it, for her to have heard such distressing things from her own mouth left her feeling terribly ashamed. "Well, we are not going to the workhouse. None of us. And you won't be digging for truffles in the woods. Go wash up, Lila. This is good news."

When the children had disappeared up the narrow staircase that led to the cottage's two bedrooms, Hyacinth took Prim's hand. "We don't have to. We can find another way if you are really afraid."

A feeling of inevitability washed through her. This was her fate it seemed, and everything that had happened up to that point was pushing her so that she would not be able to deny it. "There is no other way, Hy. And I don't want her to be afraid... or for Rowan to realize just how bad things are. Perhaps going to another place where no one knows our history, where no one remembers what our mother was will be the best thing for all of us."

"I will send a note round to the inn," Hy said.

"No. We'll go there. Both of us together and see him this evening... and we'll take Lila and Rowan with us. Until she's met him, I won't commit to anything," Prim stated thoughtfully. "She has a sense for people, Hy. If she trusts him, if she likes him even a little, then we'll know what we're doing is right. For now, we'll simply tell her she has a half-brother who wants to meet her. And if it goes well, then we'll discuss moving there."

"You're right, of course," Hyacinth agreed. "And I suppose it really ought to be up to her, at least somewhat. It'll mean far more to her life than it ever will to ours."

Of that, Prim wasn't so sure.

Chapter Five

"THEY WERE LOVELY girls... though I suppose a bit long in the tooth for that description. They are firmly on the shelf by now. The oldest must be thirty at least and the younger of the two, the termagant, can't be far behind."

"Stop it, Nicholas. I know precisely what you are about and I will not be goaded by you," Garrett said. "And they are hardly that old. Neither of them can be more than a few years past twenty, if that."

They had returned from the Colliers' humble cottage and were having a light supper in one of the inn's private dining rooms. It was simple fare, but filling and well prepared. The wine was only tolerable, but the brandy was quite good and clearly smuggled. Of course, none of it mattered. Cornelius' mind was not on the food or the spirits. It was on her. She had taken over his thoughts with a ferocious hold that he could not seem to break free of. Infatuation wasn't unfamiliar to him, but nothing so intense or instantaneous had ever befallen him before.

"But the younger one is certainly a termagant. Even as besotted as you were with her lovely hair and fine blue eyes, you must admit that!" Nicholas insisted.

"I must admit that I do not know her well enough to have formed an opinion. She appears to be protective of her siblings. But then, perhaps she finds her siblings more lovable and worthy of protection than my own," Garrett added snarkily. Had he really longed to form a connection with his brother? It was surely the most ill-advised under taking of his life. Nicholas loved nothing better than to torment him.

Nicholas laughed heartily at that, throwing his head back and giving in fully to his own amusement. Cornelius wanted to plant his fist into his brother's face for that.

In the five years since they'd first met, they'd forged a relationship that was very similar to that of siblings raised together. They laughed and teased. They shared deeper moments, as well, such as the scandal that had rocked Garrett's life and left him an outcast to the society of which he had once been a darling. It would have been easier, Garrett thought, had he been a rogue to start with. But he'd set himself apart from his father by electing to always do the right thing, to be responsible and forthright, to weigh his every action against his honor and always err on the side of honor. And because of that one fateful night, when he'd fired the pistol that ended the life of the man who had claimed to be Lord Ramsleigh, a man who had been wicked through and through, it had all gone to ruin.

The apple doesn't fall far from the tree.

He's just as rotten as his father but gives himself airs.

I heard he killed him in cold blood and then rode away pretty as you please.

Now he's thick as thieves with his bastard brother and that wife of his.

All of the ugly whispers were along the same vein. Everyone believed that the first thirty years of his life had been nothing but a sham and in that one decisive moment, his true nature, wicked and unrepentant, had come to the fore. Never mind that Randall Grantham had a pistol pointed at his aunt, Viola Grantham, the woman to whom Nicholas was now married. In that moment, when Cornelius had fired, Grantham was already squeezing the trigger. The pistol ball had struck Viola in the shoulder and very nearly killed her. Cornelius' own shot had been true. Grantham had died instantly. His only regret was that he had not fired a second sooner and spared his sister-in-law the pain and suffering of a pistol ball and the resulting fever that had raged in her for days.

There had been a feeling that night that he was on the brink of some cataclysmic change. Long before those events had unfolded, he'd felt that strange prickling sense of unease, all his senses on alert. And now, he found himself faced with that sensation once more. Whatever happened, his life would alter irrevocably. Of that much, he was certain.

"I want to see the child," Cornelius confessed. "Regardless of what the sisters decide, I'd like to at least meet her."

Nicholas frowned. "I understand that. I confess to a certain degree of curiosity myself. But your drive to create a family out of the cast-off bastards of our father puzzles me... still. What are you searching for, Cornelius?"

It was odd to hear his given name on anyone's lips. He so rarely used it. "I don't know really. An escape from the loneliness of my childhood? I might have been legitimate and the heir, but there was no sense of family or belonging. Father and I butted heads from the start and he was always far more interested in his own hedonistic pursuits than in his son. Or any of his other offspring for that matter. It isn't that he was unkind or cruel. He just simply couldn't be bothered. I don't want these other children, even if they are grown, to feel that no one would ever bother for them."

Nicholas shook his head sadly. "You cannot make up for all the ill that the world has wrought for them. It isn't your responsibility."

"Isn't it? Am I not my brother's keeper then?"

Nicholas stared at him thoughtfully for a moment and then uttered the one thing that was always a source of contention between them, "Perhaps your happiness would be better discovered in finding a woman to marry and having a family of your own rather than trying to reassemble one from the broken pieces our father left behind."

No more was said as a soft knock sounded on the door to the small dining room. The innkeeper poked his head in, a frown upon his face, and said, "My lord, I'm terribly sorry to disturb you but there is a group of young persons here who are quite insistent upon seeing you!"

Cornelius did not allow his expression to betray him. He kept it completely neutral as he said, "Yes, we're expecting them, but I wasn't certain of when they would arrive. Please have more food brought out and the necessary crockery and cutlery for them, if you will."

The innkeeper was less skilled in concealing his reaction. His bushy eyebrows climbed skyward, reaching nearly to his balding pate. "Aye, my lord. I'll see to it."

A moment later, the door opened again and the Misses Collier stepped inside with a young and gangly-limbed girl beside them. She had long dark hair that hung over her shoulders in two thick braids and a scowl upon her face that looked very much like the one Nicholas wore on occasion. Had there been any doubt of her parentage, it was quickly allayed. The youngest of the Colliers, a shaggy-haired boy with a gap-toothed smile and mischief in his eyes prompted Garrett to smile before he could catch himself.

Rising to his feet he approached the young girl. "You must be Lila. I'm very pleased to meet you."

She bobbed a slightly curtsy but said nothing. It appeared his sister was rather shy.

"Come and sit," he urged, gesturing to the many chairs that were placed about the periphery of the small room. "The innkeeper is having more food brought in if you haven't dined yet."

"Oh, no!" Primrose Collier began. "We couldn't possibly put you out or stay so long."

"It's not beets is it? I can't stand beets!"

That pronouncement, his words tripping loudly over his elder sister's protests, came from the youngest member of the Collier crew. His eyes were wide with horror and complete disgust.

Once again, Cornelius found himself smiling. "I can attest to the fact that it is very good, hearty stew made of rabbit and carrots and I think potatoes. But there is not a beet to be found."

Primrose spoke again, giving her younger brother a quelling look which seemed to escape the boy entirely. "We only came so that Lila could meet you, my lord. We did not come here to be—"

"Fed? I was going to order a second serving for us anyway. It's no trouble at all to share," he insisted. How long had it been since they'd really eaten? The younger ones were likely fed and the older sisters likely did without. That much, he was certain of. He was just as certain that the word that had been on the tip of Primrose Collier's tongue had been charity. She did not want his charity.

Lila looked back at her with dark imploring eyes. "Can we stay for dinner, Prim? It smells heavenly."

The look that passed between the two girls was one of tenderness and understanding. It was clear to him, young as Primrose and Hyacinth were, that they had been mother and father to both Lila and Rowan. Their own mother had failed them, and their respective fathers were blights on mankind, his own included in that. How many others, he wondered? How many had already been lost to poverty or illness? To crimes so unspeakable he couldn't even envision them? And all because his father hadn't felt the need to bother with providing for any children he might have created.

"If you are certain it won't be a bother, Lord Ambrose," Prim said hesitantly, her pride shrinking at the request. "We'd be very pleased to stay."

"It's not a bother in the least. It's a joy to have the company and be spared more conversation with this lump," he said, gesturing toward Nicholas. Lila didn't smile, but her lips quivered slightly as if she were on the verge and little Rowan dissolved into peals of giggles. He'd win them over one by one, Cornelius thought, even Primrose. Why that mattered to him so much was something that did not bear thinking about, not yet at least. He continued introductions. "Lila, this is my half-brother, Dr. Nicholas Warner, which unfortunately makes him your half-brother, too. I am terribly sorry about that."

Perhaps it was his teasing tone or that the girl enjoyed Nicholas' pained look. But her lips quirked of their own volition and she puckered them to keep from smiling or, heaven forbid, laughing outright. Once she'd regained her composure, she replied, "It's very nice to meet you, Lord Ambrose and Dr. Warner."

Turning to the boy, Ambrose said, "And you must be... Rowan, I believe it was?"

"You have very fine horses, my lord," the boy said. Each word was enunciated carefully and Prim ruffled his hair in encouragement.

"Thank you, I am rather fond of them myself," Ambrose agreed. "Please, everyone sit and let us enjoy this fine meal."

Once they were all seated, food had been brought and served to everyone around the small table. Cornelius spoke directly to Lila. "Do you know why I'm here, Lila?"

"Because we have the same father, my lord," she answered. "You found letters that said so."

He was surprised by how much they'd told her and more surprised with the very adult way she had replied to his question. "Yes. That's right. What you might not know is that our father was a wealthy man and he left a great deal of wealth to me and to my brother, also your brother, Nicholas."

"But he didn't leave anything to me," she said. "Because he didn't want me."

Cornelius sighed heavily. "I don't think it was that. I think that he left the bulk of the estate to me with the understanding that I would find any other siblings and be certain they were cared for. He was a silly man... our father. Details and responsibilities were something he didn't do very well with." That wasn't entirely truthful. His father had been very good with details and responsibilities but, like so many men, he felt his illegitimate offspring were the sole responsibility of their mothers. Except for Nicholas', but then it had been clear that the man's feelings for that particular mistress had been deeper than most. Perhaps, the degree to which he'd provided for the children was based on how much value the mother held for him.

"And you do well with responsibilities and details?" Lila asked.

"I do," he answered, feeling as if what he said and did not say was very important in that moment.

"And you want us to live on your estate," she replied.

"Yes. I have a cottage there where you and your sisters and brother may stay."

"But we won't live with you," Lila said firmly. "Because you don't really want me anymore than he did. I'll be a burden and an obligation, just as I am to my sisters. The only difference is that they love me."

That had not gone as planned. Cornelius stared into that forthright and curiously adult expression on a child's face and realized that he was utterly ruined.

Chapter Six

P RIM WANTED TO crawl beneath the table and hide. She could not believe how Lila was behaving. And of all the times that Hyacinth had to be struck with one of her megrims, this was the worst! For all the good her elder sister did sitting beside her, she might as well have been alone with Lord Ambrose and Dr. Warner and Lila's ridiculous statements.

"Lila, do not be rude. Lord Ambrose sought you out because he wished to meet you and because he wished to provide for you in some way. Love, even when people share blood, is not always instantaneous. I would remind you that you asked our mother to send Rowan back from whence he'd come!" Prim reprimanded gently.

"He smelled," Lila insisted.

"I offered the cottage," Lord Ambrose said, "because I thought you would be more comfortable there. Propriety would not allow your elder sisters to reside in my house because they are not my relations and I did not think you would wish to be parted from them. Regardless of that, you are welcome in my home at any time, Lila. I look forward to having you there and getting to know you."

Prim sighed in relief. Despite his momentarily poleaxed expression, he'd handled that much better than she had and he seemed to understand that it was necessary to speak to Lila as if she were an adult in spite of the fact that she clearly was not. "There, Lila! You see? Lord Ambrose is only trying to do what is best for everyone here."

"Why?" Lila questioned him further.

Prim wanted, in that moment, to choke her younger sibling. She'd finally managed to work her way around to accepting that Lord Ambrose's offer would be the best thing for all of them and now Lila wanted to interrogate the man about his motives. She looked to Hyacinth for help, but her older sister was sitting in the chair, her hand over her eyes. Her pallor was terrifying.

"Because I want to have a family, Lila. I want to know my siblings and have relationships with them. If you'd be more amenable to residing at Avondale Hall with me, then I can always arrange for a chaperone for your sisters. Perhaps that would be best," he offered.

"Viola and I could come stay after our child is born, but she cannot travel for some months," Dr. Warner offered. "Is there not another relative we can impose upon until that time?"

"We have Aunt Arabella… my father's aunt. She is… well, odd— and very old—but otherwise quite capable of the task," Lord Ambrose replied.

Prim was caught. Well and truly caught. And Hyacinth still sat silently at her side with her delicate features pinched and drawn with pain, oblivious to all that had just transpired.

"Lord Ambrose, I thank you for the offer, but it really wouldn't be proper. You hardly know us after all, and we—none of us are prepared for life in a grand estate. We haven't the wardrobe for it and would only be an embarrassment to you," Prim insisted.

Lord Ambrose cocked his head to one side, staring at her in such a way that she felt he could see straight through to the heart of her. Then he replied, "And I don't entertain, Miss Collier. There are rarely any guests at Avondale aside from immediate family and a very few close friends. Very few… I can assure you that you all will have everything you need."

Prim shivered. He was referring only to clothing and necessities. A traitorous part of her wished he meant more than that. Every minute in his presence was a danger to her.

"I think I should be the one to decide," Lila said. "After all, I'm the one who is getting an entire family in the process."

All of the adults in the room turned to look at the solemn-faced child who had made such a profound statement.

"I think it impacts everyone, Lila, but you are correct in stating that you should have a significant say in the matter," Garrett agreed. "If your sisters are in agreement with that."

"We don't really have any choice now, do we?" Prim said, but the reply lacked heat. The child making more sense than anyone had taken the starch out of them, it seemed.

"Then it seems, Lila, that it is up to you," Garrett summed up.

"I have questions, my lord," Lila said.

"And I hope that I will have answers," he replied evenly.

Prim supposed it was a rather odd thing to face interrogation from a child but he appeared to be game if it would sway things in his direction. In fact, he appeared to be remarkably calm in the face of such an unusual predicament.

"How many brothers and sisters do we have?" Lila asked.

"Well, I don't have an exact number," he answered. "There are Nicholas and you. I've found indications that there are others but I haven't yet managed to locate them. I have hired inquiry agents to look into it, however. As soon as we can manage to locate them, we will reach out to them just as I have reached out to you."

With a solemn gaze and a serious expression, she asked, "And are you going to invite them to live at Avondale, as well?"

He cleared his throat. It was clearly a stalling tactic, but then he answered her with the same aplomb with which he seemed to do everything. "It depends on what their situation is. If they are adults or if they are well situated in life, then likely not. If bringing them to Avondale would be a viable option for everyone, then certainly, an invitation would be issued."

And as long as they weren't sunk so far into a life of crime that it was too late to save them, then yes. The implication was clear in his voice and in the dubious expression he wore, though Prim understood immediately why he wouldn't wish to say anything to Lila. Some people were beyond saving.

"Will it be terribly stuffy like it is whenever we call on Lady Linden?" Lila asked. "The chairs are all hard and no one laughs. Everyone smiles like someone's pinching and they don't want to let on."

Garrett smiled. "I promise it won't be like that. I want you to be very happy at Avondale. It'll be your home. Not a mausoleum."

"What's a mausoleum?" Rowan piped up.

"It's a place where they put dead—" Nicholas offered.

Prim cut him off abruptly. "They keep old things. Very old things."

"Yes, very old," Garrett said, biting back a smile. "What do you think, Lila?"

"You don't have to make a decision right away," Prim interjected.

"I want to, Prim," Lila said softly. "I want to go and live there and see what it would be like if my father had loved mama and married her instead!"

Prim's heart broke in that moment. Lila had never been around men. She didn't know what it was like to see a man behave honorably. They were nothing more than acquaintances or strangers to her. Of course she was curious and of course she wanted to know more about him and about the father who had never bothered to acknowledge her in any way.

"Very well, Lord Ambrose. But any expenditures for me, Hyacinth and Rowan will be considered a loan only. You will be reimbursed for them," Prim insisted. *Even if she had to sell her soul to the devil to see it accomplished.* She would not allow herself to become beholden to any man for any reason. It was a hard lesson she had learned from watching her mother's life and bitter, lonely death.

"I am certain that we can come to an agreement on the terms, Miss Collier," Lord Ambrose answered. "Naturally, in light of your efforts in caring for Lila all this time, some recompense should be owed by my father and that will naturally have fallen to me."

Prim didn't answer. She couldn't. Control was slipping away from her. They would move into his home, because that was what he wanted, because it was what Lila wanted and likely needed. If he could behave honorably for Lila's sake, ensure her future in ways that she and Hy never would be able to, wasn't it worth any sacrifice on her part? Her pride and dignity were not worth depriving Lila of a future where she might be, if not a lady, then at least someone respectable. Her sister would not have to bow and scrape and be grateful to everyone who deigned to show her a kindness, even if it was only to lord it over her later.

"Very well. We shall accept your invitation to Avondale Hall," Prim replied. "But my sister and I will work while we are there. Surely there are tasks that we might be able to see to as a way of earning our keep."

"If you feel you must do so, Miss Collier, yes, a task will be found. But it is not necessary."

"It is not necessary for you, my lord. But it is for me. We have managed to survive this long without being dependent entirely upon the charity of others. I find that I am unwilling to give up our autonomy for dependence now, regardless of how generously it is offered."

He stared at her for the longest time, his dark gaze pinning her to the spot. There was something inscrutable about his expression and his study of her that left Prim uneasy. But then everything about him left her uneasy and very uncertain of what her future might hold.

Before she could say anything further, Hyacinth rose to her feet, swayed alarmingly and then collapsed to the floor.

Dr. Warner sprang into action, shouting for someone to fetch his bag. Lord Ambrose left the room immediately and returned only moments later with a dark leather bag in his grasp.

Prim knelt on the floor next to Hyacinth, cradling her sister's head as Hyacinth was taken by one of the fits that had always plagued her. It was not as bad as it had been many times before, but even then, Hy's fits were not so violent as those of some others who suffered such conditions.

"Does this happen often?" Dr. Warner demanded.

"It happens more frequently in times of stress and I fear there has been a great deal of stress lately," Prim confessed.

"And I have added to it," Lord Ambrose commented softly.

"No! Not—I mean, yes, this was unexpected and necessitated a great deal of thought and soul searching for both Hyacinth and me but that is not the sort of stress I mean. We've been struggling for months to keep body and soul together. The small amount of money that had been saved is dwindling far more quickly than we can earn the necessary funds to replace it. I had just accepted an offer to work as a maid for Lady Linden as the sewing and washing that Hy and I took in was no longer enough to meet our needs." It was a humiliating thing to confess, but Prim felt that, under the circumstances, she had little choice. If Dr. Warner could help Hy, then withholding information was hardly the right course of action.

"Sewing... lots of fine needlework, likely late into the night?" the doctor asked.

"Yes," Prim admitted.

"And do these episodes occur more frequently when you've increased the amount of work you do?"

"Yes, they do," Prim admitted. "I've long suspected that they were connected, but Hyacinth stated that it didn't matter. We had no other options to earn a living respectably."

Warner's lips firmed. "No more. These fits are triggered by the megrims and the megrims are triggered by your sister straining her eyes to sew in dim light. It cannot continue or she will do herself permanent injury."

Hyacinth's fit subsided, the tremors that wracked her slight frame fading to nothing. But she would be exhausted afterward. They always left her weak and ill for some time.

"I do hate to be a bother but if the innkeeper could be troubled for a wagon, I doubt Hyacinth will be up to the walk home. If we can get her back to the cottage where she can rest in her own bed, she will recover much more quickly," Prim insisted.

"I will have my carriage summoned and will see you all home," Lord Ambrose insisted. "It will be cramped but I am sure we can manage."

"Thank you," Prim said, once more feeling as if she were in his debt. It was a feeling she did not care for in the least.

Chapter Seven

T HE INTERIOR OF the carriage was dim, a single lamp swaying with the clomping gait of the horses and the bouncing of the wheels over the rutted lane. Hyacinth was seated beside her, fast asleep with her head resting against Prim's shoulder. Across from them, Lord Ambrose had his head turned, staring out the carriage window into the darkness.

In profile, she could study him more fully. His high forehead, prominent but straight and well-shaped nose, the jut of a strong chin and the edge of his chiseled jaw all confirmed beyond measure that was he was a far too handsome man for her peace of mind. His dark eyes cut toward her, as if aware of her perusal.

"Have I grown two heads then?" he asked.

Prim flushed with embarrassment. "I am simply puzzled by you, my lord. I find this all very strange."

A giggle sounded from above. Lila and Rowan were riding with the coachman, a grand adventure for them. He smiled at the sound, and Prim felt her heartbeat quicken.

"Have you never been around children?" she asked.

"No. I have not. I was raised as an only child. My mother passed when I very young. And my father had no interest in remarrying… he was occupying himself with other pursuits."

"It sounds very lonely," Prim admitted.

"It was, I suppose. But at the time, it was all I knew and seemed perfectly normal to me. I've glimpses now of what it is like to have a family. Nicholas teases and torments as all brothers do. But it's different from what you share with your sister. It's very apparent that the two of you have relied on one another for a very long time," he commented.

Were they so easy to read then? "When we were younger, Hyacinth protected me… from everything that she could. But as I grew up, it became more reciprocal. Now, we take care of one another," Prim replied.

"And Lila and Rowan?"

"Yes," she agreed. "And Lila and Rowan. They are my world. There is nothing I wouldn't do for them."

"Including moving to the estate of a man you do not like, do not trust, and have little to no use for," he surmised.

Prim shrugged, causing Hyacinth to stir where she rested against Prim's shoulder. If he interpreted her response to him as dislike, it was to her benefit. As for not trusting him and not knowing him, those were both quite true. "You should not take it personally, Lord Ambrose," Prim admonished. "I have little to no use for most men."

"And men have certainly given you no reason to alter that view point."

"No," she agreed, "they have not. I do not mean to insult you, but we are discussing my family. I will always put them first. And right now, I worry about your intentions for us. I worry that you will grow bored and then what will happen to Lila?"

"I can offer you assurances, Miss Collier, but those are only words. You will come to trust, in time, that my intentions toward your siblings are pure."

And toward me? The thought crept unbidden into her mind, along with the knowledge that she rather wished his intentions toward her would not be pure. Never in all her years had she encountered a man who made her aspire to wickedness. Not until he had entered their small cottage. She was cursed with her mother's blood.

An incident from her childhood came to mind, a dark and ugly one. Perhaps the very moment where her distrust of men had been born. They'd still been in their hovel in the Devil's Acre when one of the men her mother regularly entertained had knocked upon the door. Their mother had been out but he'd been insistent that he come in and wait for her. Prim could still recall the way he'd looked at her, the way he'd reached out and stroked her hair, his hands lingering too long on her shoulders. *"You've a harlot's soul just like your mother,"* he'd whispered. *"You can earn these coins for yourself, little one."*

It wouldn't be nearly so awful if she hadn't been tempted. The coins had promised full bellies and perhaps heavier curtains to hang near their small pallet to block out the chill. But revulsion had settled in quickly enough when he'd leaned in to try and kiss her, his foul breath making her retch and gag. He'd struck her then, knocking her to the floor while Hyacinth screamed and jumped on his back, pounding it with her small fists. It was then their mother had returned. She'd sent the man packing, coin or no coin, and told him if he ever returned she'd gut him and put his body in the river. Then she'd grabbed Prim up, hugged her fiercely and whispered against her throbbing cheek, *"You'll never be like me. Promise me, angel! Never be like me."*

"Where is it that you've gone, Miss Collier?" he asked, pulling her from those shameful memories that created such a terrible ache inside her.

"My thoughts are my own, Lord Ambrose, and not fit for the consumption of others just now."

No more was said as the carriage rolled to a halt in front of their small cottage. He jumped down, then helped her to alight as if she were a fine lady and not a woman far beneath his notice. While she'd intended to aid Hyacinth in the house, he lifted her sister out as if she weighed no more than a small child. "I'll carry her in. She's too exhausted to walk," he offered.

"Thank you, my lord," Prim said, though part of her felt as if she would choke on the words. It galled her to need him, to be beholden to him, and yet she was, for so many reasons already. And there would be more still to come.

Opening the door, Rowan and Lila rushed in, climbing the rickety stairs to their respective bedchambers. Lila shared the largest with Prim and Hyacinth, the three of them sleeping in one bed that was barely big enough for two. Rowan had a small cot in the hall.

"Her chamber is upstairs?"

Prim made a face. "It hardly qualifies as a chamber, but yes. We share with Lila."

He moved toward the stairs, careful to keep Hyacinth turned away from the wall, lest he should bump it. At the top, Lila held the door to the bedchamber and he stepped inside it. If their poverty was easily visible in other rooms of the cottage, nowhere was it more obvious than in their spartan room. One bed for the three of them, not a rug to be seen on the cold floor and their few gowns hanging on a single row of pegs along the far wall. At least all their underthings were freshly laundered and stored in the small chest at the foot of the bed rather than strung across the line that typically stretched from one side of the room to the other. It had given way under Rowan's attempts to swing from it like the sailors he'd seen from the wharf when they'd ventured near the river.

"You all share this room?" he asked. It was clear from his tone that he found their circumstances not just shocking but sadly deficient.

"Yes, we do. Lila is of an age where we didn't feel it appropriate for her to continue sharing with Rowan. For the last two years, she's been in here with us," Prim said. Her chin inched upward, her pride roiling up inside her as she prepared to defend their choices.

"Of course," he said. "I hadn't considered that. How any of you have gotten a single wink of sleep, packed in like that, I'll never know. You are made of far stronger stock than I, Primrose Collier. I commend you and your sister. You've both sacrificed greatly for your younger siblings. More than most would have, and with far less complaint, I think."

She'd been prepared to give him a set down. But the quiet admiration, lacking in condescension and appearing to be entirely genuine, left her uncertain of how to reply. At a loss, Prim simply inclined her head.

"I'll be off... I know it will take some time for you all to settle your affairs here. There are also things I must do in order to make Avondale suitable for all of you. I'll be leaving in the morning and I will send a carriage for you all in a fortnight. Will you need one wagon or two for your things?"

Looking around at the collection of cast-off furnishings, Prim said, "We won't need a wagon. We'll only have a few bags between us, my lord. All of these things… they are meaningless to us and it would be pointless to drag them into your already well-appointed house."

"Not as well-appointed as you might think," he replied. "Avondale is a bit rough around the edges. I think that may be why I like it. Until I see you there, Miss Collier, I bid you farewell."

Prim watched him leave with both relief and reluctance. It was not necessarily the nature of her feelings for him that alarmed her, but rather the presence of any feeling at all. For so many years, she had been entirely numb to anyone save for her siblings. That in such a short time, he'd managed to provoke attraction, anger, empathy, pride, and worse still, curiosity, was terrifying to her.

Hyacinth moved to sit up in bed, groaning softly as she did so. Prim forced any thoughts of the strange lord from her mind. There'd be time enough to dwell on him later. For the moment, she had her sister to attend to.

⚜

CORNELIUS STEPPED OUT into the night, retreating to the seclusion of the carriage. Nicholas had teased him unmercifully about Primrose Collier. The more he was in her presence, the more he came to realize that his brother's teasing was, in fact, well warranted. He found her compelling, maddening, prickly, and altogether far too appealing for his peace of mind. If he was to hold fast to his honor and abide by the code he had set for himself, she was strictly off limits, no matter what his feelings for her were. Drawn to her as he was, he'd sensed in the carriage that she was damaged. That there something inside her, some long nurtured pain that prompted her attitude toward him. To act on his desires would be to confirm her worst suspicions of him.

With a sharp rap on the roof, the carriage lurched forward and made for the inn. More of Nicholas' teasing would be in store. Of that, he was certain. But what greeted him when he arrived there was not teasing. Instead, Nicholas sat with a bottle of brandy and two glasses. At Cornelius' entrance, he poured a liberal amount of the heady liquid into both.

"What's this for?" Cornelius asked.

"Complications," Nicholas said. "Did you notice anything unusual about the boy?"

"Rowan?" Cornelius took a sip. "No. He's a typical boy."

"Well, then you should take a second look... and when you do, think about your scandal-ridden neighbor, Freddy Hamilton, Lord Samford."

He'd been too obsessed with Primrose Collier to make the connection, but having it stated so matter of factly, he could not deny it. It was clear to him immediately that Nicholas was speaking the truth. Rowan did look shockingly like Freddy and that would be incredibly problematic since there would be no way to ensure the boy did not cross paths with the reprobate who was likely his father at worst and uncle at best. From Lord Harrelson's, Freddy's uncle-by-marriage, involvement in abduction and blackmail schemes, to his crazed sister nearly murdering the new Lady Wolverton, the family was constantly embroiled in scandal. Freddy's own wife had died recently from apparently natural causes, though her death had been met with some suspicion. He was on the hunt for a new bride, an heiress, and he would not welcome having his past sins come home to roost.

Cornelius bit out a curse, something that he would typically never utter.

Nicholas nodded. "Precisely. You have a very big problem, Brother, and I don't envy you the mess that it could create."

Draining the glass, Cornelius refilled it and sank into the adjacent chair. It would be a mess. But he would deal with it when the time came along, which would likely be sooner than later.

Chapter Eight

"I DO HOPE they'll arrive at a reasonable time. Depending on where the coachman stopped for the night, they could arrive as early as breakfast or as late as tea! How on earth can one possibly prepare for guests if one doesn't know when they will arrive? It's so terribly inconvenient. I should have gone to their cottage and accompanied them here. Then there would be no question. I could have sent instructions ahead from whatever coaching inns we utilized along the way to apprise the staff of what arrangements should be made. It's just terrible, Cornelius! I detest uncertainty."

What Arabella detested was clearly silence, Cornelius thought. In inviting her to stay at Avondale as a chaperone for the Collier sisters and as someone who could teach Lila the finer points of navigating society and all she might need to know of decorum, he'd forgotten how bloody much she talked. The woman prattled incessantly until he wanted to dam his ears with beeswax and cotton just for the reprieve it might offer.

"I daresay the Colliers are quite used to making do with whatever is put before them, Aunt Arabella. Whatever can be quickly prepared will suit them very well. They are remarkably resilient and quite congenial young ladies... as for Lila and young Rowan, no doubt putting anything in front of them will suffice. So long as it isn't beets."

Arabella gasped in horror. "Make do? Suffice? Oh my word, Cornelius! The entire point of bringing the girl here, and her siblings, is to elevate them. One does not elevate people by allowing them to simply make do!"

On that score, he could not disagree. "Fine, Aunt Arabella. Have every meal prepared in readiness of their arrival. Any largesse left over will be enjoyed by the servants or distributed to tenant farmers."

Arabella blinked at him. "Well, that is excessive, but I can see no other way. I'll see to it, of course, Cornelius. I'm quite pleased that you've taken it upon yourself to locate all the children your father sired across the British Isles. I did so love my nephew, but his behavior was quite deplorable in that regard... I do like that Dr. Warner! He's quite accomplished, isn't he? And his wife is lovely. Scandalous but lovely."

She was still talking as she walked away, her words becoming indecipherable the closer she got to the door. Cornelius was left shaking his head, stunned at the woman's ability to ramble. He would be thankful when the Colliers arrived just so there would be someone else there for her to direct her monologues to.

No sooner had the though occurred than he heard the clattering of hooves and carriage wheels outside. They had arrived earlier than expected, but given that the weather had been unseasonably dry to date, it was not unusual. He acknowledged their arrival ambivalently. He was relieved on the one hand that they had arrived safely and without issue. On the other, he was not anticipating the difficulties inherent to such close proximity to Miss Primrose. Not in the least. Then there was the other matter. He knew Samford was off to Bath shortly to chase his heiress. He'd hoped that might occur before the Colliers arrived. But alas, it was not to be.

With a muttered curse, he closed the book he'd been attempting to read all morning. He'd not been able to concentrate on it to start with, now all hope was lost. It was best to face it head on. Rising from his chair, he placed the book on the table and moved toward the small entryway just off the great hall. He paused in the doorway there, waiting for them to enter. Rowan's excited chatter about castles made him smile. He supposed Avondale did look like a castle to the boy. It had been a fortified manor in days long past, but not for centuries. Still, the battlements remained though purely in decorative fashion now.

Lila's voice was quieter, softer, but still high and very childlike. The husky strains of Primrose Collier's voice were more faint, any exuberance carefully tempered as she no doubt urged her younger siblings to do the same. The butler held the door wide and the younger of the two entered. They were practically running, but stopped when they saw him, their feet skidding to a halt on the marble floor.

The two elder sisters entered behind them, moving far more sedately. They were dressed as they had been when he saw them in their small cottage. Dresses made over, hemmed and retrimmed to hide their age and wear. Neither was an appropriate garment for traveling, the fabric too thin by far for the chill of a coach. While the weather had not turned fully just yet, there was a chill in the air that hinted at the coming winter. He made a note to himself to see to their wardrobes, whatever protests they might offer. He would also need to speak privately with Primrose and Hyacinth about the situation with Rowan and the man he suspected to be the boy's father. But that could wait. For a while at least. He didn't want them to immediately regret their agreement.

"Welcome to Avondale," Cornelius said softly. "I don't recommend sliding on the marble. Jeffers, the butler, gets quite put out with it. But sliding down the banisters is perfectly permissible because it cuts down on the dusting for the maids."

"Don't encourage them," Primrose said. "You'll have them bashing their heads on the marble. I doubt Jeffers would welcome that either."

Cornelius bit back a smile at her caustic retort. "No, I suppose he would not. There you have it, young Rowan and Lila. No sliding on the marble or the banisters because your sister has said so."

"She's never any fun," Rowan said and turned to stick his tongue out at Primrose. Her only response was to lift one perfectly arched eyebrow at him in such a quelling expression that he immediately tucked his tongue back into his mouth and turned to face meekly forward.

"That's more like it," she said.

"Jeffers, have someone see to the bags," Cornelius instructed. "I'll show our newest residents to their rooms."

The butler began directing the footmen wordlessly, and Cornelius held out his hand toward the staircase. "After you."

Lila giggled and then all but skipped up the stairs, Rowan beside her. His eyes were still on the banister, no doubt mentally calculating whether or not the fun of it would be worth the scolding. As they reached the landing at the top and the hall forked in two different directions, one going to the East Wing one to the West and the broad double doors straight ahead opening onto the gallery and ballroom beyond, he caught Prim and Hyacinth's panicked looks.

"Is everything all right?"

"You said this was not a grand house, Lord Ambrose," Hyacinth said, her tone holding a slight reprimand. "I fear we have very different definitions of grand. We cannot possibly stay here."

"You can and you will," he said. "It's all been arranged. Aunt Arabella is already here in residence and eagerly awaiting her role as chaperone and social tutor for Lila. For Rowan naturally if he wishes to learn, or I suppose it would be better to say if you wish him to learn. Left to his own devices it'd be tree climbing and brook jumping, most likely."

"That is true enough," Primrose agreed, "but yes, he should learn how to go about in society, at least to some degree, so that he might be somewhat more employable in the future."

"And yet the two of you seem to be perfectly well versed in etiquette," he mused. "How is that?" He directed them down the East Wing of the house, as far from his own chamber as possible. It seemed the wisest course of action. If he was going to hold fast to his honor and abide by the tenants of being a gentleman, limiting temptation was the only way.

"Our mother's end might have been rather ignoble, but she was the daughter of a gentleman," Prim answered. "They fell on hard times, and the world is unkind to women who lack both fortune and connections."

"So it is, Miss Primrose. So it is," he agreed. They'd reached the chambers he'd selected for them. It was a second master suite, hastily redecorated to accommodate two women. "I thought you'd prefer connecting rooms. There's a small sitting room to be shared but you'll each have your own chamber."

Throwing the doors wide, he let them precede him into the sitting room. The walls were covered in a silk damask in green, the settees and armchairs covered in the same fabric. The carpet was Aubusson, in the same shade of green with bits of gold, cream and salmon woven through.

He watched them step deeper into the room, look at their sur-roundings and then look at one another. Cornelius leaned against the door frame and waited for their protests. He knew they'd be coming.

"Lord Ambrose, this is far too fine for us. We cannot possibly stay here! Perhaps there is something in the servants' quarters—"

"Are you a servant then?" he asked, interrupting Hyacinth's pro-tests. "I'll answer that for you. You are not servants. You are guests in this home for so long as you choose to remain. As such, you shall have chambers that are suited to being my honored guests."

"Lord Ambrose, I do appreciate your position," Prim countered in her sister's stead. "While I understand that servants' quarters would be inappropriate, surely there are slightly less grand chambers that we might occupy? Something nearer Lila's and Rowan's rooms perhaps where we can stay close by should they become overly rambunc-tious?"

"They'll be near enough... they are directly above you both, in fact. That was part of my reason for choosing these rooms for you. You might keep a watchful eye but also privacy for yourselves for a change. If they should become too rambunctious, as you put it, you will likely hear them before anyone else does," he offered. He knew, of course, that the real issue was their uncertainty of their place in the grand scheme of things. "These will be your rooms for the duration of your stay here. There'll be no more talk of servants' quarters. I'll leave you to get settled and, no doubt, Aunt Arabella will be descending momentarily. For that, I extend my most heartfelt apologies."

Cornelius retreated before more protests could be offered.

"HAVE WE MADE a mistake?"

Prim had been looking out the windows at the expanse of parkland and formal gardens below. Hyacinth's softly whispered question filled the room, echoing around them. It mirrored her own thoughts precisely.

"I have asked that same question every hour on the hour since we left our small cottage," Prim admitted. She crossed her arms over her chest, hugging herself for some sort of reassurance. "Whether it is a mistake for us or not, it's the right choice for Lila and for Rowan. We just have to focus on that."

Hyacinth sank down onto one of the upholstered chairs that flanked the fireplace. "You're right, of course. We must think of Lila and Rowan. I do believe that Lord Ambrose is an honorable man. I do not think he brought us here with anything but the best of intentions."

Prim believed that as well. But she also knew that even the best of intentions could fail if tested strongly enough or often enough. Her own intentions were good as well, but that hadn't stopped her from admiring the breadth of his shoulders that owed nothing to his tailor, or the long, lean line of his legs in well-fitted breeches and riding boots. Before she could ruminate on that less than cheering thought any further there was a rapid knock upon the door. They hadn't even called out for the person to enter when the door opened and a tiny, birdlike woman entered. Her silver hair was dressed in the old fashion, piled high atop her head in a mass that seemed simply too large for her diminutive form to carry.

"Good heavens! Cornelius was to inform me the very moment that you arrived and of course he did not. That man! What on earth is a body to do with him? He nods his head as if in agreement and then goes on to do precisely as he pleases. But, of course, that's neither here nor there. The younger children are settled and I've already looked in on them. And now that I'm here, I must say, Miss Primrose and Miss Hyacinth, that those gowns simply will not do. We'll need to outfit the both of you in a manner befitting a relative of an influential peer such as dear Cornelius! We don't entertain, but one never knows who one will encounter and it simply would not do for the two of you to be caught out in such a state!"

When the woman finally paused to draw a breath, both Prim and Hyacinth were simply too stunned to speak. The sheer volume of words that came out of her at one time was mind boggling as was the fact that given her decrepit state she had enough breath in her body to utter them.

"Now, the both of you get yourselves freshened up and then join me in the drawing room. I've had fashion plates sent from the best dressmakers in Bath. It's not nearly as good as having them from London or Paris, but that horrible Napoleon has ruined that for everyone. Of course, when one is in the country it's very bad form to outshine one's neighbors to such a degree. So dressmakers from Bath would likely be best after all. It wouldn't do to be the very first stare of fashion when one is rusticating, after all. Hurry, girls! We've much to do!"

They were both still gaping after her when the elderly woman had turned and gone. It was Prim who managed to speak first. "I understand why Lord Ambrose only nods and then does as he pleases. It's the only response she allows enough time for!"

"Let us hurry. If she talks that much just in greeting, I can't imagine what an actual lecture would be like," Hyacinth said.

Prim could feel her eyes crossing at the prospect. "Heaven preserve us!"

Chapter Nine

FREDRICK HAMILTON, LORD Samford, watched his younger siblings playing on the lawn with a frown. They were loud, spoiled, obnoxious, and every last one of them was a bastard. His stepmother, Lady Samford, hadn't been faithful even a day of her marriage to Freddy's late father and the four children she'd birthed after marrying the elder Lord Samford had all been sired by a different man. In truth, Freddy's only true sibling, Albert, had been banished in the wake of a scandal related to their stepmother's brother, Lord Harrelson, and his nefarious methods of stuffing the family coffers. Of course, he himself had not been entirely innocent of those schemes, but Albie had paid the price for them. To spare the family the scandal of a trial, a gentleman's agreement had seen Albie off to the East Indies where he would remain in reluctant service to his country until he died. Harrelson, ultimately, as he'd been snuffed out by one of his compatriots with a particularly nasty poison, was now gone. So was the lovely and viperous Helena, the eldest of Lady Samford's bastard children and Albie's lover.

But it was more than the whispered scandals that beset his family. It was the financial ruin that they were now on the cusp of that was the true source of Freddy's worry. Without Harrelson's contacts and skillful scheming, his blackmail and flesh peddling, Freddy was left to replenish the family fortunes the old fashioned way. He'd need to marry a walking, talking purse. But even aging spinsters with generous fortunes or horse-faced heiresses had standards, and with the family's reputation so thoroughly besmirched, not even they would have him at present.

His only hope was Wyverne's girl. Lame from a carriage accident as a child, she'd never gone out in society outside of Bath, to spare herself the cruelty of others he supposed. Wyverne himself had no reservations, he'd have thrown the girl to the wolves if it would get rid of her. But she had reservations and Freddy was left dancing to the ape-leader's tune to reassure her that he was good enough for a match despite the family scandals. Which brought him back to the hedonistic lot on the lawn. If they didn't learn to curb their wild ways, behave in a circumspect manner, he'd never get an heiress.

Of course, he was also rethinking his own strategies. He couldn't convince her that he was a nice man, willing to change his ways and live a quiet life with her. She clearly was not buying into it. Instead, he'd play the cad, make her yearn for him. Women, even aging and lame spinsters, liked the chase.

In his life, Freddy had been obsessed with two women. Isabelle, the cheapside whore he'd been willing to sacrifice everything for. Of course, in his maturity, he knew well enough that it had been her particular set of skills that had muddled his thinking. Thankfully, his father had intervened on his behalf and he hadn't debased himself so thoroughly that there was no coming back from it. The other had been Elizabeth Masters, a local beauty he'd contented himself with seducing and abandoning in favor of his last heiress. But in the wake of his many scandals, his former father-in-law had changed his will and left the bulk of his wealth to a distant relative rather than to his son-in-law. They'd thought to salvage everything by marrying Helena off to a wealthy neighbor and indulging one of Harrelson's more elaborate schemes to claim the man's wealth for their own. That had not worked out according to plan either.

Damn Wolverton and damn Helena for ruining all of it, he thought bitterly. Her heavy-handedness with her miraculous resurrection had created immediate suspicion. Impetuous, headstrong, driven by her own vanity and conceit, she'd paid for it with her life in the end.

Lady Samford entered the study. "There you are, Fredrick. I need to speak with you about a season for Camilla. I understand that there are financial constraints now, but she must be permitted to come out in society. If not, we'll never find a husband for the girl."

Fredrick pinched the bridge of his nose between his thumb and forefinger in an attempt to ward off the headache that always followed any conversations with his stepmother. The woman was bleeding him dry. "As we've no dowry for her unless I can manage to get the Wyverne girl to the altar myself, the season will have to wait."

Lady Samford frowned at that, her mouth pinching into a thin firm line. "We need to be in society, Fredrick! The longer we are out of it, the more convinced others become that all those atrocious rumors are true. We cannot allow people to believe that we were involved in all that Harrelson did or that Albie and Helena were involved in an *unnatural* relationship."

"Perhaps you should have thought of that before you indulged Helena's every whim and she became an utter terror!" he snapped. "As for the unnatural relationship, half of London knows Helena was not father's true daughter, and the other half suspects. You should have been more discreet as you whored your way through the *ton*."

She gasped in outrage. "Do not speak ill of the dead, Fredrick! Helena was all that was grace and beauty. You've no right. As for your allegations against me, better to be whore than a murderer. Or should I let it slip that it wasn't a fever that took your wife from me at all, but the pillow you held over her face?"

"You wanted my wife gone as much as I did. The pillow was your idea after all."

His stepmother shrugged. "It was only a suggestion. You didn't have to take it... and it's not as if she's missed. All she did was whine and cry about how horrible her life was here and what a terrible husband you were!"

"Well, regardless, no season for Camilla until I can bag the lame duck of an heiress," he snapped.

"If only Wolverton's fortunes hadn't been snatched from us!"

"You can lay that at your dead daughter's doorstep. If Helena had just stayed put and not allowed pettiness to get the better of her, then we could have kept Wolverton's money instead of having to return all of it to him. You'll forgive me if I'm feeling less than inclined to extoll her many virtues now."

His stepmother's expression hardened and he could see that she wanted to argue, but wisely did not. On the subject of Helena, they would simply have to agree to disagree.

"When do you see the girl again?" she demanded.

"She's in Bath to take the waters. I foresee a chance encounter with her at the Pump Room," he explained. "Or maybe the Assembly Rooms. I think my only option at this point is to convince her to elope."

"What of her father? What if he decides not to release her fortune to you for an unsanctioned match?"

"The match is sanctioned. Her father wants to be rid of her and he's readily agreed to the marriage. She's the stumbling block. I'm dancing to her tune like a marionette at the moment. But that will end now. Being good has been ineffective in landing her, perhaps it's time to be bad," he said.

"More scandal," she said with a frown. "It's the last thing we need, but without her fortune, we've no chance at reclaiming our rightful place in society. See to it. I'll reach out to some friends who might be able to arrange introductions for Camilla to eligible gentlemen."

"By eligible you mean wealthy and with one foot in the grave?"

"Precisely," she agreed. "Oh, we've received a bill from Camilla's dancing instructor. He won't return until he's paid and, frankly, we can't afford for her not to have the lessons. She'll be a laughing stock if she does go into society in her current state."

He wanted to hurl something at her. "Madame, do you not comprehend what it means to be impoverished? We can barely pay our servants much less afford dance instructors and the ridiculous number of new gowns that you've ordered for both the girls and for yourself."

"They're only merchants, Fredrick. It's not as if they must be paid," she snapped before turning on her heel to leave.

At the end of his patience and needing very much to be away from his family, if one could call the scavengers that, his only option was to ride. The relative freedom of galloping across the fields might provide some respite.

"Mathers!" he shouted.

The butler entered immediately. "Yes, my lord?"

"Have my horse saddled immediately!"

"Certainly, my lord."

IT WAS AFTERNOON and Hyacinth had pleaded a megrim to escape Lady Arabella. Prim had taken a different route and proclaimed that after being cooped up in a carriage for nearly three days, the children would never sleep if they didn't get some fresh air and exercise. To that end, she was now walking along one of the many winding paths that meandered through the estate while Rowan and Lila jumped and skipped ahead of her, their laughter echoing through the trees.

"Prim!" Rowan called out. "That's a climbing tree! Can I?"

All trees were climbing trees to Rowan, but Prim had to admit that one was a fine specimen. The branches all appeared quite sturdy and evenly spaced. "Not too high," she said, "But yes you *may*."

He whooped with excitement as Lila rolled her eyes and shook her head like someone's stuffy maiden aunt.

"Lila, why don't you pick some of those wildflowers? You can give them to Hyacinth. I'm certain it will make her feel better," Prim suggested. It would be a happy task for her as Lila had been picking wildflowers for as long as she could grab hold of one.

For herself, Prim took the opportunity to simply sit and enjoy the pale afternoon sun. It was a mild day with a gentle breeze and no rain, a rarity to be sure. The chill November air was settling in and it wouldn't be long before cold weather would be firmly upon them. Planting herself on the low stone fence that bordered the path, Prim watched her younger siblings at play. If she were to be entirely honest, she could admit that taking the children on this outing had far less to do with escaping Arabella than with avoiding Lord Ambrose. Even their brief and perfunctory meeting that morning had been charged, filled with that bizarre and undeniable connection that seemed to have existed between them from their first meeting. Prim had hoped against hope that it had been a fluke and that a second meeting with him would prove her wrong. It had not.

Keeping her eyes on Lila and one ear trained for any cries of distress from Rowan, the clattering of hooves went unnoticed until they were nearly upon her. Lila looked up and let out a piercing shriek. It was instinct more than anything else that had Prim dropping from the stone fence to the ground, flattening herself against the rocks as the horse sailed over her, its back hooves landing mere inches in front of her. She could feel the swish of its tail on her skin.

The horseman muttered an epithet as the large stallion pranced and reared. Finally, after what seemed an eternity fraught with sheer terror, the beast quieted. The rider patted the animal on the neck, muttering soothing words to him, even as his head came up and he glared daggers at Prim.

"What the devil are you thinking?"

Prim sat up, glared at him, and said, "I was thinking that I would sit on that stone fence, in full view of anyone who might approach, and watch my siblings at play. I might add that it is hardly a scandalous activity and would have offered no danger at all had you not been riding so recklessly!"

"This is private property, Madame!"

"Yes, it is private property and we are guests of Lord Ambrose," she snapped. "If you'd be so kind as to give us your name, sir, I will happily tell him how we encountered one another!"

The man's lips firmed, pressing into a hard line as his chin jutted forward in obvious displeasure. Before he could reprimand her further, Rowan and Lila came running from their respective directions. Lila immediately wrapped her arms about Prim's waist and held her tight. Rowan, their little warrior, situated himself between the man and his sisters, as if he truly meant to do battle. Tension radiated from his small body as he clenched his fists and glared up at the man who'd intruded on their pleasant afternoon.

She was so stunned that it took her a moment to really take it all in. But as she looked at him, Prim's heart stuttered in her chest. *The jutting chin and mutinous expression*, Prim realized with dawning horror. The man had looked instantly familiar to her, but it wasn't because she knew him. It was because she gazed upon a younger version of that face on a daily basis.

"You should apologize to my sister!" Rowan demanded. "A gentleman would never speak to a lady that way! Never."

If Prim had any question about whether or not the man would recognize Rowan, it was immediately answered by the slight narrowing of his eyes as they roamed over the small but fierce boy in front of him. When he'd taken his accounting of Rowan, he looked at her. His expression was measuring, weighing, all seeing, as his eyes roved over her from head to toe. She saw the recognition in his gaze, and the satisfied smirk of his lips.

"You look like your mother," he said. "Clearly, I need not worry about behaving like a gentleman. A guest of Lord Ambrose... a guest." The last was said with such lasciviousness that it was not a mystery what he believed her relationship with Lord Ambrose truly was.

Prim didn't bother confirming or denying his ugly suspicions. She'd learned the hard way that acknowledging such accusations only incited more talk instead of dashing it.

"Perhaps you'd like to be my guest?" he continued. "We'll see just how far the apple falls from the tree."

"Why would she want to come stay with you? You're mean and careless... and stupid!" Rowan shouted.

The man's eyebrows shot up. "I've a mind to show you just how mean I can be!"

Prim shoved Rowan behind her. "If you touch him, I swear to God above, I will see you dead."

He laughed then. "Maybe you're not like your mother, after all! I heard her once telling one of her fellow whores that she'd see you and your sister earning your keep in the family business. Tell me, are your rates comparable?"

"Leave us be," Lila shouted. "You're a horrid man and you don't know our mother and you don't know us. You've no reason to be so cruel other than just being a miserable person inside!"

He glanced at Lila then, finally taking notice of her. "Seems I'm not the only one whose bastards are coming home to roost." With that, he whirled the fearsome mount around and galloped away, the horse's hoofbeats echoing behind him.

"What did he mean by that?" Rowan asked.

"He meant nothing, Ro. He's just a mean-spirited and hateful man, just as Lila said. But come! We should return to the house," Prim said, hoping that her tremulous voice would be laid at the door of her fright from the horse.

"Are you injured, Prim?" Lila asked softly. "I can run and fetch Lord Ambrose to come for you if you need me to."

"No, Lila. I'm not injured," Prim replied, offering what she hoped was a reassuring smile as she looped one arm over Lila's slim shoulders. "Just a bit startled is all. The walk will calm my nerves." *And give her an opportunity to figure out what in the world she would say to Lord Ambrose.* He had to have known that one of his neighbors, assuming that the gentleman lived nearby, was either Rowan's sibling or father. He certainly had some explaining to do, regardless.

Chapter Ten

P RIM FOUND HIM in his study. It was the antithesis of everything she wanted to do and ought to do, but it was imperative that she speak to him alone and away from Arabella's incessant prattling. She also didn't want to worry Hyacinth. The last thing she wanted was for her sister to fret herself into another attack like the one she'd had at the inn. The brief walk back to the house had been spent ruminating on how best to approach the situation, on what dangers, if any, that gentleman, whoever he was, posed to Rowan. She would have answers.

As she charged in, her breath ragged from the quick pace they'd kept on their walk home, she noted the arched brow as his gaze scanned her. It was followed by a resigned sigh. It seemed he had some experience with women being displeased with him, enough to accurately read the signs and symptoms, at any rate.

"I assume there is something that displeases you, Miss Collier?" he asked, placing the quill he'd been scribbling with on the desk and closing the leather-bound book before him.

Prim had debated how to broach the subject. Ultimately, she had decided that speaking plainly and to the point would be the best option. "Is that blackguard related to Rowan?"

To his credit, Lord Ambrose did not feign innocence or ignorance. Nor did he dismiss the very abrupt question she'd just lobbed at him in a tone that could best be described as impertinent.

"Never mind," she said. "You don't need to answer that. It's glaringly apparent that he is. A person would have to be blind to miss such a marked resemblance!"

"How is that you happened to encounter Lord Samford?" he asked softly. "He's hardly the sort I'd welcome into this house."

"Lord Samford? That's his name?"

Lord Ambrose rose and moved past her to close the door. "Let's step out onto the terrace, Miss Collier, where we can discuss this without the servants overhearing, if you please."

Realizing that it was likely a wise course of action, Prim nodded her agreement and followed him to a set of wide glass doors that led outside. The terrace overlooked the park and gardens. Under any other circumstances, it would have been lovely. As it was, her mind was focused solely on the welfare of the children she'd just ushered upstairs to play.

The minute the door closed behind them, she began peppering him with questions. "Who is this man? Why is he the 'sort' you'd never welcome into this house and what will this mean for poor Rowan?"

"His name is Fredrick Hamilton. His father passed away two years back, around the same time my own did. If it is possible, they are even more scandalous than my father was… they are all certainly more lacking in conscience," he answered. "His stepmother was the sister to Lord Harrelson whom you may have heard of."

She had. Anyone living in England had heard of the high and mighty lord who'd taken to peddling flesh like a Seven Dials abbess. That was Rowan's family? He was connected to some of the worst and most scandalous criminals in all of Britain? And she'd literally brought him to their doorstep.

"Is it just the scandal that taints them or is there something about Lord Samford himself that inspires your distaste for him?" she asked. If the man's behavior toward her was any indication, he was the worst sort of villain.

"It's very likely that he had knowledge of, if not involved to his eyeballs, in the schemes of his uncle. Then there's the matter of his brother and half-sister. If she was his half-sister. Legally, she was recognized by the previous Lord Samford though Lady Samford's fidelity has always been suspect."

"And what was this relationship?" Prim asked with a frown.

"It's believed that they were lovers," he answered bluntly. "Believed by most, known by me. I saw them together. They would sneak about on the estate and I stumbled upon them in rather compromising positions more than once. And quite honestly, Miss Collier, there are men and women who exist in this world who are simply not good. They are not capable of being good. Mr. Severne is one. Lord Samford is another. How is that you encountered him?"

"He was riding. Rowan was climbing a tree and Lila was picking wildflowers. I sat on a stone fence to watch them. I suppose he came up too quickly to abort the jump," she replied. Her hands were clenched together in front of her. She was too stoic for wringing them like some helpless miss, but the urge was there nonetheless.

"Jump? He was riding that beast of his?"

She was unprepared for the question. "If by that you mean a very large, very black and very terrifying stallion, then yes. I was very lucky to have heard him approaching when I did. I threw myself to the ground and aligned myself as closely to the fence as possible. I was very fortunate. Will that good fortune continue, Lord Ambrose?"

"What do you mean, Miss Collier?"

"Is this man a threat to Rowan?"

WHAT SHE HAD described filled him with absolute horror. She had very nearly been killed by Samford's reckless disregard for anyone other than himself. Of course, if he hadn't been so adamant in his desire to avoid the temptation of her company, he might have warned her about him and spared her both the terrifying incident and now the uncertainty regarding the questions of Rowan's parentage.

"You will be safe here, Miss Collier, and your siblings will be safe here. I give you my word on that."

"It isn't as simple as Rowan being related to him, is it? He is Rowan's father isn't he?" she demanded. "He made a comment—" She'd broken off abruptly, clearly more upset by it than she wished to reveal.

Fear knotting his gut, Cornelius asked, "What did he say to you?"

After a long pause, the silence growing taut between them, she turned her face away and said in a clipped tone, "He said that I looked like my mother. Clearly he knew her and knew her well."

He had the distinct feeling much more had been said than that. "He will not bother you again. I know that he rides across my lands from time to time, despite knowing it is frowned upon. I will send word that it is to halt immediately. And if he should attempt to approach you, your sister or the children, you must tell me immediately. I will take care of this issue, Miss Collier, I assure you."

"Did you know before we came here?"

It was an accusation and he knew the answer would displease her, but he was unwilling to lie to her. "Nicholas pointed out to me the strong resemblance between Rowan and Samford that night after you all left the inn. But it was only a suspicion, it was not confirmed."

"Now it is," she snapped. "We've brought Lila here on the promise it would improve her life and now we may very well have placed Rowan in danger. You should have told us, Lord Ambrose, before we came here. You should have let us make that decision on our own, with all of the facts laid out before us."

He knew that. He'd known it all along. But it had been selfishness that had kept him from it. He'd wanted her there, along with Lila and the others. Still, he could admit, at least to himself, that everything he had done had been an effort to get her close enough that he might explore the feelings she stirred in him. Then he might determine what course of action to take in regards to them.

"Yes, I should have. But I did not. All I can do now is make amends and be certain that you are all safe from any harm," Cornelius promised. It was more than obligation. Keeping her safe was imperative for him in ways that he could not fathom, much less explain. "I can assure you, Miss Collier, that if I had thought the danger posed by the question of Rowan's paternity outweighed, in any measure, the benefits you would all receive from being here, I would have told you."

"Therein lies the problem, Lord Ambrose. It wasn't your decision to make. I understand that you are Lila's half-brother, but we are her family. We are the ones who've been there for her from the moment of her birth, working and sacrificing to keep body and soul together after our mother's death. I understand that a man in your position is not used to having his authority questioned but, in this regard, any decisions regarding Lila's welfare will be deferred to Hyacinth and me. As it has always been."

Cornelius watched her turn, skirts whirling, and march from the terrace and through the room beyond. She was in high dudgeon and he could not blame her for it. He'd made a tactical error and he could only pray that it would not cost him further.

Chapter Eleven

"THE NERVE OF that man!" Prim snapped.

"Lord Ambrose or Lord Samford?" Hyacinth asked pertly.

Both. "Lord Samford, of course. That knowing smirk when he said I looked like Mother—and the dirty look of him as he made those remarks about being Lord Ambrose's guest! I despise men, Hyacinth. I despise them all."

Hyacinth sighed and patted the settee beside her. "Come and sit, Prim."

Prim knew what that meant. It would be one of Hyacinth's infamous heart to heart chats where hard truths were uttered in the gentlest of tones. She was in no mood for it. "What?"

"Mother was, without question, one of the most beautiful women I have ever beheld," Hyacinth began. "And I say that objectively, my vision not colored by my love for her. Because I see her faults as well. She was as weak as she was beautiful. She fell in love with every man who batted an eye at her because she was constantly looking for a man to save her when men, by and large, are only ever out to save themselves."

Prim blinked at her sister's plain speaking. Typically, Hyacinth rarely ever spoke of their mother's shortcomings. "Is this supposed to make me feel better, Hy?"

"Prim, you do look like our mother. You have her delicate features, her lovely hair, the same spark is in your eye that she had, and of course, her enviable figure... what you do not have is her same weakness. In that regard, Prim, you are as unlike her as night is from day. But that may be a weakness in and of itself. Do not be so opposed to help that you refuse it on principles we cannot afford."

Prim rose and paced the floor. "I haven't. We're here, aren't we? Against both of our better judgments, I might add."

"Yes, but not without resentment, Prim. You're waiting for him to show you the ugliness he holds inside him, ugliness that you believe exists not because of his own behavior but what you've seen in others. Do you truly believe Lord Ambrose is anything like Lord Samford?"

Of course, she didn't. But perhaps she wanted him to be. It would make it easier to despise him, easier to harden her feelings toward him. Every time she looked at him, she was struck anew by how handsome he was. But more than that, she was swayed by the kindness she sensed in him, by this unimaginable need inside her to be closer to him. He had granted them an opportunity to better their lives when no one else ever had. Even the employment offered by Lady Linden had been nothing more than a feather in the woman's cap, something she could boast about to the other ladies of the parish when it came time for them to sit around a tea table and compare their good works. It was an unkind thought, but not an untrue one.

"I dislike being beholden to him, Hyacinth. I cannot change that. I dislike being beholden to any man." Pride was the one thing she'd always possessed in abundance and it was the one thing they could least afford.

"Beholden implies he expects repayment or some sort of reciprocal arrangement, Prim," Hyacinth countered. "And I think you do him a disservice to assume that what he has done thus far and will do in the future is anything more than generosity. Your pride will wound you both if you are not careful."

Hyacinth rose to her feet. "I'm going to check on Lila and Rowan. They are both far more observant than I would like and I am terribly afraid that after their encounter with Lord Samford today that one or the pair of them might put two and two together."

Guilt washed through Prim that she hadn't thought to do the same. "It was a very brief encounter. I'm certain they'll be fine."

"I'm certain they will, too, one way or another," Hyacinth replied as she sailed out of the door to their suite.

Alone, Prim put her hands over her face and tried to make some sense of her feelings for and about Lord Ambrose. It wasn't as if she knew him very well, after all. She'd spoken to him that day at the cottage, in the carriage as they brought Hyacinth home that night and now here, after their arrival. Three encounters with the man did not account for the strange tingling she felt when he looked at her or for her desire to avoid him so desperately. Why was he different from any other man she'd ever known? He certainly didn't fawn over her or fall over himself as other men of her acquaintance had. Nor did he grasp at her and try to touch her inappropriately the moment they were alone. He'd never been less than a gentleman. It was that which set him apart and that which also made him a danger to her.

Prim rose once more and crossed to the window, looking out. She didn't do well with uncertainty and they were in a position where everything was uncertain. Their home was unfamiliar, their position in the world altered but in ways she couldn't fully comprehend yet, and all of that had been wrought by a man whose nature was unpredictable to her.

A soft and unsatisfyingly mild curse escaped her lips.

FREDRICK HAD RETURNED home in a temper. What the hell were Isabelle Collier's bastards doing at Avondale? Of course, he knew that Isabelle had kept company with the elder Lord Ambrose. Had he gotten a bastard on her, as well then? Thinking of the dark-haired younger girl, it was possible. It still didn't explain why the current Lord Ambrose had fetched all his father's sins to the bosom of the family home.

Another and far more disquieting thought formed in Fredrick's mind as he stalked toward his study and the brandy that awaited him there. Perhaps, it hadn't been Ambrose's idea to bring them there at all. Perhaps, they had inveigled their way there through their own machinations. He'd always been a stickler. Despite the gossip and that one incident where he'd shot the bounder, Randall Grantham, Cornelius Garrett had spent the entirety of his life avoiding scandal. Was that what prompted their invitation to Avondale? Were they blackmailing the man? Was he next?

"That's it," Fredrick muttered aloud as he poured the brandy. "That chit and her bastard siblings mean to bleed Ambrose dry and once they've done it, they'll come for me next."

He thought of the Wyverne girl and all her lovely money slipping through his fingers. Between his own siblings' wild behavior, Harrelson's flesh peddling, his stepmother's blatant infidelities, having his own bastard living next door would be the nail in his proverbial coffin when it came to snagging her. Lame, with a figure that some would call *ample,* she represented his last hope of obtaining the necessary wealth to keep his estates afloat and avoiding the public humiliation of selling off parcels of land while bailiffs swept the house for valuables. He'd put a pistol ball in his brain before he'd suffer that indignity and since death by suicide held no allure for him, that truly wasn't an option.

So get rid of him. The insidious whisper in his mind sounded shockingly like his late uncle-by-marriage, Lord Harrelson. It was certainly what he would have done. Harrelson had never let a little thing like murder or infanticide stand in his way when it came to getting what he wanted. He'd kill the lot of them and Ambrose, too, if he got in the way, Freddy decided.

An expression of determination, of resignation, crossed his face as he sipped the spirits and pondered the best method to murder his own flesh and blood.

Chapter Twelve

BEFORE THE DINNER hour, a selection of gowns had been sent to their rooms. It was obvious from the cut of them and the color that they belonged to Lady Arabella. It was also equally obvious, that while finer than anything either Prim or Hyacinth owned, the styles were at least two decades out of fashion. Still, they donned them without complaint. If that was what Arabella wanted them to wear for dinner and if it would maintain the peace, then that is what they would do. Or so Prim thought, until she had the gown on and caught sight of her reflection.

"Good heavens. I'm spilling out everywhere. I look like an untended dairy cow!"

Hyacinth laughed. "You look lovely. Bountiful, yes, but lovely. And I've seen fine ladies wearing significantly less."

"We're not fine ladies. We're the maids who help fine ladies don their scandalous garments," Prim shot back. "I've never had so much of myself on display in the entirety of my life."

"No doubt Lord Ambrose will be so far away at the grand table it will not matter," Hyacinth reassured. "And poor myopic Lady Arabella will simply squint at the very lovely blur you make."

Prim did laugh at that. Recalling how the elderly woman had peered at them through a quizzing glass she kept draped about her neck, she couldn't help but be amused.

"All right. Let us go below and face what will surely be a humiliating evening. Perhaps our manners will be so atrocious they'll never invite us to dine with the again."

"Our manners are fine. Mother made certain we'd know what forks to use and how to interact at a fine table, whether we ever sat at one or not," Hyacinth replied indignantly.

"But they don't know that," Prim said conspiratorially.

"I refuse to pretend to be more of a bumpkin than I am just so you may retain your hermit-like tendencies," Hyacinth rejoined as they left their chambers and descended the stairs.

The children were dining in the nursery that night in the company of one of the maids who was, based on the peals of laughter they'd heard coming from the room, their new favorite person. It had been Lord Ambrose's suggestion and Prim could only assume that it was because he meant to discuss the situation relating to Rowan and Lord Samford.

They found Lady Arabella in the drawing room and, much to Prim's chagrin, Lord Ambrose was with her. They appeared to be in a rather heated conversation. Or rather, Lady Arabella appeared to be having a conversation and Lord Ambrose appeared to be having a quietly heated response to it. His expression could only be described as annoyed.

Immediately, Arabella stopped haranguing him for whatever it was and said in a lilting tone, "There you are, my dears! Heavens, those gowns look lovely on you! Naturally, they won't do for company but for dinner at home with just the four of us, they are quite all right. I was just telling dear Cornelius here that I must get you both to Bath for fittings with a decent mantua maker. London would be better, but that would require more than a day trip and, sadly, Cornelius has turned off London altogether since the scandal!"

"What scandal is that?" Hyacinth asked softly.

"Oh, my dear! He had to shoot that awful man who had tried to murder dear Viola! You've met his half-brother, Nicholas Warner, of course. Well, Viola is his wife. And, of course, she was married before and has the most delightful little boy, Tristan, but her late husband was a terrible sort. So scandalous. Even my dear late nephew, poor Cornelius' father, would have naught to do with him. And heaven knows my nephew was no stickler for morality! But I digress, Randall, the bounder's nephew—"

"Enough!" Lord Ambrose shouted, rising to his feet. "It's an old scandal and hardly worth repeating. I killed a man, but he was one who needed killing. That is all that need be said of it. Now, we shall go into dinner."

There was a finality to his tone. It was clearly not a subject that he wished to address and certainly not one that he wished to have discussed in front of him. That much was obvious from his shuttered expression and the firm set of his shoulders as he stalked forward and offered Lady Arabella his arm.

Prim fell into step behind him, Hyacinth at her side. She felt a pang of sympathy for him because she had no doubt that if he had killed a man, there had been little other option for him. But it was also quite clear that the weight of it pressed heavily upon him. And Lady Arabella was the oldest and silliest goose in all of England, it seemed, for not being able to pick up on it.

"What do you suppose that's all about?" Hyacinth whispered.

"We're all entitled to our pasts, Hy. And our secrets," she replied.

The dining room was beautiful, but not nearly so grand as they might have imagined. The table was small and circular, surrounded by upholstered chairs. There must have been numerous leaves for the table as there were at least eight additional chairs to match that were placed along the walls of the room. The table itself was laid with crystal and intricately-carved silverware, as well as fine porcelain. A small centerpiece of various hothouse flowers was nestled in the middle of the table. It was a low centerpiece, one that would not obscure anyone's vision of her. As obscene as her gown was standing, it was so much worse when seated.

She would be directly across from him. Based on the rules of etiquette as she understood them, Lady Arabella would be to his right because of her rank. Hyacinth would be to his left because of her status as the eldest of the two of them. Which meant that she, Prim, would spend the evening sitting directly across from him with her bosom on display like a tavern wench. *For heaven's sake.*

When they were seated, the first course was served. The soup was divine, but she hadn't expected less. As she savored each bite, she felt the weight of his gaze on her. It created a pleasant warmth in her, an awareness and tension between them that surely even Arabella must have picked up on. As Hyacinth glanced from one of them to the other, Prim was well aware that her sister had detected it.

As if to break whatever spell had been cast, Hyacinth directed his attention away from Prim for the moment. "What do you intend to do about this Lord Samford, Lord Ambrose?"

"I have already written him and expressed in no uncertain terms that he is not to step foot on my lands again, for any reason. And that if, at any time, he importunes anyone who is a guest here, he will be forced to deal with me directly," he said.

"You surely cannot mean you would challenge him to a duel?" Prim demanded.

"I can mean that, Primrose. And I will, should it prove necessary. I am hoping that for once in his miserable life, Lord Samford will choose to do the decent thing and simply let that be the end of it," he said simply.

"What in the world is all of this about?" Lady Arabella demanded. "I feel as if the lot of you are speaking in riddles."

"It was nothing, Aunt Arabella," Lord Ambrose lied. "Just a minor misunderstanding with Lord Samford today. He's forgotten how to mind his manners and speak to ladies. It's taken care of."

Prim knew instinctively that he didn't wish to say anything to Arabella because Arabella was patently incapable of keeping a secret. The woman prattled on incessantly about everything.

Peeking from under her lashes, she stared back at him, at his chiseled features and the sweep of his dark hair over his forehead. It made her heart flutter uncomfortably. Picking up her glass, she made to sip her wine and then immediately thought better of it. Attributing her reaction to the large quantities of wine that flowed freely with the meal, while patently untrue, offered her a respite from the dreaded truth of her attraction to him. Prim put her glass down decisively.

"Is the wine not to your liking?" he asked.

No. It isn't. I might become a drunkard and throw myself at your feet. "The wine is delicious, my lord. But neither my sister nor I are used to imbibing quite so freely. I think it best to proceed with a bit of caution."

"Oh, my goodness. Yes. Yes, indeed!" Arabella gushed. "I must say, Miss Primrose, both you and your elder sister show remarkable good sense. So very unlike many of the young women of my acquaintance. A bunch of silly gooses. Geese? Oh, dear. I can't think of which is correct! Do you know?"

"I think it hardly warrants conversation," Lord Ambrose said as he beckoned to the footman. "Have a pot of tea fetched for the Misses Collier."

"Thank you, my lord," Prim said stiffly, once more feeling out of sorts at his thoughtfulness. It reminded her of her earlier conversation with Hyacinth about the true nature of the man and how much she wronged him by treating his every word and gesture as if it were suspect.

"We are very nearly family. I find it preposterous that we should stand on such formality here. You must call me Cornelius, or Ambrose if you prefer it," he said.

Ambrose. She would not call him by his given name. That was too intimate by far.

"And you must call us by our given names, my lord—Ambrose," Hyacinth interjected. "It would be much more convenient than constantly wondering which Miss Collier was being addressed."

"That is all well and good," Arabella began, "But it cannot be entertained in company. If we were to have guests, they would think it most irregular. I cannot even imagine what sort of household they would presume us to be!"

"We are very unlikely to have guests, so I daresay it will not matter," Ambrose replied. "As to being in company and also seeing to your wardrobes, I have made arrangements to see you all to Bath the day after tomorrow. Nicholas will be joining us there so that he might offer advice on procuring an appropriate pair of spectacles for you, Hyacinth. With the correct lenses, we may be able to avoid future spells such as the one you suffered at the inn."

"Oh, no! That's too much, my lord. Really! Since I've not been doing all the sewing like I was, I haven't had another one—"

"Thank you, Ambrose," Prim interjected, cutting Hyacinth's protests short. Of all the things he'd paid for and of all the things that he was willing to be so generous about, that was the one that she desired above all things. "It will be lovely to see Hyacinth in her new spectacles and to know that my sister's health is finally being attended to in a proper fashion."

⚘

CORNELIUS WAS RELIEVED that it wouldn't be a battle to see to the elder Miss Collier's vision issues. Had the need been reversed and if it was Primrose who required spectacles, he doubted that her response would have been to acquiesce so easily. They would order clothing for all of them, get books and toys for the children, and while there, he would pay a visit to the Vale townhouse. His neighbor, a man who had his own axe to grind with the Samford, Lord Wolverton had married Vale's adopted sister and they were currently all in town together. While he and Wolverton had not always seen eye to eye, under the circumstances, he was fairly certain he could count on the other man's assistance.

It was an odd thing to look forward to going into society. He was so used to being gossiped about, to stares and whispers, that he had avoided such things for himself. But he found himself eager to spoil the Colliers a bit. Not just Rowan and Lila, though having heard their laughter echoing through the halls earlier, their exuberance for life was infectious. To see Primrose and her sister in gowns that were made specifically for them, likely something they'd never experienced in their lives, was terribly appealing.

The meal continued, each course served and cleared as they continued to converse about all the things that would need to be done for the children. Rowan's love of horses made him a prime candidate for riding lessons. Lila would need to learn as well though it was clear that her heart wasn't truly in it. A governess would be hired but he had not wanted to do that without the input of the elder sisters. He'd stepped on their toes enough already.

As the last course was cleared, Arabella rose. "We will adjourn to the drawing room for dessert and leave Cornelius to his brandy and cheroots."

He didn't want them to. The urge to countermand Arabella's edict and join them was just strong enough to give him pause. It wasn't just that he was enjoying the company, or the conversation. *It was her.*

For the entirety of the meal, he hadn't been able to tear his gaze from her. They were both beautiful. But there was something about Primrose Collier that drew him, that called to something inside him. Indulging his attraction to her, even in such a harmless way as extending his opportunity to look upon her in a purely platonic setting, was imprudent at best. At worst, it would only weaken his resolve to resist the temptation of her. Of course, it might have been the height of conceit to think she would welcome any advances from him or that she might be equally tempted. He'd made the decision that, at some point in the future, she would be his wife, but not before she was ready to be. He didn't want to do anything that would force her hand and make her resent him.

Cornelius had prided himself on being the kind of man who would never force himself on an unwilling woman or seducing an innocent who might not fully understand what was happening. He knew any number of men who called themselves gentlemen who would not hesitate to indulge in such practices, but that was not him. Still, there was something in Primrose's reaction to him that made him think, perhaps, she might not be unaffected by him. She was cautious with him, aware of him in much the same way he was aware of her.

"Unless, of course, you'd care to join us, Cornelius," Arabella offered.

There was something in his aunt's tone that alerted him. Even more curious, she'd actually paused to allow him to respond. He met her gaze and noted that, while she still squinted, there was a smug and knowing tilt to her wrinkled lips. The old woman, blind as a bat and silly as a goose, had figured him out.

"No, Aunt Arabella," he declined. "While I have no interest in cheroots, as you well know, I do have some things to attend to and a brandy sounds wonderful."

He rose as the women did and bowed his head in their directions. "Good evening, Hyacinth, Primrose."

They walked out and his eyes followed them. It was going to be difficult maintaining any semblance of indifference, but he had no choice. If he allowed himself to slip, even once, and think of her as his, he'd never have the strength to let her go. And despite his determination to have her, it was obvious to him that Primrose was equally determined not to be had.

Chapter Thirteen

I T WAS THE wee hours of the morning and Prim couldn't sleep. The bed was comfortable, spacious, and warm. Three things she'd never experienced simultaneously. Yet she'd tossed and turned from the moment she had laid down. Was it the strangeness of having a bed to herself for the first time in her life? Their new and unusually luxurious surroundings? Or was it Lord Ambrose, lying in his own bed under the same roof?

Prim, despite the small untruths she'd clung to at dinner, by her nature, was honest with herself and with others. It was the latter. She'd been aware of his gaze upon her all during dinner. She'd been equally aware that the warm feelings that had flooded her had only a little to do with the wine she'd imbibed. He was too attractive by far, and it was clear that his interest in her was rather marked. If she were to be entirely honest, she would admit that she'd been unaccountably drawn to him from the first moment he'd entered their small cottage.

He was not the first handsome man she'd ever encountered, to be sure, nor the first to express interest in her. But she found him compelling in a way that unsettled her, because it seemed to be somehow beyond her control. Frustrated, she tossed and turned for a few moments more before giving up entirely.

Pushing back the bedclothes, Prim rose and reached for the wrapper draped across the foot of the bed. Shrugging into it, she belted it tightly as she slid her feet into her worn slippers. She didn't wake Hyacinth. The last thing she wanted was to face her sister's curious expressions and answer any questions about what might be happening between her and Lord Ambrose.

Nothing. Nothing was happening between her and Lord Ambrose.

Perhaps if she uttered that to herself frequently enough she could will it into being.

To combat her wayward thoughts and her sleeplessness, Prim did what she always did. She went to check on Rowan and Lila. Their rooms were on the floor above, flanking the nursery and schoolroom. Easing out into the hallway, she noted that there was enough moonlight filtering in from the large Palladian windows at either end of the corridor to light her way. Making her way to the stairs, she climbed them slowly, keeping one hand on the banister at all times. The last thing she needed was to trip, fall and wake the entire household.

When she reached the nursery, she opened the door and looked around. The small schoolroom that had been set up in front of the windows was perfect for the children. Many of the toys that were present were for children much younger than Rowan and Lila, but they were also ages old. Had they belonged to Lord Ambrose? It was strange to imagine him as a small boy. He would have been beautiful, of course, just as Lila was.

Easing toward the room to the right, she opened the door as quietly as possible. Lila was sleeping peacefully. Lying on her back, her dark hair carefully braided and draped over the pillow, it was one of the few times she would ever look tidy. Smiling at the thought, Prim closed the door and crossed to the other room where Rowan slept. Unlike his sister, he was sprawled across the bed with arms and legs tangled in the covers and a soft snore escaping his parted lips. Easing inside, Prim smoothed the covers over him once more. It was a losing battle, but she at least wanted to do what she could to ensure that he'd be warm through the night.

Tiptoeing quietly from the room, she closed the door behind her and left the nursery to return to her own chambers. If she were brave enough, she'd go below stairs to the library and read. But despite Lord Ambrose's welcome and Lady Arabella's assurances that they should treat Avondale as their home, she wasn't quite prepared to make so free of it yet.

She was halfway down the stairs, watching each step carefully, when she became aware of another presence. Lifting her head, she found Lord Ambrose standing at the foot of the stairs.

"Is everything all right?" he asked softly.

"Yes," she replied, her own voice couched just as low in the stillness around them. "I only went to check in on the children."

"And are they resting more comfortably in their new environment than you are?"

Prim blushed. "We are very comfortable here, my lord. Our accommodations are lovely and will meet all of our needs beautifully."

"I see," he said, as he lifted one foot and placed it on one of the steps before him and leaned against the banister.

It was a masculine pose, one that drew her gaze to the firmness of his thighs still encased in evening breeches. Prim looked away, once more uncomfortably aware of the warmth that suffused her in his presence.

"If it isn't your room that keeps you from sleeping, Primrose, what is it?"

"Lord Ambrose—"

"Cornelius," he corrected. "I watched you at dinner. But then you know that, don't you?"

Her breath shuddered out. "This cannot be. Whatever this awareness is between us, we cannot indulge it."

"But you acknowledge that it exists?"

She sighed wearily and crossed her arms over her chest. "Yes. I admit it. I find you attractive. But that doesn't mean I have to act upon it. I am not a slave to my impulses... and neither are you."

He no longer leaned nonchalantly. He pushed away from the banister and climbed the few steps between them until he stood on the one directly below her. He was still a bit taller than her but they were close enough to being eye to eye that she found herself trapped by his gaze and unable to look away.

"I have never been a slave to my impulses. My entire life has been devoted to ignoring them, in fact. But until I met you, truly I wasn't aware that I had impulses," he admitted gruffly. "Never in my life have I found myself so captivated by someone with just one look. I keep telling myself not to act upon it. Not to acknowledge it. And then I find myself alone with you here, and good sense flees."

She could smell the brandy he'd imbibed, not so strongly to imply that he was drunk, but enough to know he'd indulged in it. "Your good sense, but not my own," she replied. "I won't be your mistress."

"I never asked you to be," he retorted quickly.

"I am not my mother. I am not a woman so weak and desperate for love that I will lower myself to be used by a man while convincing myself he is my savior. I may be attracted to you, I may feel drawn to you in some way... and our proximity is a complication. But not an insurmountable one. I only have to remind myself of what there is to lose."

"And what is that?"

"Pride. Dignity. Self-respect," she answered.

He lifted his hand so that the backs of his fingers traced the curve of her cheek. "I have those things in abundance myself. I am finding them to be poor company."

Perhaps it was the darkness around them, the hush of the large house as all its other inhabitants slept that heightened the feeling of intimacy. There was no escaping it.

The touch of his hand on her face was nearly her undoing. It was soft, tempting. The gentleness of it had her leaning into it, into him, pressing her cheek more firmly against his hand. In return, he cupped her face gently and tilted it up. Somehow, he'd stepped closer to her, until only scant inches separated them. Her gaze dropped to his lips, framed by the shadow of whiskers. She wanted to feel his lips on hers, she realized. She wanted him to kiss her more than anything and, because of that, she knew she could not allow it to happen. Prim turned her head, looking away from him and breaking the spell. "We cannot do this."

"No," he said. "We cannot."

There was something in his tone, anger and resentment, but above all, disappointment. She dared a glance at him. Their gazes met for just a second, locked, and then he broke away. Abruptly, he turned on the stairs and walked away from her, never even glancing back.

Shaken, as much by that delicate touch as she was at the anguish she'd heard in his voice, Prim watched his retreating form for just a moment and then fled quickly to her own room.

AMBROSE ENTERED HIS chamber and only by sheer force of will avoided slamming the door. All of his determination to ignore his attraction to her had vanished in a single second. Alone in a darkened corridor, he'd descended on her like some unscrupulous Lothario. Seeing her there in the moonlight, the silvery glow of it bathing her skin and highlighting the dark fall of her hair, he'd been entranced. It could be the brandy. Heaven knew he'd imbibed far more of it than was wise in the hopes of numbing his lusts and falling into a dreamless sleep.

Her words flitted through his mind. They were connected, far more than she realized. They shared a bond few others would understand. The both of them were equally determined to be as unlike their respective and very fallible parents as possible. She was haunted by the specter of her mother's dishonor just as he was tormented by the fear that he was, at his heart, the same sort of reprobate his father had been.

Biting back a curse, he stripped off his evening clothes and let them fall to the floor. His valet would find them in the morning and be utterly beside himself, but Cornelius was beyond caring. He felt bound by them, constrained.

The cool air bathed his skin, offering some respite from the lust and brandy-fueled fever that consumed him. He'd come so close to kissing her there on those stairs. He'd wanted it more than he'd wanted his next breath. If he were entirely honest with himself, he still did. Every time he saw her, was near her, he felt it more, that connection between them. And with just enough brandy in him to muddy his judgment, he'd very nearly done the unthinkable. One taste of her lips and he'd be a man lost.

Scrubbing his hands over his face, Cornelius made his way to the wash basin and poured some of the chilled water into the bowl. Splashing it over his face, he struggled to regain some sense of equilibrium. He was more shaken by the encounter than he wished to admit, and was torn between wishing more had occurred and wishing it had not occurred at all.

She'd be on guard against him, as well she should. One of them needed to retain some sense and, at least for the moment, he clearly was not capable. Seeking his bed, Cornelius slid beneath the coverlet and prayed for a dreamless sleep, one that would not be haunted by visions of her as every night had been since first they met. But as he lay there, staring up into the darkness, sleep would not come.

"WHAT DID YOU discover?" Freddy asked. He'd set one of the footmen to charm a maid at Avondale and find out whatever he could about the plans of Lord Ambrose and the brood of bastards he'd taken up with.

"They're to go to Bath day after tomorrow, my lord. But only for the day. They're to set out early on what I'm told is a shopping excursion," the footman said. He was a greedy and ambitious fellow. It was the very reason that Freddy had selected him for the task. "Seems those young women showed up with naught but rags to wear and the children, too."

Freddy shrugged. He'd seen them, of course. He knew what they were wearing. Gowns too old and so often mended that it was a miracle even the strongest thread might still hold them together. But the girl had been a beauty. Was she as lusty as her mother had been, he wondered? It was tempting to have her, but risky.

"Can you get into their stables without being seen?" Freddy asked.

"I can," the footman said. "What do you want me to do, my lord?"

"Loosen the pins on the wheels of their coach. Not enough for them to notice, but enough that they'll meet with some misfortune on the road. A coach loaded with people and a snapped wheel should eliminate at least one or two of my problems."

"Yes, my lord."

Freddy frowned. "You're being awfully agreeable and yet I haven't even offered you payment for these extra duties. Why is that?"

"The butler is aging, my lord, and soon to be pensioned off. I might only be a servant, but I'm not without ambition," the footman said.

Freddy nodded. "See this task done… the lot of them gone from this earth, and you will have the position you desire. But betray me, tell one soul what we're about, and I will see you in hell."

"Certainly, my lord," the footman answered. "You have my loyalty."

"Your name?"

"Harcourt, my lord."

Freddy smiled. "At least it'll sound grand when you're a butler. The elder girls need to die, but kill the boy first. I need him gone before I marry the Wyverne girl. If the carriage accident isn't successful, a more direct approach will need to be taken. Do you understand, Harcourt?"

The footmen with lofty aspirations nodded and slipped from the room.

Freddy reached for a decanter of brandy and poured himself a generous portion. It was a minor setback. Once the bastard was wiped from the face of the earth and they had nothing to hold over his head, he could proceed as planned. He would not fall into the ruin of poverty and misery that his family seemed determined to drive them all into. With his late father's spending and gambling, with Albie and Helena's courtship of gossip and social ruin, they'd all done their damnedest to see the family in penury, ostracized from the very society that they should otherwise have ruled. Whatever the cost, he would see them returned to the position that was rightfully theirs, and nothing and no one would stand in his way.

Chapter Fourteen

PRIM HAD MANAGED to avoid Lord Ambrose for most of the day. She'd even pleaded a headache of her own to get out of going down to dinner. But having spent the entirety of her day hiding in her room, she was restless. Once more, it was late in the evening and she was roaming the halls. If there was a part of her that hoped for another encounter, the more reasonable and fearful part of her quashed it easily enough.

Easing up the staircase as she had the night before, she was at least fully dressed and not wearing a threadbare nightdress and wrapper. Entering the children's rooms, she checked on Rowan first and then on Lila. Outside the door to Lila's room, she heard a masculine voice, deep and rich, followed by her sister's answering giggle.

Dozens of memories, ugly and terrifying, swamped her, flooding her with fear. Fear that she had failed, fear that she had put Lila in the path of a predator, fear that she had misjudged him so thoroughly. But as the conversation on the other side of that door continued, she realized she was once more coloring him with brushes dipped into the foul colors of her own past.

"Do you think Rowan will be a good horseman?" Lila asked, her voice muffled through the door.

"I think he will be a fine horseman," came Ambrose's reply. "I think we may put him on a donkey though. They are as hardheaded as your brother and will be less likely to get into mischief if mischief is what he desires."

"Mischief is all Rowan ever finds!" Lila said emphatically.

Her heart no longer pounding and the bile once more settling in her stomach, Prim knocked softly on the door and Lila bade her enter. Opening that door, she found her sister seated on the floor before the fire, playing with a doll and Lord Ambrose seated before the window.

"I had thought you would already be abed," Prim said.

"I got a new doll," Lila said, holding up the toy with pride. "It was sent from Bath by Dr. Warner and his wife, Viola. They sent Rowan a wooden horse."

"I see," Prim said. "That was very nice of them. Tomorrow, I'll help you and Rowan pen thank you letters to them."

Lila smiled at that and went on playing with her doll. Prim's gaze darted to Lord Ambrose who was looking at her speculatively. "Now, Lila, I think it's time for bed."

"I'll leave you to it then," Ambrose said and rose. He walked over to Lila and kissed the top of her head in an affectionate and easy gesture, one that was completely innocent and made Prim feel ashamed for what she had thought of him.

When he'd gone, she helped Lila change into her nightclothes, braided her sister's hair and tucked her into bed with her new doll at her side.

"Why did you come in, Prim? You know I can get myself ready for bed," Lila asked.

"I do know that you can. But I just want to be sure you're happy here and that you're settling in. Do you like Lord Ambrose, Lila?"

"I do. He's very kind… but he's very lonely, I think. He has sad eyes."

It was an astute observation from the girl. "I think you might be right."

"You thought he was a bad man, doing bad things. That's why you came in here," Lila said.

"I did, but only for a moment," Prim admitted. It was nearly impossible to lie to Lila. The girl had an uncanny ability to see through people.

"Like the bad men that used to come see Mama."

"You cannot possibly remember that!"

"But I do," Lila insisted. "I remember because you'd hug me tighter and make me stand behind you."

Prim blinked against the tears that threatened. "It seems you do remember. Well, it was only a moment of panic. I know he's not like them. But why was he here?"

"To bring me the doll," she said. "Apparently they arrived during dinner."

"Oh," Prim said, everything beginning to make sense. And he wouldn't have trusted the task to a servant because he would have wanted to see Lila's and Rowan's faces when presented with new toys specifically for them, something that was not a broken cast-off from another child. The ugliness of her own mind was a terrible thing to be confronted with.

"Well, now I feel even sillier," Prim said with a smile so patently false it wouldn't fool anyone, especially not her incredibly astute younger sister. "Go to sleep, Lila, and I'll see you in the morning."

Lila reached out and closed her arms around Prim, hugging her tightly for a moment as she whispered, "We're safe here, Prim. Lord Ambrose won't ever do anything bad to us… and he won't let anyone else do anything bad to us either. Do you believe me?"

"I do, Lila. But sometimes I get scared anyway, because there are a lot of bad people in the world, and bad men especially. But I know he isn't one of them."

Lila settled back against the pillows, her doll clutched to her side. What a strange life they had lived that she could look so innocent and yet possess such an uncanny wisdom and ability to read others.

"Good night, Lila. I'll see you in the morning."

"Good night, Prim."

Prim snuffed the candles and slipped from Lila's room. Out in the hallway, she stopped. Ambrose waited for her there, leaning against the banister once more. But his expression was hard, angry. *Hurt*, she realized.

"What did you think I was doing in there?" he demanded.

"I didn't think you were doing anything," she denied in a heated whisper.

"Didn't you? I saw the look on your face, Primrose. I saw the accusation in your eyes. There are half a dozen establishments in London that I can name off the top of my head that cater to the proclivities you just assumed I was inclined to. I'd have hardly had to go to the trouble of bringing you all here and establishing you in my own house!"

Prim looked away, not quite able to meet his gaze, as she said, "I didn't think that of you, Lord Ambrose. But I will admit to having a moment of panic at hearing a man's voice in my sister's room. Not yours. Any man's. By virtue of my own experiences with men at Lila's age, I can attest that not everyone is honorable. But that isn't about you, my lord. That is about us, my sisters and me, and even little Rowan, and where we come from—what we have endured and seen. So you'll forgive me for offending your delicate sensibilities by having a moment of doubt and fear. The simple truth is, it had absolutely nothing to do with you."

⊱❦⊰

IN SO MANY ways, he wanted to hold on to his anger. It made it easier. But her explanation was at once so understandable and so maddening that he could not continue to be angry at her. He understood. For the longest time, after he'd been forced to kill Randall Grantham, any loud noise would make him jump, anything that even sounded remotely like the report of a firearm would have sweat beading on his skin and his heart racing. The invisible scars were always the deepest and those that caused the most lingering pain.

It was maddening to him to know that she'd had no one. That she'd been a young girl, the same age as Lila, and had to fend off the advances of grown men. But there was the other possibility, that perhaps she hadn't been able to fend them off, that she'd been hurt by those same men in ways that he would never be able to understand and never be able to heal.

"I'm not them, Primrose. She is but a child and she is my sister. Those things are sacrosanct to me. Do you believe that?" His tone and his words were demanding, still tinged with the highly charged emotion between them.

"I do believe it," she said, meeting his gaze directly for the first time. "And I am sorry to have offended you."

Silence grew, stretching between them as they stood there in the dimness of the corridor, their eyes locked with one another. The servants would all be below stairs tidying up after supper or seeing to their own meals. They were essentially alone on the third floor but for two children sleeping in the rooms beyond. Finally, when it had drawn out so long that they were forced to break eye contact, Cornelius spoke and uttered something that nearly broke him. "I'm sorry, too. I'm sorry no one was there to protect you when you were Lila's age. There should have been."

"It was never your father," she said. "I don't want you to think poorly of him in that regard. He was always kind to us. Absentminded, but kind. Mother would often have protectors who were gentlemen... and things were better then. We'd live in better places, have clothes and enough food. But it was those times between, when she was forced to work the streets like so many other women, that was when things were really terrible."

"Like when you were living in the Devil's Acre?" Cornelius asked. He knew the answer and, in truth, there was little else that needed to be said between them, but he was reluctant to let the moment end. She was more open, whether out of guilt for what she'd believed of him for that split second outside Lila's room or because the rush of unpleasant memories had left her vulnerable. He couldn't say. He just knew that he was reluctant to see it end. It was probably a terrible thing of him to exploit it, but she was so guarded, it was perhaps the most honest moment that had passed between them.

"Yes," she conceded. "It was while we were there. Nothing ever happened... truly. But there was a night when a man came to our room looking for my mother and she had not yet arrived home. He offered me the coins that were intended for her."

He felt ill at the thought of it. "How old were you?"

"Ten or eleven, I think. Too young for what he was asking but old enough to know that he might get impatient and leave and we needed those coins. I was tempted... very tempted. Desperate. But I couldn't. He had rotting teeth and horrible breath and when I smelled it, I retched. He struck me then, at the precise moment when my mother entered. She threw him out, coin or no coin, and pleaded with me to never be like her. I've tried very hard to live up to that promise, Lord Ambrose. It's never been difficult until now. And that is why I don't think I can stay here with you. When Lila feels more comfortable here, I will leave. I can get a job as a governess or companion and no one would think it odd. Not even Hyacinth, though she'd likely suspect my true motives for leaving."

"I don't want that for you." The protest was instantaneous. No one knew better than he did that women in such positions were vulnerable, far more so than she might suspect. Hadn't his own father seduced one of his governesses?

"But it's what I want for myself, Lord Ambrose. I'm not the sort of girl a man like you marries. And I couldn't live with myself if I allowed myself to be any other sort... so leaving is best. But it'll be a while yet."

She started to walk away but he couldn't let it end like that. Reaching out, he caught her arm. The touch was gentle, just enough to halt her but not enough pressure that she couldn't break free and move on if she chose to.

"I can't be here like this with you," she said simply. "It's tempting fate in ways that neither of us ought to."

"You are precisely the sort of girl a man marries, Primrose. Do you really think it would matter to me?"

"That I have no fortune? That I'm a bastard? That my mother was a whore? That you are a titled gentleman who has a duty to perpetuate the prosperity of your estates? I think if it doesn't matter to you, Lord Ambrose, you are a fool," she said.

"There are worse things to be than a fool."

She laughed at that. "Such as?"

"Alone. Unhappy. Miserable and desperate to feel a connection to another human being. I've felt all of those things, Primrose. I'd take being a fool any day," he said.

"But I wouldn't. And all those ugly things I thought of you to-night... I'll think them again. Because I can't help it. Because that's a part of who I am now. And every time I think them, it would hurt you again. How long would your foolishness last then, my lord? Not very long I suspect. It would all too quickly be replaced with regret. And that's something neither of us should have to live with."

She walked away, moving past him and down the stairs while he stood there, staring at the door to the nursery and trying to fathom how in the world to fix the mess of everything.

Chapter Fifteen

F OR THE SAKE of comfort, they were taking two carriages into Bath. But it wasn't just the comfort of not being packed in atop one another. It was so that he might avoid Miss Primrose Collier and to avoid having to revisit the occurrences of the night before in his mind. On that score, it had failed miserably. He'd been unable to think of anything else. She'd been two nights in his home and on both nights, they'd had unchaperoned encounters in the corridor. And while he hadn't done anything dishonorable, he hadn't told her the truth of his intentions, that he wanted her for his wife. He'd hinted. He'd made veiled references, but she'd dismissed them out of hand obviously not thinking he could be serious. And now if he told her, she would think he was only trying to keep her small family together to benefit Lila.

All the reasons she'd laid out for how inappropriate she would be as a choice for his bride were true. And he gave a damn for none of them.

Regret weighed heavily on him. He regretted what he had done, but just as deeply regretted what he had not. That first night, he'd stood there, close enough to kiss her, the desire to do so burning inside him. And she'd turned her face up to him, clearly anticipating the same. For just a moment, she had wanted that kiss as well, until good sense and reason had prevailed. And the second night, he should have told her. He should have adamantly refused her notion of taking a job as a governess or companion and explained to her in no uncertain terms that her place was with him. But he had not, and now the time for action was past and there was a chasm growing between them.

She'd been distant and aloof at breakfast, to the point that even Hyacinth had sensed it and frowned thoughtfully at the both of them.

At nearly midday, they were well on their way to Bath with Primrose and Hyacinth in the carriage with Rowan and Lila while he rode with Arabella in the second coach. As per her usual, she had filled the silence with her incessant chatter.

"I must say, I rather like the girls. Naturally, Rowan and Lila are a bit much to handle at my age, but they are still delightful children. I am pleased at how well-mannered they are despite their rather unconventional upbringing. I do not think that it will be difficult at all to get the girls launched into society and find them husbands. I assume that is your plan, of course. To find them husbands?"

"I do not have a plan for them, Arabella. They are perfectly capable of making plans of their own," he answered, pinching the bridge of his nose between his thumb and forefinger. She exhausted him. Always. He loved her. A kinder woman he'd never known, and yet, she talked more than any ten people. He honestly didn't know where she found the breath.

"Well you must have, Cornelius! Surely you were not so limited in your vision to have brought them here with no thought as to what they might do? I do hate to be the bearer of bad news, but I am an old woman. I will not live forever. Lila is your sister, so if she remains with you, so long as her parentage is acknowledged, there will be no difficulty there. And Rowan, being a boy child, will be fine. But those young ladies, and despite the nature of their births I do believe that we cannot call them anything less, cannot remain with you given how loosely they are connected to you in a familial way! They must have either husbands or employment in respectable households. Without it, they would be as ruined as their poor mother had been. I blame your father, of course. I did adore him, but he had such short-sightedness when it came to the women who flitted in and out his life, never thinking of the damage he might be doing or what he should do for them to ensure their futures."

"Aunt Arabella, they have been here for only a few days and you are hardly at death's door at the present. Can we not discuss this at some other time once everyone has been properly outfitted and had an opportunity to settle into their new surroundings?"

She huffed out a breath, her disapproval quite obvious. "My eyes are not so keen as they once were, Cornelius, but I am not blind. It is plain to me that you have some sort of attraction to the younger girl. She's lovely enough to warrant it, I daresay. And I can find no fault with her manners or bearing. If you choose to pursue her for an honorable attachment, then I certainly will not interfere. But if you do not have honorable intentions toward her—"

"I have no intentions toward her," he said firmly. "None." It was a lie. He did. But until he had some inkling of how to proceed, the last thing he needed was to have Arabella meddling in it. She'd never be able to keep the information to herself regardless and she would run amok telling everyone.

Her expression relayed just how dubious she found his statements to be. "Really, Cornelius! Intentions or not, can you promise me now that you will never behave in an ungentlemanly manner toward Primrose Collier while she is under your roof?"

"This is not a conversation I mean to have with you, Arabella. Leave it be," he snapped.

"No. I will not. I refused to marry in my life, Cornelius, precisely so no man would ever be able to tell me what to do... that includes you," she replied archly. "Now, I know that you have always lived your life according to convention and to your own moral compass which necessitated doing precisely what your father never would, but I am going to tell you something about the Garrett men. Your father was the aberration. Most of them are singularly monogamous creatures. Their passions can be stirred as easily as any man's, but once their hearts are engaged, all women, save for the objects of their affections, will cease to exist. Would it really be so terrible if Primrose Collier was the object of your affections?"

Not if she might not return those affections. Given what she'd seen of men in her life, what she'd witnessed of her mother's degradation and the difficulties they'd experienced in their lives because of her fall from grace, would she ever be able to harbor such tender feelings for him? He didn't know and, while he'd never have considered himself a coward, he was terrified to find out.

Cornelius did not have an opportunity to offer an answer. There was a loud commotion from the front carriage occupied by the Colliers. The sound of screams, animal and human, as well as the loud crack of splintering wood, rent the air.

Their own carriage halted abruptly, the horses whinnying in protest as they were pulled up sharply. Suddenly, the carriage went careening off to the side.

"Oh heavens! We're all about to be killed. Highwaymen," Arabella gasped. "We've been set upon by highwaymen!"

"We've likely been set upon by a lame horse or a broken wheel," Cornelius said sharply. "Calm yourself, Arabella, while I go check on the others."

Climbing down from the carriage, he surveyed the scene before him with his heart in his throat. The first carriage was on its side. One of the rear wheels had snapped off entirely. The other was still attached but mangled. The front wheels were both tilting inward, the axle obviously destroyed. Broken bits of wood and torn leather littered the road. The horses had broken free entirely and were across the small stream on the opposite bank from where the wreckage lay.

Cursing under his breath, he approached the carriage cautiously. "Primrose? Hyacinth?" he called out. "Are you injured? The children?"

"Rowan and Lila are fine," Hyacinth called out. "But Prim is injured."

His blood ran cold. Carefully climbing up, listening to the wooden side panels groan under his weight, he prayed it would hold long enough to at least get everyone out. Peering down into the destroyed interior of the carriage, he found himself shaken far more than he cared to admit.

Rowan was closest, so Cornelius grasped the boy's arm to give him a hand up. But Rowan, being the excellent climber he'd boasted of, did most of the work on his own. Lila was next. She was just a slip of a thing and light as a feather. Hyacinth was not much bigger than her. Prim would be a different matter altogether because she was completely unconscious.

"How on earth will you get her out?" Hyacinth asked.

"I will. Rest assured," he vowed and then disappeared into the darker interior of the broken vehicle. He crouched beside her and felt her pulse. It was steady and strong beneath his fingers, but the rivulet of blood that trickled along the side of her face was cause for alarm. Head wounds could be tricky.

"Primrose?"

She groaned lightly, a slightly groggy sound. But at least she had some awareness of her surroundings and was responsive. Feeling along her neck and shoulders for any breaks, he then checked her limbs. Finding nothing, he placed his palm against her cheek and said her name again, much more firmly. "Primrose Collier?"

Her eyes opened and then she closed them again with a cry of pain.

"I know it hurts… is it just your head?" he asked.

"Yes," she said on an anguished whisper.

"I'm going to have to put you over my shoulder, Prim, and climb out of the carriage. It overturned. Do you remember?"

"The wheel snapped," she said.

"Yes, it did," he replied. "I need you to stay awake if you can to make sure not to bump your head any further while we extricate ourselves from this."

"I can climb out," she protested. "Just hand me up."

"Are you certain?" he asked. It was impossible to keep his skepticism at bay.

Her eyes opened again, half-mast, and she glared at him beneath her lowered lashes. "I will not be hauled out of here like a sack of grain. I can manage at least part of it on my own."

Why that was so bloody important to her, he didn't know. But if it would get her out of that darkened wreck so that she could be properly examined, he'd do it. "Fine. Let me help you up. You may be lightheaded."

Cornelius helped her to stand. She stumbled slightly, falling against him. He caught her, keeping her from doing greater harm. "Do not push yourself into taking foolish risks, Primrose. Let me carry you."

"The opening is too narrow, Lord Ambrose," she protested. "You'll injure yourself. If you can just push me up to the opening, then Hyacinth and Rowan can help me the rest of the way."

Uneasy with the decision, he said, "Place your hands on my shoulders." When she had done so, he stooped low and clasped his arms about her thighs, lifting her up the open door. Hyacinth and Rowan were there, hauling her up the rest of the way as he continued to support most of her weight. When she'd managed to wiggle through enough, he let go of her. He missed the contact immediately. It wasn't even about the sensual aspect of it, though later he would likely be tormented by the memory of how lithe and supple her thighs had felt beneath his hands. For the moment, however, he just missed being able to touch her, to assure himself that she was well.

When the Colliers had moved away from the topsy-turvy door of the coach, he hoisted himself up and then clambered down to where Arabella was fanning herself exaggeratedly and working her way into a fit of the vapors. Prim was leaning heavily against Hyacinth while Lila pressed a makeshift bandage to the head of the coachman.

"What shall we do, Cornelius?" Arabella began. "We cannot all possibly fit into one carriage and heaven knows that we cannot be left here alone while you ride away for help. We'll be killed on the road by brigands! Brigands, I tell you!"

"No one will be left behind and we can most assuredly all fit in one coach. It will be cramped, but we will not be going far, simply turning around and returning to Avondale," he stated emphatically.

"Forgive me, Lord Ambrose, but we are nearly halfway to Bath and I know that your brother, Dr. Warner, is there with his wife. Might we not go on ahead to him?" Hyacinth asked. "I'm very worried for Prim."

Cornelius dared a glance at her and noted immediately that Primrose's pallor had become ashen and she was not doing at all well. She leaned weakly against her sister and the blood seeping from her wound appeared to be flowing far more freely than any of them had first realized. She was also favoring her left arm, which was quite worrisome. Was it fractured after all? Had he missed it when he did such a cursory exam or had it occurred while she was being hoisted out?

"I will take one of the horses and ride with Prim to Wolfhaven Hall which is but five miles away," he said.

"Without a saddle?" Arabella asked, utterly shocked.

"I've ridden bareback before, though it's been some time," he admitted.

"But these are carriage horses and not used to being ridden!" Arabella protested.

"I'll be careful, Arabella. These particular horses have been used for riding and pulling a coach, so it won't be a completely foreign notion to them. In the meantime, you all will pile into the remaining carriage and make your way on to Bath. You can put the injured driver on the floor where he will be jostled about the least. There is no better man to have at the reins than Collins here," he said, referencing the driver of his own coach who was still working to calm the team of horses that had been attached to his own carriage. "When you arrive, send word to Nicholas and have him come to Wolfhaven to tend Primrose there."

"I'm hardly an invalid," Prim began, but as she stepped away from Hyacinth to make her point, her knees gave way and she began to sink.

Cornelius caught her. "Certainly not an invalid, but even you can admit you are not in the pink of health at this moment."

"I'll get the horses," Rowan said and then went tromping through the creek to collect the two.

"Get back here," Hyacinth shouted.

"They're carriage horses, Hy," the boy protested. "Docile as lambs!"

"Carriage horses that have been through quite a scare and could easily bolt or rear. You'll not go a step further, young man!"

Cornelius was impressed with how stern and parental she sounded. Considering that Hyacinth was only a few inches taller than Rowan, it was doubly impressive. Lowering Prim to the ground where she could lean against the busted carriage, he said, "You will stay there and I will fetch the horses."

She started to nod in agreement, thought better of it at the first small bit of movement and then spoke, "Yes. I will wait right here."

Cornelius left her then, waded through the stream and across to the opposite bank. Luckily, the stream was not too deep or swift moving. Using the broken reins that were still about the horses' necks, he led them back. Tethering them both to a tree, he made short work of loading everyone else in the remaining intact carriage and seeing them off. To the driver he said, "Collins, be very careful with them. If you get a sense of anything wrong, stop for help. Don't try to push on."

"Aye, my lord," the driver said. "I'll see they get there safe and sound and get Dr. Warner back to you quick as can be."

Ambrose watched the carriage rolling out, weighed down with all its occupants. It wasn't intended to carry so many, but it would do, he thought. They had no other choice.

Alone with Prim, he looked down at her. "Now that they're gone, tell me the truth. How badly are you injured?"

"I don't know. I think my shoulder is... well, not where it ought to be. I struck it and my head on the side of the coach when it rolled," she admitted. "It isn't my head that's making me weak and faint. The pain in my shoulder is unbearable."

A dislocated shoulder was not life threatening. On that score, he was relieved, but he knew from firsthand experience just how painful it could be. That she was not wailing and screaming with it was testament to her strength of character. Likely it had far more to do with her not wanting to upset her siblings than anything else.

Cornelius reached for her, hauling her up by her uninjured arm. Leaving her standing there, he retrieved the horses and mounted one of them, holding on to the reins of the other. She couldn't ride bareback so she'd have to be pillioned with him.

"Under the circumstances, I think you must ride astride for safety. Place your foot on mine and use it to step up," he instructed.

She did so. As she stepped up, he grasped her uninjured arm and hoisted her the rest of the way up. It wasn't graceful in the least, and the horse protested the unfamiliar weight of both of them on its back, but there was little choice in the matter.

When she was positioned before him, her back to his chest and her head tucked in just beneath his chin, Cornelius nudged the horse forward. The companion horse fell in step beside it, as if they were both still bound to the same vehicle. Cornelius was torn between wanting to gallop ahead and needing to maintain the slow, sedate pace to prevent her further pain. Damned if he did and equally damned if he did not, he contented himself to hold her close and make steady progress toward their destination.

Chapter Sixteen

WITHOUT A SADDLE, it had not been a smooth ride. Every bump and jolt had made her stiffen in his arms, a hiss or whimper of pain escaping from her lips. At some point, she had blessedly slipped into unconsciousness, the pain simply too much to bear. It had been a relief on one hand, to know that it would ease her suffering in some way. At the same time, it was quite worrisome. He feared that her head injury might be worse than he first believed.

When they finally reached Wolfhaven, the butler opened the door and his eyes widened. "Lord Ambrose! Lord Wolverton is away!"

"I am aware... we've had a carriage accident and she's too gravely injured to go further. My aunt and the others have gone on to Bath and will send back Dr. Warner to attend her. For now, I need a bedchamber for her and laudanum if you have any on hand."

The butler nodded. "Of course, my lord. Please come inside. The young lady?"

"Her name is Miss Primrose Collier. She is a family connection," he offered by way of explanation. The truth was far too convoluted and not really any of the butler's concern. "Thank you for opening Wolfhaven to us. In her current state, I did not think she could stand the journey to Avondale."

"Certainly, my lord. Certainly. Bring her in and we'll take her upstairs to the gold room. It has been aired out recently when Lord and Lady Vale stopped for a visit."

Cornelius followed the servant through the wide carved doors and into the great hall. They climbed the stairs to the second level and then traversed the length of the hall to a suite of rooms in the section of the house that had clearly been recently redecorated. He placed her on the bed and stepped back, staring down at her. What was he supposed to do with her now? His knowledge of medical procedures was shockingly limited, not to mention that his own emotional state was likely rendering his decision making abilities poor at best.

"I'll have the maids retrieve a nightrail from her ladyship's things," the butler said. "They can get her changed into something more comfortable and then we may begin assessing which of her injuries require immediate tending... if you are in agreement, that is, my lord."

Of course he was in agreement. His own mind had completely frozen and he was unable to think of a single thing beyond the fact that he'd managed to get her there. "Yes, of course. I know she has taken a nasty bump to the head and her shoulder is out of joint. Have them be careful of it."

"Yes, my lord. All will be taken care of."

He was reluctant to leave her, reluctant to entrust her care to others, and yet he knew he had to do so. Backing away from the bed and toward the door, he stepped out into the corridor but went no further. He would not go far from her in her current condition, a condition that he felt responsible for. It had been his carriage, after all. If it had been properly maintained or checked carefully prior to the journey, the accident might never have happened. She would not have been injured and the lives of everyone else in the carriage would not have been endangered.

Two maids passed him to enter the bedchamber, borrowed clothing draped over their arms. He could hear them talking inside as they tended to her. After a few moments, they emerged again and he didn't bother to knock as he turned and once more went through that door.

The blood had been washed away from her face and most of her hair, leaving a large bruise visible to him. The dark, angry spot just above her temple was a stark reminder of just how close she had come to perishing. Recalling the wreckage of the splintered carriage, it was a wonder that she hadn't been more seriously injured or even killed. It was a wonder still that she was the only one who had been seriously injured.

Her eyes fluttered open then and she looked up at him. "This is a fine mess, isn't it?"

He laughed in spite of everything. "I do believe that is a grand understatement of the facts, Miss Primrose Collier."

"How long it will take for Dr. Warner to get here?"

"Are you in a great deal of pain?"

She sighed, a grimace of discomfort crossing her face. "My head hurts, but is bearable. It's my shoulder that's truly horrible. I think the laudanum is beginning to work though. I'm sorry for being such a bother."

"You're not a bother, Primrose. I am sorry for not taking more care with your safety. It was my carriage, after all, that was in such a sad state of repair that the wheel snapped and resulted in your being injured in the first place."

She frowned at that. "I don't understand why the wheel snapped. The road was in good condition, and I heard the driver say he'd gone over everything carefully the day before and both coaches were in tip-top shape. I know that accidents happen, but—"

"But what?"

A frown marred her features. "It seems silly, but I can't help thinking of our encounter with Lord Samford. What if... what if he decided that he doesn't want Rowan near enough to create difficulties for him? The resemblance is so marked that anyone seeing him would know without question what his parentage is!"

"I can't imagine that he would take it upon himself to do such a thing... not because I think him above it, but because I cannot see him being bothered with it. His reputation is such that having a child out of wedlock would not be a surprise to anyone. If he were thinking to remarry, it might be an issue. But otherwise, it is hardly worth his notice."

Her gaze was less direct, her expression more lax. It was clear that the laudanum had begun to work. "And is that how Lila was viewed by your father? Hardly worth his notice?"

"Sadly, yes. I do not say that to be cruel, Primrose. And it is not in any way an indictment of Lila, Rowan, your mother, or any other poor woman who finds herself in such a terrible situation. It is an indictment of such men who act without honor."

"And was it honor on the stairs the other night that kept you from kissing me?"

It was definitely the laudanum that prompted such a question. Her speech was somewhat slurred and very slow. Cornelius looked away from her then. He would answer her, because it was very unlikely that she would recall it anyway. "Yes. It was honor. I will not be like my father or Lord Samford and his ilk. Why would you ask that, Primrose?"

"If your honor forbids you from kissing me, it is because you see me as a woman too far beneath you for honorable intentions," she admitted, and her lower lip trembled slightly, as if such an admission was painful for her. "I ask that question, Lord Ambrose, because I need to remind myself, especially now when we are alone together, of all the reasons I must hold firm to my own resolve in your presence. Women have honor, as well, you see? I am as determined to be different from my mother as you are determined to be different from your father."

"It is not that you are beneath my station, Primrose. It is not even that I am not a good prospect for marriage, though that is certainly true. There are scandals attached to my name... a long history of them. Most can be laid at my father's door. But the worst can be laid at mine. My intentions toward you are not what you would believe and now is not the time to discuss them."

"And what have you done that is worse than your father's utter disregard for the children he fathered?"

Would it alter the way she viewed him? It ought to, he thought. "I killed a man."

"You said that before. An innocent man?" she asked.

"No. He was anything but."

"I see. And did you do this to save others?"

"I thought I did. I did not know when I fired my own pistol that the second one he possessed was already spent," he admitted.

"That does not make you evil, my lord. Or even scandalous. It makes you very brave and very troubled, I think."

He said nothing in response, but nothing was required. On the last word, her eyes had closed once more. She slept peacefully, the laudanum easing her pain and lulling her into a deep sleep. Free to do so, Cornelius eased himself onto the edge of the bed. Cupping her cheek tenderly, once more savoring the silken texture of her skin and the warmth of it beneath his hand. His attachment to her was growing disproportionately.

It seemed as if the instantaneous attraction he'd felt for her was deepening into something more. Despite her sometimes prickly nature, he saw her for what she was. Frightened, and yet fierce as she sought to protect herself and her family. He admired her for that. Respected her for it. Those things, admiration and respect coupled with the stunning beauty that he could not deny, were creating far more difficulties for him in keeping his feelings in check than he had anticipated. She was in no way ready to accept his suit and with each passing moment, he was sinking deeper under her spell.

A noise behind him alerted him to the presence of the butler. The man cleared his throat in a somewhat scandalized manner. Cornelius rose and turned to the encroaching servant. "I think it best if she sleeps until Dr. Warner arrives to set her shoulder. Otherwise the discomfort will be too much."

"Yes, my lord. I could not agree more. The cook has prepared a poultice to reduce the swelling of her injury. The maids will be here to apply it momentarily."

There was a wealth of censure in the man's tone, despite their difference in status. Cornelius did not take umbrage as the butler was clearly in the right and he quite wrong.

"A fire has been laid in Lord Wolverton's study, my lord. There is brandy there or tea can be served if you so choose."

"Tea shall do nicely. Under the circumstances, I should keep my wits about me lest I forget the proprieties," Cornelius offered by way of assurance.

"Just so, my lord," the butler agreed. The maids entered then, dipping into curtsies even as the butler held the door open for him. The implication that he should leave could not have been more pointed, or more correct. He should leave and he should endeavor to keep as great a distance between them as possible. But he would not. Of that, Cornelius was certain.

Chapter Seventeen

I T WAS EVENING when Prim awoke. The pain was bearable, or so she thought. When she moved, it exploded in her shoulder like a ball of fire. It arced outward, racing down her arm and toward her neck as she cried out.

"You mustn't move yet, Miss Collier. We have not yet set your shoulder... I had hoped the laudanum would keep you under a bit longer until it was done."

The voice belonged to Dr. Warner. Gingerly, she turned her head in the direction from which he'd spoken. "I can't stand it much longer. Can we not just set it now and be done with it?"

"It'll be excruciatingly painful," he warned. "I don't think you understand what you're asking."

"I do," she said. "It'll take too long for the laudanum to work again and it only makes me feel sick. Quicker is better, I think."

Dr. Warner approached the bed, standing near enough that she no longer had to turn her head to look at him. "Better for you, Miss Collier," he said. "But it appears that your current condition might very well be the death of my dear brother. He has paced the floors until there may well be a hole worn in Wolverton's new carpets."

She groaned softly as she tried to draw herself up further in the bed. "He feels responsible for what happened, but I do not believe that he is."

Warner nodded. "No. I heard about your suspicions, that you believe Lord Samford to be involved in this accident. I do not disagree with you that he is capable. We'll discuss it further, my brother included, once we've set your shoulder. Take the laudanum, Miss Collier."

Reluctantly, Prim accepted the glass of liquid he handed her. The small amount of milk laced with the laudanum was bitter on her tongue, but she drank it down quickly. Her stomach rebelled and it took all of her will not to cast up her accounts right there. She managed to narrowly avoid that humiliation, but only just.

Within mere minutes, the dizziness began again. The room seemed to dip and sway about her. The door opened and she heard the deep tones of Lord Ambrose's voice. She did not speak to him, but instead let the lethargy of the laudanum overtake her, lulling her into a strange state between wakefulness and sleep.

The men approached the bed and she felt their long shadows falling over her. In her drugged state, past and present mingled. It was no longer Dr. Warner and Lord Ambrose who loomed over. It was the horrible men that her mother had entertained between her more affluent protectors, those men who had made advances toward her, toward Hyacinth, who had engendered such fear in her of men and of being touched by them.

When they reached for her, their hands clasping at her arms, she screamed out and began to thrash. But it was an imprudent move. Despite the drugs, the pain was shocking in its intensity. It suffused her so completely that she could do nothing but scream her agony. The wail echoed throughout the room, the sound of it deafening, until it drifted off to nothingness and blackness consumed her.

"DO NOT FAINT."

Cornelius glanced up at Nicholas' tight features. "Men do not faint."

"Lovesick calves do and you, my brother, are a lovesick calf."

Cornelius drew his gaze away from his brother's teasing face. He knew that Nicholas' words were intended to ease the unbearable tension that had fallen over the room with her godawful scream.

"Let us please set her shoulder and be done with it," Cornelius said firmly. "The pain is unbearable for her, but it is the laudanum that brings back the ghosts of her past. I think they do more damage."

"Hold her steady. Whatever you do, do not let her move," Nicholas instructed.

Bracing himself for what was to come, Cornelius placed one hand on her uninjured shoulder and then across her rib cage, just beneath her breasts. Under any other circumstances, touching her so would have been a fantasy come to life. The need for it in that particular moment left him not only cold but filled with dread. They would hurt her, necessarily, but it still pained him to think of it.

As Nicholas lifted her injured arm, she whimpered softly. The sound that escaped her when he pressed down and forced the joint of her shoulder back into its natural position was something Cornelius would never forget. Ragged and animalistic, it all but gutted him.

In all, it was done quickly. Nicholas set the joint and then quickly bound her arm to her side so that she could not move it and re-injure herself. For his part, Cornelius was simply in the way. But with that, he still could not bring himself to leave her. His brother was correct in his earlier assessment. He was a lovesick calf. No woman had ever affected him as she did. And it wasn't simply her beauty. As extraordinary as it was, it had drawn his attention, but it was not the thing which held it. There was a strength in her that he found compelling. She was guarded and cautious; a woman who had seen the worst that men had to offer.

He wanted her to know that they were not all the monsters of her youth, that good and honorable men did exist. It was imperative to him that he be counted in that number by her. But his motives were not entirely altruistic or pure. He wanted her. Craved her. Longed for her. His desires and his intentions could not have been further apart, but he very much feared that desire would win out. Perhaps he was not so different from his father, after all. His baser urges were not without sway over him, despite everything he'd believed about himself to that point.

Finally, Cornelius turned and left the room. He sought the solace of Wolverton's library and the brandy he knew he would find there. It was only moments later that Nicholas followed suit. Silently, he poured a second glass of the heady liquid and passed it to his half-brother.

"What do you mean to do about her?" Nicholas asked.

"I mean to see that she is well cared for and can recuperate in comfort once we can safely transport her back to Avondale," Cornelius replied.

Nicholas placed his glass on the desk with a soft thump. "That isn't what I meant, Cornelius. You realize that, despite the necessity of them, your actions have left her in a very vulnerable position socially? And not just Miss Primrose, but Lila. You wanted to acknowledge her, to one day launch her into society and see her make a suitable match, did you not?"

"That is still my plan!" Cornelius protested. "This changes nothing!"

"And when people begin to whisper that she is not your sister but your daughter and that Prim is not her sister but her mother? When people cast aspersions on her siblings and she is forced to defend the both of you?"

"It is obvious that Prim is not nearly old enough to be her mother!" Cornelius snapped in reply.

"And gossip is always founded in truth, isn't it?" Nicholas' chiding response hung between them. They both knew the truth of it. Gossip and fact often shared few commonalities.

"What would you have me do then?"

"Marry the girl, Cornelius. It salvages her reputation and yours. It will prevent ugly gossip from tainting Lila later on when she goes into society... the situation of having the elder Colliers residing in your home was barely respectable to begin with, even with Arabella present. Now there is simply no other way."

"Her station makes no difference to me... but it will open her up to even more censure from others. They will say horrible things about her," Cornelius replied. It wasn't enough to make him refuse the option outright, but when he considered the pain it would cause her to be labeled an opportunist and social climber, it did give him pause.

"Perhaps they will... but would they be as horrible as having the entire world label her your whore?"

Cornelius whirled on him then. "My God, but you are maddening!"

"Whatever sins their mother might have committed," Nicholas continued, "those girls were raised with the manners and morals of gentility. Somehow, even in all that they witnessed, they managed to hang on to that. You could take her into society. Anyone who looked at her would understand why you gave not one damn for her station or her fortune. Any gossip would die down. Unless you do not wish to marry so far beneath you."

"I give not a single damn for such things! As well you know!"

Nicholas nodded. "Would it be so horrible to be married to her? Clearly, you have a care for her."

No. It wouldn't. It was the thing he wanted more than anything. But it was not solely up to him, and therein lay the crux of the matter. Cornelius sighed. He had never thought to marry at all until he met her. What woman would wish to tie herself to a man who was devoting his life to locating all of his father's bastards, after all? Then there was his own personal scandal to consider. The murderous son of a profligate womanizer who'd died of a diseased liver from drinking himself into ruin. What on earth did he have that any woman would wish to be bound to?

"And if she refuses?" Cornelius uttered the question softly, not meeting his brother's inquisitive gaze.

"She may... and for reasons of her own that have little enough to do with you. But I think she can be swayed to the point of reason when it comes to how her choices might impact her younger sister. Can your pride survive such a blow? To have a woman marry you not because she wants to, but because it's best for someone else?"

If the woman were Primrose Collier, it wouldn't matter. He would spend his life ensuring that she did not regret the decision.

The thoughts came to him with such clarity that Cornelius was startled by them. But he didn't doubt the utter conviction behind them. "My pride can survive it," he answered softly.

"I can't stay. I must get back to Viola. But I will return the day after tomorrow and see if it is safe for her to be moved. If so, I'll assist you getting her back to Avondale," Nicholas said. "It would be best if you secured her agreement as soon as possible."

"When she's awake and not addled by laudanum, we will discuss it," Cornelius agreed.

There was a sharp rap on the door and his driver, who had kept his promise and brought Nicholas to Wolverton in record time, entered. He had been tasked with clearing away the wreckage of the carriage.

"Forgive me, Dr. Warner, Lord Ambrose. I don't mean to inter-rupt... but I reckon you both need to see this."

"What is it, Collins?" Nicholas asked.

"It's the pin what held the wheel in place." The driver held it in his outstretched palm. It was easy enough to see, even from a distance, that it had been sawed nearly in half.

"It was cut to ensure it would break in transit," Cornelius said. Recalling Primrose's question from earlier, he had to concede that she had been correct in her assessment of the situation and that he had been presumptuous in dismissing her concerns.

"So, this was no simple carriage accident. Someone tried to kill you," Nicholas said.

Cornelius glanced up at Nicholas' obvious distress at the thought. "I don't think they meant to kill me. I think it was an attempt on the life of Primrose Collier and perhaps young Rowan. She suspected as much."

"Who would do such a thing?" Collins asked, shocked. "It's wom-en and children that don't have a half-pence between them!"

Cornelius didn't take umbrage at the driver inserting himself into the conversation. Collins was more than a coachman. He'd served in the Royal Navy with Nicholas and aboard a ship that dealt in more nefarious activities later on. Nicholas had implored Cornelius to take the man on and provide him with reputable employment. Whenever he and Viola traveled, they often borrowed Collins as their driver as Nicholas still feared there might be some sort of retribution from her father.

"Rowan's father," Cornelius replied, "Lord Samford. They encountered him while out for a walk. Apparently, Brother, you were not the only one to note the uncanny resemblance between Rowan and the man who sired him. It likely does not help that, by all accounts, Primrose is the image of her mother. The connection would have been an easy one to make given the evidence before him."

"Damn and blast it," Nicholas cursed. "Well, if you needed a better reason to marry her than her reputation, her life ought to count for something."

"What the devil does that mean?" Cornelius asked.

"It means, you halfwit, that while Samford might not think twice about killing the daughter of a known prostitute who happens to be living there on your charity, killing the betrothed or the wife of a lord would be viewed as a far weightier offense... one that could see him hanged, despite his title."

Cornelius knew it to be truth. He despised it, but there was no denying that the world they lived in placed greater value on those with prestige than those without.

"I'll discuss the matter with her when she wakes... though I doubt she will like it."

"She doesn't need to like it," Nicholas said. "She only needs to agree to it."

Chapter Eighteen

HER BRAIN WAS still fogged with laudanum when Prim woke again in a room that was fully dark. Confused, more than a little disoriented, she fought off the encroaching panic. Not even a sliver of moonlight penetrated the heavy curtains that draped the windows. But even as she peered into the darkness, she was certain of two things. She was not at Avondale Hall and she was not alone.

"You're awake. I can tell by the sound of your breathing."

The voice from the darkness was achingly familiar to her. Cornelius Garrett, Lord Ambrose. A part of her was immediately put at ease. For as much as she trusted anyone, she trusted him. But another part of her experienced a heightened awareness of the fact that they were alone in a darkened bedchamber together. And if memory served her correctly, they were in a house that was only lightly staffed at the moment because the inhabitants were away.

"I am awake," she admitted, as memories of the day's events suffused her. The horrible sound of splintering wood and the screams of her family echoed by the screams of the horses as the carriage tipped and rolled. Then it was all lost to a haze of pain and laudanum, though moments of that were stark in their clarity. He'd stayed with her, helped her and soothed her when she required it. It created a maelstrom of emotions within her, most of them far too tender and far too tempting for her peace of mind.

She heard him rise, his boots striking the wood of the floor as he crossed to the fireplace. The dimly glowing embers suddenly blazed to life as he stoked the fire. The light from it cast his hard features in stark relief in the darkness. She could see the firmness of his jaw, the hard jut of his chin, the strong line of his nose and the high sweep of his forehead. He truly was a man too handsome for words and far too handsome for her peace of mind.

"Your shoulder has been set. It's bound and should be moved as little as possible. If you need to get up, I will help you."

She did need to get up and she desperately needed to relieve herself but, clearly, she would die before allowing him to help her with that. "If you could help me sit up and then have a maid fetched to assist me... I would be very grateful."

"Of course," he said and moved back to the bed.

She had thought that he would simply help her to sit up. Instead, he lifted her in his arms and carried her easily to one of the chairs before the fire, tucking the blankets about her.

"I will remain outside the door. The laudanum may have lingering effects," he said and then disappeared into the hallway beyond the heavy door.

A few minutes later, a sleepy-eyed maid entered the room. With the girl's assistance, Prim managed to see to her most pressing needs and was once again seated before the warmth of the fire when Cornelius entered the room again. With the shadow of his whiskers framing his sculpted lips and highlighting the hard planes and angles of his face, he was intensely masculine in a way that made Prim far too aware of their differences. The maid looked at him, blushed, and scurried out like a scared mouse. Clearly, Primrose was not alone in lacking immunity to his brand of masculine charm.

"Must you do that?" she asked.

"Do what?" he replied.

"Send the maids into a tizzy with a look!"

He frowned, his confusion quite obvious. "I don't recall looking at her."

Explaining that he hadn't looked at the maid and that, instead, the maid had looked at him would only stroke his ego. That was the last thing that needed to happen.

"Of course not," Prim said, for lack of anything better to add.

He eased himself into the chair across from her. She could see that he was tired. There were hollows beneath his eyes. His hair was tousled as if he'd been running his hands through it.

"How long have I been asleep?" she asked.

"It's after midnight. Nicholas gave you the laudanum and set your shoulder at four."

Nearly nine hours. Had he stayed with her the entire time? "Have you not slept at all?"

"I dozed," he answered. "I wanted to stay close if you needed anything."

"There are servants for that," she pointed out. "You need not have attended me personally!"

"The footmen are in residence in Bath with Lord and Lady Wolverton. The butler who is running the house is an ancient pensioner who forfeited his retirement to do so. There are a handful of housemaids and an aging cook on staff at present," he answered. "They could hardly lift you from the floor to the bed if you fell from it."

"Did I fall from it?" she asked.

"No. But you were thrashing about and very nearly re-injured your shoulder. They could not have held you."

Phantom memories of his hands on her, pressing her back against the bed and of soft, soothing whispers in her ear flooded her mind. Were they actual memories or just fantasies offered up by her traitorous mind? "I see."

"There are things we must discuss, Primrose. Things that cannot wait."

"Such as?"

"You have been alone with me… for far longer than society would forgive."

"I am not in society," she pointed, "So it hardly signifies."

"You are not now. But Lila will be eventually. There will already be many factors set against her… she does not need the scandal of having her paternal half-brother's ruin of her maternal half-sister to be among them," he stated matter of factly.

"Who will know that we have been alone together, Lord Ambrose?" she demanded.

"Anyone that Aunt Arabella was imprudent enough to mention anything to. Anyone that the servants here at Wolfhaven gossip to. You forget, Primrose, that my name is scandalous. All of society views me as a murderer, despite the circumstances in which those events occurred. Everything I do is subject to gossip," he insisted.

"What are you suggesting?"

"That when you are well, we shall travel to London immediately and be married by special license," he answered succinctly. "It's the best way to avoid scandal and to ensure that Lila does not suffer any consequences for this folly."

"That's a terrible reason to get married." The protest was quick to her lips, but no less true. There were many reasons they shouldn't wed. Too many to list, if she were to be perfectly honest.

"There are other reasons," he suggested.

"Such as?" Prim demanded. It was ludicrous. She was ill-prepared to be the wife of gentleman, much less a lord. And he had no real wish to marry her. He desired her. Of that, she was certain. It wasn't vanity or conceit. She recalled easily enough how beautiful her mother had been and how men had responded to her. And she knew that she looked like her mother. But beauty was not a blessing to her mind. It was a curse. Beauty was something others longed to exploit or to possess. Her nature would allow her to submit to neither of those things.

"You were correct in your earlier assessment... the carriage did not overturn as the result of an accident. The pins holding the wheel in place had been cut nearly clean through. I believe that Lord Samford was responsible," he explained. "The man is in debt up to his eyeballs and if what Nicholas said is true, means to snag himself an heiress. Having his by-blow for a neighbor is apparently more objectionable to him than I might have imagined."

"That is a reason for us to leave, Lord Ambrose, not a reason for me to marry you and stay forever," she snapped.

"Protection, Primrose. Without the protection of my name, you and your brother would not even warrant an investigation into your deaths should something terrible happen. But if you become Lady Ambrose, and young Rowan becomes the brother-in-law and ward of a peer, that would make the stakes infinitely higher for Samford."

She didn't like it. But then the truth was rarely ever a pleasant thing. Her mother's life was a cautionary tale, after all. The daughter of a gentleman, when her father had passed away, she had married unwisely to a man who squandered her meager fortune and got himself killed in a duel. Penniless and alone, with only her beauty and her body for currency, her path had been set.

"What about Hyacinth?"

"Your sister may remain at Avondale for as long as she wishes. I am not a villain, Primrose. I would not deny you, Lila or Rowan the family that you know and love," he insisted.

"And would this be a real marriage or a marriage of convenience?"

He said nothing for a long and taut moment, but his eyes glittered in the dim glow of the fire. "Is a marriage of convenience what you desire?"

There was a wealth of meaning in that question, most of it impart-ed by the roughened and graveled tone of his voice. What she desired and what she could allow herself were entirely different things. "I don't know. We know one another so little."

"It will be a real marriage, Primrose. I will be your husband and you will be my wife... but I will not pounce on you the moment we leave the church, if that is your concern. You may have time. You may get to know me as you wish."

Saying no wasn't an option. Even questioning whether or not it was the best course of action had only been to humor her. She'd do anything that was required to ensure her family's safety, even if it meant forfeiting her own. And if there was one thing she was entirely certain of, Cornelius Garrett was a danger to her. The walls she'd built around herself, to protect herself and to cage that part of her that longed for adventure and excitement and passion, those walls all but trembled in his presence and had from the moment he'd stepped into their little cottage.

"Then we are betrothed," she agreed solemnly.

"So we are, Primrose. So we are."

Chapter Nineteen

F REDDY ENTERED THE Assembly Rooms wearing the same cool and slightly condescending smile that he adopted for all social gatherings. His late arrival was by design. He'd wanted Miss Wyverne to wonder if, perhaps, he did not intend to show. As much as he needed her fortune, he would never be the sort of man who would kowtow to a wife. It was best to begin with her knowing that, fortune or no, she was the lucky one in their arrangement.

Pausing inside the door, he waited to be announced. His name echoed throughout the chamber. If people whispered more than they once had at his entrance, if a few turned their backs entirely, he didn't much care. He wasn't there for them anyway.

Casually clandestine, he scanned the room and found his quarry. Wallflowers were never difficult to locate, after all. She wasn't an unattractive girl, but she was quite plain. Her unremarkable brown hair was swept back from her rather unremarkable face in a style that was much too severe to ever be flattering. Wire framed spectacles perched on the end of her nose and her gaze was downcast, fixed on her hands folded primly in her lap, resting on the pale ivory muslin of her gown.

Seated, her figure was not objectionable, at least. She was neither fat nor rail thin, and had pleasant enough curves. But her limp, when she walked, and the cane she was forced to use obviously detracted from any of her more redeeming assets. But he wasn't there because he was smitten with her. He was there because he required the hefty marriage settlement that would accompany her. He'd have bedded an ogre at that point if it would get the creditors off his back.

Freddy appreciated the power of anticipation. Miss Wyverne knew why he was there. So did her father. But he saw no reason not to reclaim some of the power for himself. Instead of walking directly to her, he made it a point to speak with friends and acquaintances, to flirt for a moment with a woman who had once been his lover. Even as he continued to move in her general direction, he made no effort hurry there.

"Oh, good heavens! Lord Samford, how wonderful to see you here!"

The exclamation came from behind him. Turning, he smiled at the sight of Leticia Posenby. She was a friend of his younger sister's, out a year before her, and the silliest of silly geese to ever grace society. She hadn't sense enough to know she should not be so obvious in her regard for him. But he'd use it to his advantage.

"Miss Posenby, I am delighted to find you here. Tell me your dance card is not yet full!"

"It isn't. I'm free for the next set," she said.

She was likely free for all the sets. Pretty but dull, she lacked the wit or the fortune to be truly successful in society. But she was pretty enough and graceful enough to spark envy in Miss Wyverne. That was all he required of her.

"Then we shall dance with more joy and abandon than any other couple present," he said.

She blinked up at him, dazed. "Oh, dear. That sounds delightful."

"It will be, Miss Posenby," he vowed. "It will be."

Offering the girl his arm, he led her toward the dance floor and didn't bother to look back at Miss Wyverne. He didn't need to wonder if she was watching. He could feel her piercing gaze on his back. Facing Miss Posenby, he smiled with all the charm he could muster, uncaring that he was making her feel as if he had intentions toward her or a tendre for her that simply did not exist. She was a pawn, after all, and pawns were meant to be sacrificed.

SHE HAD REFUSED more laudanum. Despite her obvious pain, she'd been far more distressed by the confusion it caused than by any physical discomfort at the result of her injury. Cornelius had given up arguing the point and conceded that she could skip it provided she could go back to sleep without it, but if she were awake for more than an hour, she'd take another dose of the foul liquid. That agreement had been hard won.

Now, as he watched her slumber fitfully, Cornelius felt the corners of his lips tug upward in a reluctant smile. No doubt she had willed herself to sleep. If there was one thing he was quickly learning about Primrose it was that she had a will of iron. The thing he remained confused of was whether she feared all men, just him, or if it was something in herself that prompted her panicked response. Regardless, he'd seen the fear in her eyes and he had to wonder if it was something they would ever truly overcome. For his part, most of the women of his acquaintance were overjoyed at the prospect of marriage. Or perhaps it was simply the prospect of weddings? Maybe the marriage itself took second place to lavish breakfasts, cakes and a new gown and pretty posies.

Women were an enigma to him, but none more so than the one he was now set to marry. Marriage. He had only a faint recollection of his parents together. From what he could recall, his father and mother had been fond of one another, but he could not say whether his father had been faithful to his mother or whether she had even desired that he would be so. It obviously had not been a great love, but he didn't think they were entirely without regard for one another. Though in the aftermath of her death, his father's self-destructive behavior and willful hurling of himself into every form of debauchery might have been grief. Or it might simply have been the freedom to do so without a wife to embarrass and scoldings to suffer.

Love wasn't something he'd considered as part of his future, but marriage hadn't been either. For what it was worth, he desired her, he admired her. He found her compelling and intriguing. But he didn't know if that constituted a foundation for love or simply infatuation. Regardless, he hoped that they would at least deal reasonably well with one another and not embark on a life of misery and strife together. As goals went, it was modest, but only on the surface.

Cornelius didn't know how to be close to people. It was one of the many reasons that he was so astounded and curious about the relationships between the Collier siblings. He didn't have the same ease with Nicholas as they did with one another. He had few close friends aside from a few school chums he now saw very infrequently. It had seemed easier in the aftermath of the scandal to simply remove himself from society other than that of his newly found half-brother and the few individuals that were part of Nicholas' circle.

In retrospect, it was easy to identify the cowardice in his actions. The word burned in his mind, representing a weakness in himself that he despised. It was also one that he meant to eradicate. If his plan to secure the safety and security of Prim's future, as well as Lila's and the others, they would have to go back into society. The more people who knew her, the more people there would be to question if something terrible should happen to her, was all for the better. She needed enough attachments within the *ton* that she would become untouchable for Samford.

The thought of Samford made him furious. With his earlier fear for her, the shocking realization that they'd very nearly been murdered while in his charge, he hadn't yet let the emotion of it all take him over. But in that moment, had Samford been in front of him, he would have put a pistol ball in the man just as he had Grantham five years earlier. To protect her, he would do what he swore never to do again. He would take a life if need be.

Prim stirred, rolling from her back to her uninjured side. In the process, she came to face him, offering ample opportunity to study the delicate symmetry of her features. Yes. He would do whatever was required to protect her. And perhaps they did not love one another, but she was not immune to him. Of that, he was certain. Whatever the source of her reluctance to embrace the carnal aspect of their marriage, he would conquer it. Because somehow, in the short span of time he had known her, possessing her had become as imperative to his continued existence as the very air that he breathed.

Chapter Twenty

L ORD AND LADY Wolverton returned to Wolfhaven just as Prim and Lord Ambrose were preparing to depart. Prim hadn't been quite certain what to expect, having invaded the home of an earl and his countess. But the remarkably pragmatic Lady Wolverton was a revelation.

"Oh, dear. We need a traveling gown for you. That will never do. And mine would look like they were made for a child on someone with your enviable figure," Lady Wolverton said softly as she tugged at her lower lip in a thoughtful manner.

"I will be fine in the gown borrowed from your maid," Prim insisted. "You've been far too kind already."

Lady Wolverton waved a hand dismissively at that. "Do you know that my husband rescued me running from my abductors in the woods that bordered this estate? Then, his late wife's clothes were still here and could at least be cut down for me to wear. Sadly, we've gotten rid of all her things—for obvious reasons—and now I wish I had at least kept some of them. They would have fit you perfectly… because you cannot leave this house in the company of the lord you are betrothed to looking like a housemaid."

Prim's eyebrows rose in shock. "I did not tell you that we were betrothed!"

"My dear, you have spent two nights unchaperoned in this house with Lord Ambrose. Of course you are betrothed. He is a gentleman and anything less would be unacceptable," the countess said softly. "Now that I think on it, I believe that I have some things stowed in one of the other bedrooms that belonged to my sister-in-law, Eliza-beth! She's much closer in stature to you. They are somewhat out of date and had been intended as a gift for my maid as they would not fit her own. I'll have them fetched and we'll get you turned out in a somewhat presentable fashion."

"It isn't necessary, Lady Wolverton. We are only returning to Avondale."

"We are not, actually," a deep voice interjected from the door.

Prim looked up to see Lord Ambrose standing there. The sunlight filtering in through the windows struck the dark waves of his hair, showing the hints of copper hidden in the depths of it, along with a few stray strands of silver. "I don't understand... are we to head for Bath then?"

"No. We shall go on to London. I've sent word to Aunt Arabella and to your sister to apprise them of our plans. They will join us in London before the week is out," he answered. "Wolverton was kind enough to lend us the use of his carriage. Something about repaying an old debt, I believe he said."

Lady Wolverton smiled rather enigmatically. "Your father was a very dear friend to my husband," she offered by way of explanation. "Will there be a large wedding, Lord Ambrose, or a private ceremo-ny?"

"Private, I think," he said. "Though I daresay a wedding would not be remiss. Perhaps, we shall plan a celebration of our nuptials at a later date. If so, we shall be certain to send an invitation to you and your husband."

"Am I to have no say in this at all?" Prim demanded, furious that he and Lady Wolverton seemed content to discuss the matter as if she were not even present.

Ambrose glanced over at her. "You already did have a say... and you said yes, for reasons we both are well aware of. I don't need to remind you, Primrose, that it is in everyone's best interests to behave expeditiously."

He didn't, of course. She remembered that conversation only too well. With it came the memory of another encounter, the one with Lord Samford and the cold hatred in his eyes when he had spared a glance at Rowan. "Of course."

"There is a modiste on Bond Street… Madame Le Faye. You will go to her and tell her that I have sent you. She will find something appropriate for Miss Collier to wear as a bride. It would not do for her to marry a peer in a cast-off gown," Lady Wolverton said.

"We will see to it," Ambrose answered. "If you are free, Primrose, I thought we might walk for a moment in the gardens before we depart."

"Of course," she agreed, wondering what pressing details he did not feel he could reveal in front of their hostess.

Lady Wolverton draped a borrowed shawl over Prim's shoulders, the fine paisley a sharp contrast to the rough woolen dress that one of the maids had given her to wear as her traveling costume had been beyond repair.

Following him from the room, she stayed close to him on the stairs, taking them more slowly than necessary. But as she was still feeling somewhat dizzy from the blow to her head during the carriage accident and from being abed for two days, it was a welcome respite. Once they were clear of the house, walking along a graveled path in what had obviously once been a lush formal garden and was well on its way to returning to its former glory, Prim stopped. She stood in the center of the path and demanded, "What was so pressing and what required such discretion, Lord Ambrose?"

"As we are to be married by the end of the week, Primrose, I think it is time you called me by my given name… Cornelius."

"Tell me what has happened, Cornelius," she insisted.

"I've received a letter from Nicholas just this morning, delivered by one of his grooms who rode out before dawn to bring it here. Samford has gone to Bath. That is why we are making for London now. It's better to move quickly before he has a chance to regroup and plot another attack. Apparently, there was quite a scene at the Assembly Rooms last night. He miscalculated the desperation of Miss

Wyverne to be his bride and his tactics to inspire jealousy in the girl have apparently turned her off him entirely, according to the gossips at any rate. That means he will have to persuade her, somehow, that he's not the bounder he appears, or he'll have to find a new heiress altogether."

"Then he will be entirely too busy to pay any attention at all to Rowan or to me! There is no need for us to proceed with this farce," Prim stated. If that sentiment prompted a spark of disappointment to bloom within her she would not give it credence by acknowledging it.

"On the contrary, Primrose. There is every reason to continue as planned. If he can turn the tide with Miss Wyverne, any further setbacks would surely prove permanent. That makes Rowan's existence, and yours, an even greater threat to him than before. Fredrick Hamilton is an innately vain creature, Primrose. He is wicked to the core and assumes that all others are like him. He will never cease to see you and Rowan as threats because, if the tables were turned, he would be using that information to its full financial advantage."

There was a universal truth in his assessment. Wicked people always saw their own wickedness in others. It was that which allowed them to continue their misdeeds without guilt or fear of reprisal, because they believed, inherently, that they were "normal." Hadn't she witnessed that herself as a child with the men that her mother would entertain? Men who would look at her with their wicked intentions written plainly upon their faces and their seemingly impervious beliefs that she welcomed such attentions.

"I see. Then we shall proceed as planned," she conceded, ignoring the renewed fear she felt at the prospect as well as the conflicting relief. Her thinking was so muddled by him that she no longer knew what she wanted!

He reached into his pocket and produced a small leather-covered box with an ornate clasp. "I returned to Avondale this morning and retrieved it. The ring belonged to my mother. It was one of her favorites and I thought it would suit you."

Prim released the clasp on the box and raised the small coffin-shaped lid. Inside, nestled on a bed of velvet, was a pretty gold band set with a generously-sized sapphire ringed by small diamonds and flanked by pearls. It was the loveliest thing she'd ever seen. It would certainly be the loveliest and most valuable thing to ever grace her person. "It's too much!"

"You don't like it then?"

"Of course, I like it! It's beautiful… but this ring is worth more than I can possibly imagine."

"I didn't give it to you because of its worth, Prim. I gave it to you because my mother treasured it. And when I was a boy, she told me that I should one day give it to my bride."

His bride. "You should not have to marry me out of obligation. You should be able to marry who you choose, where your heart leads," she whispered hoarsely. "Your mother would likely have been mortified to see you tying yourself to the bastard daughter of a doxy!"

"I am marrying as I choose, where my heart has led me. I will finally be part of a family, as I've always wanted. As to the other, you are not your mother. Her sins are no more yours than my father's are my own."

"And yet we both struggle to atone for them, do we not?" Prim walked away from him then, easing herself down onto the small stone bench nestled against the hedges. "You behave properly and above reproach because you've no wish to be compared to a man who couldn't be bothered to behave appropriately or responsibly in his life. And I—"

The silence continued for a moment, until he prompted, "And you what, Primrose?"

"And I avoid men. I avoid being alone with them. I avoid conversation and flirtation and entanglement. I have spent my life doing everything I can to discourage their interest because I am terrified that I will make her mistakes and find myself in some dingy room begging for the scraps of a man's love or worse—bartering my body and the shattered bits of my soul for a few coins."

Those words, the broken admission that she'd dared only whisper to her sister, hung between them. Not even the distant sounds of birds calling could break the spell of silence. After a long moment, he took the box from her, lifted the ring from it and placed it gently on her finger. When he did so, he finally spoke, his words a solemn vow. "That will never be your fate, Primrose. On my soul, it will not be. You may count on one thing... I will see to your welfare. You and your siblings."

"It isn't a rational fear," she said. "Just as yours isn't. You won't suddenly turn into your father... drinking and whoring your way through life. But it's always the dark thing hiding in the shadows of your mind, isn't it?"

"It is," he agreed. "There are few people who understand the complications of loving others who cannot love themselves. It's a hard thing to watch people you love slowly destroy themselves. And yet we both have. Perhaps that is the thing that will allow us to find some peace in all of this. We are in a unique position to understand one another, Primrose."

Prim touched the ring that now rested on the third finger of her left hand. The weight of it was unfamiliar but not uncomfortable. "I suppose we are. It is a better basis for building a life together than many have."

"It isn't only that, Prim. And it isn't only obligation."

There was something in his tone that alerted her, something that called to that part of her that had stirred so readily that night on the stairs. Turning her head to meet his gaze, she was not surprised to feel his lips on hers. The kiss itself was, perhaps, the most normal interaction they'd shared as a betrothed couple. Yet it rocked her to her very core because her blood rushed and soared in her veins. There was no room for fear. No room for guilt or shame. There was only him, filling up her senses and blocking out all the world. Nothing else existed— past or future. There was only the present and the taste of him on her tongue, the scrape of his whiskers against her skin, and the feel of his arms closing around her, always gentle and mindful of her injury, but nonetheless insistent.

When he drew back, his breath caressing her lips and his forehead dropping to press against hers as their breath mingled between them, one word came to her mind. Inevitable. That moment of surrender and his presence in her life had been inevitable. It was as if the fates themselves had arranged it.

Chapter Twenty-One

F REDDY CURSED UNDER his breath as he climbed the steps to the Wyverne house in the Royal Crescent. He had misjudged Miss Wyverne it seemed. She had more pride than he had accounted for and was not nearly so enamored with him as he'd initially assumed. He wondered if, perhaps, there wasn't more to it than that. Perhaps, she did not seek the company of men because she preferred the company of women? She was a bluestocking, an ape-leader, and many of them were devotees of Sappho. None of that mattered. She could have had the face of a donkey and it would have made little difference.

Now he found himself in a position that he despised. He would have to apologize and beg her forgiveness. That or he would be forced to find another way to shore up his family's failing finances. Frankly, they didn't have the time for that. If he didn't make the necessary payments, everything that was not entailed would be seized by the bailiffs to pay his debts. There was no one left to borrow from and nothing left to sell that wouldn't lend credence to the rumors that the family was deep in dun territory.

With a posy in one hand and a box of chocolates tucked beneath his arm, he lifted the heavy knocker and let it fall with a metallic clank. Almost immediately, the door opened and the painfully thin figure of the butler appeared before him.

"Lord Samford for Miss Wyverne," Freddy said.

The butler's expression never altered. "Miss Wyverne is not at home, Lord Samford."

Not at home. Yet as he'd walked up the street, he'd seen two of Miss

Wyverne's friends admitted. In other words, she was not at home to him. She was done with him entirely it seemed, as the gossips had suggested once she'd left the Assembly Rooms the night before.

They would see about that. "If you could give these to her," he said and produced a letter from inside his coat. It was both an apology and a patently false explanation. She might believe it. She might not. But in that moment, Freddy decided one thing. He would marry her. Whether she agreed or not.

If he dragged her off to Scotland, she'd have little choice in the matter. Heiress or not, she was still lame, still rather homely and plain. If her reputation were ruined, no one else would ever have her no matter how rich she was. But first, there was another problem to take care of. He'd received word just that morning via the unlikely source of Cornelius Garrett's aunt. The dotty old bird was incapable of keeping her mouth shut and she'd been blathering to everyone who would listen about the carriage accident that very nearly killed them all. His bastard brat was still alive and so was the sister. That would have to be remedied. Later, after he'd settled things with Miss Wyverne, he'd attend to the matter. He wasn't about to set his finances right by tying himself to a hatchet-faced wife only to turn a portion of the rewards over to blackmailers. No doubt, as soon as word of his marriage came out, the demands would begin.

INSIDE HER FATHER'S luxurious townhouse, Kitty Wyverne stared at the gifts laid before her by their aging but dedicated butler. She'd harbored no illusions about Lord Samford. His reputation had preceded him. But she would happily have ignored the gossip. It wasn't even a requirement that he love her. But she would not consent to be courted by or married to a man who would publicly humiliate her. She'd recognized his behavior the night before as an attempt to manipulate her. But she lived with Samuel Wyverne and no one was a greater master of manipulation than he. Her efforts to find a husband were so she might escape her father, not tie herself to someone just like him.

"He's very handsome, Kit," Judith Villiers offered in what was intended to be a helpful manner.

"So was Lucifer," Kitty replied sharply. "I allowed his attentions in the beginning because I hoped he was different from what I had heard of him. He has proven now that he is not. You need not fret, Judith, for my heart was not involved."

Judith shook her head. "I don't know how you do that! You are impervious to the attentions of men. If a man as handsome and charming as Lord Samford were to pay court to me, I'd make an utter cake of myself."

"It's easy enough to be impervious when he danced attendance on a silly girl right in front of me," Kitty answered. "I've heard rumors, as well. I knew his family was in debt, but it appears to be far worse than I had initially believed. I'm not opposed to marrying a man who is poor and swayed to it by my fortune, so long as he is kind and I think we can have a pleasant life together. Lord Samford showed me last night that he is not that man."

Across the room, Sally Carter looked up. "I heard something else about him... it was from a maid in the Ambrose townhouse. She's cousins to one of our parlor maids and she said that there were whispers that the youngest child in a family named Collier, who have become wards of Lord Ambrose, is the spitting image of Lord Samford."

"He would not be the first gentleman to sire a child out of wedlock. At least Lord Ambrose is offering to care for them. No doubt, his father contributed to the birth of at least one of the sibling group," Kitty mused. The previous Lord Ambrose had been rather notorious for such exploits.

"If you're willing to overlook scandal, then Lord Ambrose might be a good prospect for a husband," Judith said. "He's very handsome, as well!"

Kitty did not roll her eyes, but she only just managed to refrain.

Judith was obsessed with male beauty. And male ugliness. And masculinity in any form in between. Never in all her life had she known someone more desperate to marry. "If you say one more man is handsome, I swear, Judith, I will turn you out of this house and never let you enter it again."

"Well, he is! I know there was that awful scandal and the rather questionable death of that Grantham fellow but, by all accounts, Grantham was a scoundrel! It sounds to me as if Lord Ambrose should be lauded a hero instead of a villain. And he's nice, Kitty. He's always pleasant and kind whenever I've had occasion to encounter him, though admittedly that has not happened frequently in the last few years. He's avoided society altogether since that nasty business."

"I've met Lord Ambrose on multiple occasions and he has little to no interest in me. I'm not even sure he was aware of my presence," Kitty said. "No. Lord Ambrose will not do. I'll settle on someone soon enough." She had to. If she didn't find someone by the end of the year, her father had stated unequivocally that he would find someone for her. Their criteria for selecting a bridegroom were quite different.

"We'll go to the Assembly Rooms again tonight. Perhaps you'll meet someone there," Sally offered. "And it can't hurt."

No, it couldn't hurt anything more than her pride. Just one more night sitting in a corner, watching others dance and flirt while she was ignored. "Fine. We'll go."

Chapter Twenty-Two

THE JOURNEY TO London was a difficult one. They were nearing the end of their first day. Every jolt of the carriage had caused agony. As the vehicle lurched into the inn yard, Prim was biting the inside of her cheek to keep from crying out with the pain.

"This was too much for you," Cornelius observed.

"It doesn't matter," she said. "Time is of the essence and we cannot afford to coddle me."

"I'll procure rooms for us if you wish to wait here."

It was only the two of them. They'd elected not to borrow a maid from Lord and Lady Wolverton or to return to Avondale and fetch one. The lighter they could travel, the quicker they would be able to get to London and get the deed done. Theirs would not be a joyous wedding, but a perfunctory thing to achieve and be done with. Perhaps their lack of joy and anticipation of the wedding itself would not carry over into the marriage if they were lucky.

After Cornelius climbed down from the carriage and she was alone, Prim let out a deep shuddering breath. Without the carriage being in motion, there was some relief from the pain. She was at least not being jolted and jostled about.

Easing back against the seat, she stretched experimentally, trying to ease the kinks from her back without causing further pain to her injured shoulder. It was only moments later that Cornelius returned.

"There is only one room available," he said.

"We are already courting impropriety, Cornelius. I hardly think it matters," she said. She trusted him to be a gentleman. Despite their kiss in the garden just that morning, she had no fear of him. If nothing else, that kiss had confirmed for her that she could trust him. He had kissed her, but done no more, though given how his kiss had affected her, he certainly could have. It was something she had struggled with from the beginning. Her response to him seemed to defy her will and her sense.

"Let me help you," he said, offering his hand to assist her down from the carriage.

The warmth of his fingers on hers was a welcome jolt of pleasure to ward off the misery of the aches and pains that wracked her. Stepping down, her legs trembled as her feet touched solid ground for the first time in hours. He placed her hand on his arm and Prim was grateful for the support as they made their way into the crowded inn.

The innkeeper glanced at them, but said nothing. A serving girl scurried in their direction. "Follow me, my lord, my lady," she said.

My lady. It would take some adjustment. And while they were not yet wed, she understood the necessity of allowing the innkeeper and staff to believe so.

Following the girl up the narrow stairs, they were led to a room tucked under the eaves of the building. It was small, the bed as narrow as the one she had shared with Hyacinth for so many years. A fire had already been laid in the hearth and the chill was abating. Before the fire were a small table and two rather rickety chairs. While it lacked luxury, it was neat and tidy.

"I'll bring up a tray shortly with tea, bread and cheese. There might be a bit of stew left from dinner. If so, I'll see to it, as well. There's fresh water for washing yon," she said, and gestured toward a wash stand tucked into the corner near the fire. With a quickly bobbed curtsy, she was gone.

Alone with him, Prim wasn't quite sure what to do. How did one proceed in such a situation? He had been a perfect gentleman and had made no advances toward her at all. Yet it was such an intimate thing to share a chamber with a man, even without any real impropriety occurring.

"I'll go below while you wash off the dust of the road. Lock the door behind me, Prim. This is a respectable inn, but there were some rough-looking characters in the tap room. I'd rather not put their morals to the test," he said.

"Of course," she agreed with a nod.

He looked at her again for a long moment, the silent stretching between them. Finally, he asked, "Do you need my help?"

"With what?"

"With your gown," he answered. "Given your injury, I wasn't sure you could manage it alone."

She would. Regardless. The very idea of having him assist her with such a personal and incredibly intimate task was more than she could bear. "I'll be fine," she replied. "I can manage."

"Very well. Lock the door," he reiterated and then was gone. The soft snick of the door closing behind him echoed in the small space.

Immediately, Prim did as she'd been instructed and crossed the narrow room to turn the key in the lock. The sound of the tumblers clicking into place spurred her to action. With difficulty, she managed to shed the heavy cloak that had been draped about her shoulders. In the last few days, the weather had turned. Late-autumn was upon them and it held the portents of a bitter winter.

The simple day dress she wore, quickly altered from some things left behind by Lady Wolverton's sister-in-law, had a bib front that was thankfully easy to manage without having to remove her arm from the sling. Pouring water into the basin, she scrubbed her face and neck, washed her hands and then made for the valise in the corner that Lord Ambrose—Cornelius—had brought up with them. Another borrowed garment, a wrapper of velvet and silk that was old and worn but still much finer than anything Prim had ever owned, was hastily donned.

She was just sitting down in the small chair before the fire to attempt to brush the snarls from her hair, when there was a soft knock at the door.

"It's me."

She recognized his voice immediately and moved to let him in. As she stepped back from the door, he entered bearing a heavy tray. He'd apparently intercepted the serving girl in the corridor.

"That smells divine," she said, inhaling the aroma of the stew.

"There isn't much of the stew, but with the bread and cheese it should suffice." He'd placed the tray on the table as he replied. "Let me wash the dust off and then we'll dine."

Prim nodded and moved away from the fireplace, crossing the room to the small valise that Lady Wolverton had provided, stuffed to overflowing with borrowed things. She needed nothing from it, but she hadn't wanted to stand so close to him. Distance was impossible to obtain in the small room, but she needed it desperately.

A glance over her shoulder revealed that he'd stripped off his coat of superfine and his waistcoat, leaving him in just his dark breeches and a white lawn shirt. The fabric stretched taut over his shoulders as he leaned forward to wash his face. Prim looked away quickly. It was foolhardy to tempt herself further.

When he finished, he returned to the table and began divvying up their supper. He placed an earthenware bowl filled with the steaming mutton stew and a large hunk of bread in front of the chair she'd so recently occupied. "Eat," he said. "I know you're starving and you need the nourishment to heal properly."

Prim was too pragmatic to balk at the command, though a part of her felt compelled to do so. He was right. And she could appreciate, though it pained her to admit it, that he was not being autocratic out of arrogance but out of concern for her. She could feel the exhaustion from their journey creeping in on her. Her muscles ached and trembled with it.

Easing into the chair, she waited until he'd served himself and then they ate in silence. It was a surprisingly comfortable silence. Perhaps because they were both tired and hungry, the need to indulge in social niceties for the sake of it had been replaced by the tending to more basic needs.

When he'd finished, Cornelius leaned back in his chair. It creaked rather ominously prompting him to raise one eyebrow.

Prim felt a giggle building inside her. It bubbled up, impossible to contain. "The look on your face!"

CORNELIUS LISTENED TO the soft peals of her laughter and found himself enchanted by the sound. A smile tugged at his lips. If it took him falling on his arse and sacrificing his dignity to hear it again, he'd happily do so.

"These chairs do not keep one from sprawling on the floor... they simply delay it. I feel as if the seat will give way any moment," he offered. His comment had the desired effect and her laughter continued.

After a moment, when she'd managed to compose herself, though her lips were still curved in the sweetest of smiles, he said, "You should take the bed. I'll sleep on the floor."

"You can't possibly!" she protested immediately.

"I've slept on floors before, Prim. Not often and I do not enjoy it, but I assure you it will not wound me to do so."

"Where, Cornelius? There isn't room! Not unless you wish to sleep half-under the bed!"

It was true. The room was small. Even if he pushed the table and the rickety chairs that accompanied it up against the far wall, there was still little room.

"I will manage," he replied.

"I will take the floor. I'm not nearly as tall—"

"Absolutely not!"

"Why ever not? I can attest to the fact that when Hyacinth was restless or ill, I often slept on the floor!"

"I am a gentleman, Primrose. Despite my behavior this morning in the garden... I will not allow a woman, especially one who is injured, to sleep on a cold hard floor in my stead! What sort of man would I be?"

"One who can walk upright tomorrow instead of like a hunchback," she said pertly.

"It will be fine. Now, I believe as I entered the room, that you were attempting to brush your hair and finding yourself not up to the task," he said. "I'll help you and perhaps fashion a braid for you that won't give way through the night."

She wanted to protest. He could see it on her face, but the desire to have her hair free of snarls must have outweighed her reasons for protesting. After a long moment, she rose and retrieved her brush from near the washstand and placed it in his hand. "It'll be worse tomorrow morning if we don't see to it tonight," she said. "Thank you, my—Cornelius."

It had been a slip of the tongue for her, an amalgamation of his title and his name. Regardless, he found he rather liked being called her Cornelius. But he didn't comment on it. The tentative peace between them was too fragile for that. Rising to his feet, he moved behind the chair she'd just reclaimed. It was, on the surface, a simple and mundane task. But the reality of it was completely different. Feeling the silken strands of her hair sliding through his fingers, brushing against the soft skin of her neck, it took all of his control and significant willpower to restrain himself.

The kiss from the morning had replayed itself in his mind dozens of times. Every time he looked at her, he thought of it. And now, touching her, he was desperate to repeat the experience again. But it was not the place or time. She was beyond exhausted and they both needed rest.

Finally, the task was done and he stepped away and she rose. He watched as she moved toward the bed and turned the covers back.

"We could share the bed, Cornelius," she said.

And he'd surely die of wanting her. He could well be the first man in history to shuffle off the mortal coil from the complications of unfulfilled lust. "That is preposterous."

"We're to be married, Cornelius. And you yourself stated that this will be a real marriage. We will be sharing a bed soon enough."

He would be honest with her. It was something he had decided from the moment he had accepted the fact that their only course of action was to wed. He would not have lies in his marriage. "I am attempting to hold fast to my honor and be the kind of man that I have always striven to be. But you are more tempting than you realize, Primrose, and I am far weaker than I ever thought," Cornelius confessed.

"And I am too exhausted to be seduced, Lord Ambrose... even by you," she said. "We will sleep. And if you attempt to do anything more than that, I will toss you onto the floor and you may sleep with your feet in the hall and your head under the bed if necessary."

It was his turn to laugh. "Fair enough," Cornelius agreed. It was going to be a hellish night, but he would survive it. Possibly.

Chapter Twenty-Three

PRIM AWOKE SLOWLY. It wasn't quite dawn yet, but the darkness was beginning to fade, replaced by a cool glow that promised morning was soon to come. She was warm, impossibly so. And she realized that the heat was emanating from the body beside hers. Opening her eyes, she found herself staring at the whiskered jawline of her husband-to-be. He lay on his back, one arm above his head and the other draped across his abdomen. The fabric of his shirt was stretched taut over the muscles of his arms and chest.

As if he felt her gaze upon him, he stirred, turning his face toward her.

"Good morning, Primrose," he said, his voice gravelly with sleep.

"Good morning, Cornelius."

After those initial greetings, they fell silent once more. Prim looked away first, her gaze drifting back up to the ceiling where it traced a meandering crack in the plaster that she had not noted before. Anything was better than looking over at him, and thinking about just how close they were, how she could feel the press of his hip against hers and the unbearable heat of his body burning through the thin fabric of her chemise.

Finally, after a long moment, Cornelius broke the silence. "This is a bit awkward, isn't it?"

She smiled at that, relieved that he was at least willing to acknowledge it. "It is. I didn't really think about this part of it when I suggested you should sleep here with me last night."

"For what it's worth, I'm glad I didn't spend the night on the floor.

It's rather cold in here now that the fire has died out."

It had been offered companionably, no censure, no double en-tendre, no presumption of anything more than she was willing to give. "Thank you, Cornelius," Prim said softly, overwhelmed by his kindness, his understanding and the fact that, perhaps for the first time in her life, she felt she might be able to trust someone who was not her sister or brother.

"For what?" he asked.

"For being a gentleman. Not just by birth but by deed. I don't think I've ever encountered a man quite like you and I don't know what to make of it."

He frowned, his brows drawing together in consternation. "Prim-rose, I'd like to say that I'm unique, but the truth is I'm not. There are other men in the world who are honorable and good. It pains me to think that your life has seen you encounter so few of them."

"I think I've seen the worst side of a lot of things," she said. "But I let myself forget that is only one side of it."

He rolled onto his side, facing her. "It's an easy enough thing to do," he said. "For the longest time, I saw only my father's flaws. They were many in number. But he had the capacity for kindness as well, and a sense of fairness that I never really understood about him until I saw the way he stood by Lord Wolverton when he was accused of the murder of his first wife. My father was steadfast in his belief in Wolverton's innocence, and rightly so, when everyone else believed him guilty."

"He seemed like a very kind man and Lady Wolverton seemed lovely, as well. Generous and giving… and not in that false, pious and self-aggrandizing way that Lady Linden had been."

"Lady Linden was the woman you were going to work for as a house maid?" He asked.

She grimaced. "Yes. I didn't really want to work for her but I felt we had no choice. We were struggling to keep food on the table and taking in sewing only went so far. Hiring me was simply a good deed for her to boast of to the other ladies in the village. It was some sort of strange competition between them to see who could outdo the others with their charitable contributions or acts of mercy. I shouldn't complain. If it hadn't been for those women we would not have survived in Devonshire as long as we did."

They grew silent then, the moment stretching between them. The awareness of just how near they were, of just how few layers of cloth separated them. Finally, he rolled away and stood up.

"We should get up and begin the day's journey," he said. "We've a long way yet to travel and it won't be easy for you."

"Yes, I suppose we should begin the day," Prim agreed. The tension that now existed between them had seemed to develop spontaneously, a split second of awareness shattering the companionable quality of their conversation and turning it into something strained and loaded with portent. But she didn't mind, she realized. That tension brought with it anticipation and that anticipation, maddening as it might be, was also strangely exciting and felt just a little bit wicked.

He rose first, climbing from the bed, donning his coat in one swift movement and running his hands through his hair. Within less than a minute, he was out the door, muttering something about breaking their fast. Once more, Prim was left in privacy to dress.

CORNELIUS DIDN'T SLAM the door. He did, however, cross to the opposite wall and press his forehead against the cool plaster and pray for some end to his lust-fueled torture. Lying there beside her in that bed, feeling the softness of her body next to his, and all the while making inane conversation so that she wouldn't see just how terrible his thoughts were.

God, but he wanted her. He wanted her like he'd never wanted anything in his life. For a man who'd never known desperation, he'd taken to it like a duck to water, it seemed. He'd been in a constant state of it from the first moment he'd set his gaze upon her. Every encounter only made it worse. Not a minute of the day passed that he did not ache for her.

But it wasn't just desire. As much as he wanted to make love to her, he wanted her to be his to touch, to hold, to care for. She was so impossibly strong, had such determination and fortitude, and yet he wanted to give her the opportunity to count on someone other than herself.

"Get food, Cornelius. Get the food, get the carriage ready, and be done with this before you go mad," he muttered to himself and banged his forehead lightly against the wall. Perhaps a small bit of head trauma would dull the misery of unrequited lust and camouflage the fact that he'd transformed into a lovesick calf.

No sooner had he finished his pep talk than one of the serving girls rounded the corner. She paused long enough to look at him as if he were a madman and then gave him the widest berth that the narrow corridor would permit.

"Perfect," he muttered. "Just bloody perfect."

Chapter Twenty-Four

THEY HAD REACHED London. It had been yet another long and wearying day on the road, trapped in the confines of the carriage with the man who was to be her husband, though they hardly knew one another.

She should have been happy. Marrying a man of wealth, privilege and prestige would afford her the kind of life that she and Hyacinth had dreamed of as children. How many nights had the two of them lain on that small pallet in the corner of the single room that had been their home when they were small girls and whispered of such things? Even then it had been nothing more than a fantasy. As a small child, Prim had recognized the extreme unlikelihood of her life ever undergoing such a transformation. Princes and handsome knights who came riding up on white horses were only stories for children. While she might have been only a girl of seven at the time, she had not been a child. No one who witnessed what she and Hyacinth witnessed there could ever be described as children. That word implied a kind of innocence and hope that neither of them had been able to cling to in that place.

Prim shuddered slightly, recalling the dark desperation of those days. She didn't often allow herself to think of them. Drawing herself back to the present, she surveyed her surroundings carefully.

It was evening, the lamp lighters meandering the streets to light each one in the better neighborhoods. For Prim, it was a revelation. She was seeing a section of London that she never had. Less than a mile cross country, though significantly more through the winding streets of the city, from the hovel where she and Hyacinth had lived for so long with her mother and then with Lila as a baby, it was difficult to imagine that they were in the same city. There were parks and green spaces, perfectly manicured and lovely even in the fading light. The houses were bright and cheerful, candles and oil lamps gleaming through the windows.

While the air was still thick with smoke from thousands of chimneys, it was not the dirty, dingy and terrifying city of her memory. Not in Mayfair at any rate.

"You act as if you have never seen London before," Cornelius said softly, his deep voice filling the small space of the carriage.

It had been at her behest that he'd shared her bed the night before. It had not seemed such a remarkable thing in the moment. She had been sharing a bed her whole life with her sisters and with Rowan. Practicality had inspired her decision, but had she known just how different it would be, how much it would increase her already dangerous awareness of him to be in such close proximity, in such an intimate space, for so long, she would never have suggested it.

"I suppose in some ways I have not. I daresay, I could take you to the Devil's Acre and you would seem as if you had never seen London either," she replied. It wasn't a reprimand, but an observation. They were from completely different worlds, despite their current circumstances, and could not have had less in common in terms of their experiences in life.

"Touché," he replied. "It's a miracle the lot of you survived that place. Not just the criminal element. But it is rife with disease."

"Any place where people live in such cramped quarters is rife with disease." Prim looked out the window once more, noting a woman walking by on the arm of a man. There was something about her, the tilt of her head, the too loud peal of her laughter—she was not his wife. *A mistress perhaps. A courtesan or a demirep. But not a respectable woman.* "Perhaps there is not such a great difference between the Devil's Acre and Mayfair, after all. Men are still men and women are still a thing to be bought and bartered, it seems."

Her comment must have rattled him for he turned to gaze out the window himself at the passing couple. Trapped as they were in the slow moving evening traffic, they were still in view. "Not all men are without honor and not all women who have entered such a life have done it blindly. There are no absolutes in this world, though I once thought that to be true."

There was something sad in his tone, something that hinted at regret. Curious, Prim asked, "And how is that you came to recognize your grave error in judgment?"

"My father... he was not a good man. He was thoughtless, irresponsible, bent on self-destruction. And yet he was generous to a fault. He would help any man he considered a friend, or any woman. The fact that he has not cared for all the children that he sired was not out of miserliness or meanness or lack of feeling. It was simply that he forgot. That something shiny, or more likely someone pretty, was in front of him, and other things passed to the back of his mind. Never to be thought of again, unless someone broached the topic."

"And you think that does not make him a bad man?"

"No. I've come to the shocking realization after judging him so harshly for most of my life that I think my father was a lonely man. Everything he did was an attempt to distract himself from that, to mask the pain of it with women and drink and carousing. He was not a good man, but he was not an entirely wicked one either."

"And you, Cornelius Garrett, Lord Ambrose... what manner of man are you?" Prim demanded. She had her own thoughts, but she knew that he was tortured by his past. It would likely color his answer.

"I am a murderer. Regardless of my reasons, I took another man's life."

"A man who was a threat to those you cared for! What of the soldiers at the front line? They kill in battle, for king and for country, and to save their brothers-in-arms. Would you hold them to the same standard you are marking for yourself?"

"It's hardly the same," he protested.

"It's hardly different," Prim insisted. He seemed determined to view himself poorly, no matter what was said. "You should take some of the mercy you are so willing to grant the memory of your father and spare some for yourself. You are no less deserving of it."

"And are you no less deserving of it than your mother was? Do you not judge everything you say and do by the distance you wish to keep between her fate and your own?"

His words had been a challenge, tossed out between them and demanding an answer. Prim's lips pursed for a moment, and then she replied, "Touché."

"We are not at war, Primrose. Despite our barbs, I would not have it be so... but these are painful subjects. The wounds are deep and jagged, and I think, for now, best left alone," he said.

"Perhaps you are right. What are we to do now? I've never been married. I don't even know where to start," she admitted.

CORNELIUS SMILED IN the ever growing darkness inside the carriage. It was a peace offering, an olive branch in the form of a change in subject. He'd take it gladly. "I shall take you to Madame Le Faye tomorrow... and while you are being fitted for gowns and all the necessary fripperies, I shall set about procuring a special license and making an appointment at a church. Do you have a preference?"

"I've never been to church all that much either," she admitted. "Certainly not in London. We'd have been tossed out given how notorious my mother was and the fact that we were dressed little better than beggars. It doesn't matter. You choose."

"St. Martin's in the Fields is close by and smaller than St. Paul's to be sure, though not as grand."

"Grand hardly matters," she replied breezily. "We are unlikely to have guests, after all, outside of family."

It shouldn't have been that way for her, he thought. So much of her life had been cheated already. Poverty, working from dawn till dark to provide for her siblings, worrying constantly about how to survive without sacrificing herself fully to the demons of her past—and now she would have a havy-cavy wedding to a man she barely knew. Regardless of how their marriage was to begin, he hoped that as it continued, they would find some contentment with one another at least.

"We will schedule the ceremony for three days hence," he said. "That will give you time to have something suitable to wear prepared for you and also for your siblings and Arabella to arrive."

"And in the meantime, we reside in your townhouse without a chaperone," she mused.

He didn't want to be insulted by it. But the nature of his intentions and the nature of his true desires were just disparate enough for him to recognize that her wariness was wise. "There are servants in the house. You will be perfectly safe, Primrose."

"Safe isn't the issue, Cornelius. I'm not afraid of you. But if the point of our marrying is to avoid scandal, it hardly seems wise to court it."

"Most people have not yet returned to town. We have another two weeks at least before the season begins in full. It won't be an issue," he explained.

"And Lord Samford? Do you think he'll figure out where we've gone?"

Cornelius was counting on it. They might remain unobtrusive for the time being, but as soon as the ceremony was complete, the gossips' tongues would wag so fiercely they might manage to clear London of its fog. But the carriage was slowing further, easing to a stop before his townhouse on Curzon Street. The last thing he wanted was to be heard discussing the man on the street. It would only fuel the fires of his suspicion and paranoia.

"We will discuss it more over dinner, Primrose. I think when it comes to conversations about the threat he poses, we should be as circumspect as possible."

"But you said no one was in town—"

"I said most were not in town. There are always outliers and those are typically the men who prefer the debauched entertainments that can only be found in the city. Those same gentlemen are the ones Lord Samford would be most likely to associate with... I can't stress the importance of not antagonizing him further."

"Further? I never antagonized him at all! He nearly ran us down with his horse and then managed to put two and two together to determine that Rowan was likely his son! Then he tried to murder us! We are the innocents here!"

"Yes," Cornelius replied, "you are. And I want to protect you both from him. Your very existence, and Rowan's, is antagonizing to him... not because you have done anything wrong, Primrose, but because he has. No man likes to be reminded of his misdeeds. He is unhinged. We should both remember that when considering how to deal with him."

His words seemed to have some effect on her. The jut of her chin lessened, the tension in her seemed to dissipate to some degree.

"I apologize for being so quick of temper." Her words were uttered stiffly, a clear sign that she was not someone used to apologizing. "I have grown weary in my life of those who would victimize someone and then blame that very victim for their misfortune."

"To be entirely clear, I hold you blameless in everything. I should have been more vigilant and less narrow in my thinking when it came to Samford and the depths to which he would sink." He said nothing further. The carriage had halted entirely and he could hear the driver as he jumped down from the box. Within minutes the carriage door was open, the steps were in place and he was climbing out onto the pavers before his home. Turning back, he offered his hand to Primrose to assist her. She took it, her fingers cool against his hand as she accepted his help.

The door opened as they climbed the steps and the butler he employed for town appeared. "My lord, we did not expect you."

Cornelius' eyebrow shot up. "It was an impromptu journey, Headley. I'm afraid we've had a bit of an accident and my betrothed was injured. The journey has quite exhausted her."

"Betrothed?" the butler repeated, his tone clearly uncertain.

"Yes, Miss Primrose Collier and I are to be married posthaste. In the meantime, you'll have a room prepared for her and a hot bath drawn, as well."

The butler made no movement. He simply stood there and blinked at the pair of them.

His own temper flaring then, Cornelius asked, "Is that a problem, Headley?"

The butler cleared his throat and stepped back, no longer blocking the entrance. "Of course not, my lord. I'll see to it once. We will endeavor to make Miss Collier as comfortable as possible during her stay here."

Cornelius stepped aside and allowed Prim to enter before him. He gestured to one of the footmen. "See Miss Collier to my study and have a fire laid there. We shall have tea while the appropriate preparations are being made."

When Prim was out of sight, he turned back to the butler. "Her tenure, Headley, not her stay." Cornelius corrected. "She is not a guest in this house. This will be her home. And in two short days, she will be mistress here. It might be something to think on before you insult her further."

The butler's sour face pinched even further. "It was not my intent to give offense, my lord. I most humbly apologize. It was only the shock."

"That I was betrothed or that I was betrothed to a woman whose standing is not my own?"

Headley turned to face him then, his posture stiff and unrelenting. "If I may speak freely, my lord?"

"Please do!"

"It was a shock to see you announcing your betrothal to a woman who came and went freely from you own father's bedchamber!"

"That was not Primrose, Headley. It was her mother."

"That is more than a family resemblance, my lord. No two people could be so alike unless they were twins!"

Cornelius sighed. "My father has been dead for seven years, Headley. And he had not been involved with the woman you are remembering at that time for more than five years. Which would have made Primrose Collier roughly eight years old at the time. Think on it."

Abashed, the butler's head jerked toward the study door. "You mean to marry the daughter of your father's mistress?"

"I mean to marry *that* woman who has raised one of my father's illegitimate children at great cost to herself. Miss Collier's siblings, the elder Miss Collier, Hyacinth, young Rowan and Miss Lila—my own half-sister—will arrive within a day or two. I expect all of them to be treated with the same dignity and respect you would show Prinny himself. Is that understood?"

"Yes, my lord," the butler replied, but his tone was clipped and it was clear that he still held his poor opinion of Primrose firmly.

"I've tolerated your insolence in the past, Headley, because you worked for my father and tolerated his proclivities. This is not an instance where such tendencies will be indulged or ignored. Do as I've said or leave the service of this house." With those parting words, Cornelius turned and stalked away, leaving the servant gaping after him.

Chapter Twenty-Five

KITTY STEPPED DOWN from the sedan chair with the porter's assistance. She had her cane, but with the uneven cobblestones, it was still a relief to have someone there. Most times, she didn't require assistance, but her leg had been paining her as of late.

"There you are, Miss," the porter said. "Shall I wait for you?"

"I'll be in the book shop for some time and then I must go to the milliner. If you've another fare, I wouldn't want you to miss out on it. I should be done with all of my shopping by two if you wish to return," she said.

He was a younger man, but pleasant and never forward on any of the occasions when he'd transported her. For that reason alone, Kitty wanted to reward him.

"I'll be here, Miss. Thank you," he said and was off.

Kitty turned to face the row of shops and the impatiently waiting Sally and her maid. Judith was supposed to have met them, as well, but the younger woman was nowhere to be seen.

"Where has the silly wretch gotten off to?" Kitty asked.

Sally rolled her eyes. "Heaven knows. A man might have smiled at her on the street and sent her into a dead faint. Perhaps, she fell into the Avon and he had to enact a dashing rescue?"

"I certainly hope she did not," Kitty snapped. "It's freezing. He might catch his death."

Sally laughed. "We shouldn't be so mean. I do love Judith dearly. She's just so man crazed that I sometimes question her good sense."

"Well, I want to be crazed for Udolpho. I've heard they are at

Treadway's," she said, referencing the book shop they often frequent-
ed. "My father found my last copy and tossed it in the fire."

Sally's eyes widened. "So how far did you get? It's very salacious!"

"I hadn't gotten to anything resembling salacious," Kitty admitted
forlornly. "Is it terribly wicked?"

"Yes… and delightful," Sally said. "Come, we'll get you a copy.
And we'll buy some boring treatise on how to preserve botanical
specimens."

Kitty frowned. "If I wanted a book like that there are plenty in the
library already!"

"You don't want the book, silly! You want the cover. There is a
clerk at Treadway's who will, for a half-pence, switch the book covers.
You can read all about wicked Udolpho and no one will be the wiser."

Kitty grinned. "Unless they ask me how to preserve a botanical
specimen. Then I'm afraid I'd be caught out entirely. But it's worth the
risk!"

The two of them were still giggling as they entered the
bookseller's and selected their items. They had taken them to the
counter to pay when Judith stumbled in. Her cheeks were flushed and
her eyes bright.

"Who have you been flirting with?" Sally asked sharply.

"No one. I was running to get here because I was late," the other
girl replied. It was clearly a lie.

"Never mind," Kitty said. "It doesn't matter. I'm certain he was
imminently unsuitable and that you will come to your senses once
we've got some food in you. There's that tea shop a few doors down
with those lovely cakes!"

Sally groaned. "I'll take the tea. But I cannot have the cakes. My
gowns are already too tight. Papa has refused to let me take a sedan
chair anymore. He insists that I walk everywhere now as I've become
too plump and he refuses to buy me anymore new gowns when I've
failed, yet again, to land a husband."

"Which one is the clerk who'll switch the book covers?" Kitty
asked.

Sally frowned. "He's not here. I wonder if he was sacked for his transgressions."

Kitty placed the copy of Udolpho on the counter before the shopkeeper. "I suppose I'll just have to take my chances."

With her purchases wrapped, they left the bookshop and made for the tea room. Judith kept glancing nervously over her shoulder.

"Do you think we're being followed or are you simply hoping for it?" Sally asked her.

Judith turned her head sharply to face forward. "I was only looking because I thought I saw someone I know. Must you be so suspicious, Sally?"

Kitty frowned. Judith was behaving oddly, even by the standards they held for Judith which were somewhat more lax than they might otherwise have been. "Are you well, Judith? You seem unusually distracted. Perhaps today is not a good day for our weekly outing."

Wallflowers, spinsters, bluestockings. They were called dozens of equally unappealing names. At the end of the day, it meant their social calendars were very bare. They attended balls in the evenings, though most never even noticed their presence, but few people called on them during the day. It was one of the many reasons that they'd taken to having weekly visits in one another's homes and shopping excursions such as their current one.

"I was reluctant to say anything, Kitty, but I'm not feeling just the thing. The idea of tea and cakes is making me rather ill. Do you think we might stroll down by the river first? Some crisp bracing air might be just the thing!" Judith said.

"Of course!" Kitty agreed instantly. "Of course, we can. Are you certain you wouldn't rather return home?"

"Oh, no!" Judith said quickly. "I had a terrible row with my stepmother before I left the house. That's likely why I don't feel well now. Going home would not improve the matter at all."

Kitty nodded while behind them Sally rolled her eyes. Sally and Judith were forever sniping at one another. Kitty loved them both, though at times she could have gleefully knocked both their heads together. But they all did have one thing in common—difficulties with their respective families. Unwed. Unwanted. Quickly approaching an age of being utterly unmarriageable. The three of them were embarrassments.

Keeping an arm around Judith, they walked toward the busy area before the baths and the abbey, where they could look down at the weir. As they neared Pulteney Bridge, Kitty became aware of the surreptitious glances that Judith kept making toward the road.

Judith was many things, but an accomplished liar was not one of them. While her friend might very well have had a row with her stepmother, Kitty was almost certain that was not why she was acting so strangely at the moment. On the verge of asking her friend what was actually going on, the sound of an approaching carriage startled her. It was close. Far closer than it should have been. With the head of her cane draped over her wrist and her other arm looped through Judith's, she was stuck, unable to make a speedy retreat. But the carriage did not run her down, as she'd feared. Instead, it halted near enough that when the door opened, a pair of strong hands emerged from within and grabbed at her.

Kitty fought, slapping at the grasping man who hauled her into the vehicle, but hindered as she was by her limp, by Judith and the heavy and cumbersome weight of her cane, her efforts were ineffectual at best. Hauled into the hired carriage, sprawled on the dirty floor, it took her a moment to get her bearings. It was so dark inside, that her eyes were having difficulty adjusting. But as she did, she turned and caught sight of an all too familiar face.

"What have you done?" she demanded.

Fredrick Hamilton, Lord Samford, smiled though no warmth from that expression ever reached his eyes. "I'm ensuring that our match can continue, Katherine."

"Kitty," she corrected. "I despise being called Katherine. Though under the circumstances, I think you should probably continue to address me as Miss Wyverne."

"I don't think that I will. You see, this carriage is bound for Gretna

Green. I mean for us to be married, Kitty."

Kidnapped. She'd heard stories of such things happening to other young women, especially those upon whom a fortune rested in the balance of their matrimonial state. But they were beautiful girls, typically, or so young and meek that to abduct them would not be a challenging task. Somehow, she'd always believed herself immune to such threats. Clearly, she had been mistaken.

"I'll refuse!" she uttered vehemently. While she'd already made her decision about Lord Samford, his current behavior hardened her resolve. He was a scoundrel through and through.

His smile faded, hardened into something ugly and dark. He leaned forward, and grasped her face in his hand, tugging her toward him. It wasn't a gentle gesture. Each of his fingers dug painfully into her flesh. The grip, hard and bruising, was inescapable. When they were eye to eye, only inches separating them, he spoke again. "No, Kitty, you will not. You will comply or it will go very badly for you. As it stands, I'm willing to let you remain chaste until our wedding night. Truth be told, I am not so eager to bed you. But I will. And if I must do so before bestowing the honor of my name upon you, I shall. I will ruin you so thoroughly no other man will ever have you, fortune or no. So cooperate and spare us both that indignity."

He let her go abruptly so that she fell backward onto her bottom, her back striking the edge of the carriage seat. Kitty's lips parted with shock and her gasp of pain. Had he truly just threatened rape as a means of securing her hand in marriage? "You are a monster," she whispered. He wasn't a scoundrel at all. He was something infinitely worse, something that in her sheltered existence she did not have a name for.

"If necessary," he said. "I can be kind. I can be pleasant, as well. But mark me, Kitty, I am willing and perfectly capable of being the antithesis of those things. What you get from me, Kitty, is determined by what you give. Cooperation and compliance will ensure that this is pleasant for both of us. Rebellion and obstinance will make things very uncomfortable for us both. More so for you than me, I'd wager, however."

"Or you could just marry someone who actually wanted you! Like that girl at the Assembly Rooms," she snapped.

"She's a twit. And a penniless one. I need your fortune, Kitty. And I mean to have it. I'll do whatever is necessary and inflict any torment upon you that I must to get it. Think about that before you test me further," he warned.

If she'd been able to run, if her leg had not been such a hindrance, she could have jumped free of the carriage and sought help from the crowds. But he'd been smart about that, much smarter than she'd ever given him credit for.

Judith.

Judas was more like. Her friend had betrayed her for him. The girl she had trusted and welcomed into her home so many times had intentionally led her to that place so that he might abduct her and force her into marriage.

"What did you do to Judith to sway her to your cause?"

Samford smiled. "I did nothing. I offered her a smile. I told her she was pretty. I told her what a shame it was that you'd wind up old and alone… but that if you were my wife, and she was your friend, I would feel honor bound to help her secure a worthy husband. Loyalty often wavers in the face of such pathetic desperation."

Had it truly been that easy? Had one of her best friends sold her out for the promise of matchmaking? Kitty didn't want to believe it, and yet she couldn't shake the feeling Lord Samford had been more honest with her in the last few moments inside that carriage than in all the weeks she had known him.

With every passing second, they moved further and further away from anyone who might be able to help her. She had no hope of outrunning him. She had no hope of being able to propel herself far enough from the carriage to be able to successfully extricate herself from his kidnapping scheme. Physically, she was at a loss. But Kitty did not let that deter her. She would escape him, but she would do it by being smart and keeping her wits about her.

The one thing she was certain of was that she would rather die than become Lady Samford.

Chapter Twenty-Six

S TANDING BEFORE THE mirror in Madame Le Faye's shop, wearing a dress that had quite obviously been made for another woman and that was being hastily pinned so that it might be altered to fit her, Prim felt rather lost. She wanted her sister with her. Never had she felt the need for Hyacinth's gentle guidance more so than in those moments. Surrounded by lovely and oh-so-very-costly things, she felt terribly out of her element.

"It's a lovely gown on you," Madame said. "Pale colors are fashionable but they flatter few women truly. But with your eyes and your hair, which seems to be every color all at once, it is good."

Madame's French accent was a terrible imitation. Prim was fairly certain that she knew more French than Madame Le Faye did. But the woman was kind and very accommodating.

"Thank you, Madame Le Faye."

The woman smiled, and made one circuit around the small dais that Prim stood on for the fitting. "Yes. And this gown fits your figure to perfection. The woman it was originally made for, she did not come back for it… I think her family took her away to Bath to try and catch a husband for her there. I believe there is less competition. It would never have done for her, anyway."

Prim frowned. "Why not? It's a lovely dress."

"She has a limp… light fabrics such as this, drape and sway with movement. It would have emphasized her shortcomings. I tried to tell her mother that, but she was insistent that her daughter be dressed in the latest fashion plates. The girl needed velvet and wool, brocade…

160

fabrics that bring grace to their wearer, not fabrics for whom the wearer must provide the grace."

Prim felt like she should defend the girl, but it wasn't as if Madame Le Faye was saying it mean spiritedly. She spoke matter of factly and, in truth, seemed distressed that the girl might have been forced by her mother to wear a gown that would not flatter her.

"Bath, you say? Might I ask her name? Perhaps when we return there, I can thank her."

"I do not see why not. It was Miss Wyverne," Madame Le Faye said as she plucked at a small pleat where the bodice and skirt met, adjusting it minutely.

Miss Wyverne. It seemed to Prim that their paths were destined to cross. Surely it could not be coincidence that they kept circling around one another?

"I believe we have common acquaintances," Prim managed. "I shall make an effort to make her acquaintance myself."

"Lovely girl," Madame said distractedly, still adjusting the fabric. "Pity about her limp. And about her mother."

"Is her mother ill?"

Madame looked up, startled. "Oh, no. Not ill. Just horrid. I think we have the necessary measurements for the dress. It will be ready and delivered to you by tomorrow morning at the very latest. But now we need to get you into something for today. There is a round gown. It is not so grand, but it will do and should require no alteration at all to fit."

Once more, Prim found herself being stuffed into another dress. It was a simple day dress of dark blue wool. It was fine, though rather plain, but Prim preferred it to everything else she'd been forced to try on. She didn't want to think what Lord Ambrose might have offered Madame Le Faye to take the very gowns she had sewn for others and use them for Prim's own wardrobe. It was likely costing the earth.

By the time her shopping expedition was done, she had a stack of packages that would have been taller than Rowan had he stood next to it. New corsets, petticoats, shifts, and stockings had all been selected.

Next was a trip to the milliner for bonnets, hair ribbons and gloves. Then it was off to the cobbler for shoes. Strict instructions had been left on what she was to return home with. It felt so strange to buy things for herself.

Prim honestly couldn't remember a time in her life when she had ever owned a single gown that had not first belonged to someone else. Though considering the poor Miss Wyverne, perhaps that was still true. It seemed everything Madame was passing to her had been commissioned by the other woman before she'd been whisked away to Bath.

"It seems odd that she left London in such a hurry with all of this waiting for her," Prim commented.

Madame Le Faye leaned in closely, as if she had a secret to whisper, though it was unlikely that Madame had ever whispered anything in her life. "Her father is putting her in the path of a potential suitor... trying to get her married off. Lord Samford. I heard her talking about it with her friend who accompanies her here. She was not pleased."

"She's unwilling to marry him?" Prim's heart sank. The poor girl. It was bad enough to be blinded by a man like Samford, to have his charm mask the truth of his character until it was too late. But for her to know that he was not a man to be admired or desired, and be forced to wed him regardless—it was just terrible.

"I heard her say that he was not a man to be trusted and that she feared he was more like his family than he admitted. Horrible people they are!"

Madame said nothing further because the bell over the shop's door tinkled. She scurried away to greet her patrons, leaving Prim there to contemplate what had been said. From her perch on the dais, she heard Madame's overly warm welcome.

"My lord, welcome back. I know you will be very pleased with all that we have selected," the modiste gushed.

Cornelius' answer was uttered in a much lower tone, harder to make out. Still, Prim found herself relieved to hear him, to know that he was near. That alone was alarming to her.

Stepping down from the dais, Prim smoothed the skirts of dark blue wool and left the fitting area for the store front. Cornelius looked up as she entered, his gaze traveling over her in a way that was familiar, and quite appreciative, but it did not have the effect on her that such glances normally would. From any other man, it would have been met with a firm set down. From him, it only created a warmth that suffused her.

"It's very flattering," he said. "I'm pleased Madame could provide you something so quickly. The other gowns?"

"One will be delivered first thing in the morning, and the other two the following day," Madame said. "Any further commissions will be the following week."

"That will do for now," Cornelius agreed. "Add another two dresses identical to the one she's currently wearing."

"Color, my lord?"

"Something vibrant. Jewel tones, I think," he said.

"I am capable of making decisions on the colors of my own dresses, my lord," Prim said, inserting herself into the conversation as much to remind them of her presence as to intercept his high-handed decision making.

"Then what colors would you prefer?" he asked.

"Something vibrant... and jewel toned," she admitted. "I abhor pastels."

"Perhaps a lovely peacock blue and then the other in amethyst?" Madame offered. "I already have the fabric but it has not been marked for any other commissions."

"That will do nicely." Prim had made her point and she wasn't going to cut off her nose to spite her face. It was terribly vain and horrible of her to be so excited about new gowns, but she was. And she wanted desperately for Hyacinth to have the same.

CORNELIUS NOTED THE high color in her cheeks. It was obvious that she was cheered by her new clothes, but he could see something in her eyes, some hidden worry. "Come. We'll get some tea before we tackle the milliner's shop," he suggested. Primrose answered with a nod, picked up one of the many shawls that Madame Le Faye had insisted she required and draped it over her shoulders.

There was a small tea room only a short distance away. Walking there with her hand on his arm, she remained curiously silent.

"Are you unhappy with Madame Le Faye's wares?" he asked.

"Not at all. I love my new gowns. I wasn't sure if I should say anything here on the street or wait until we're in the tea room, but there's likely a greater chance of being overheard there than here," she admitted. "These gowns were made for Miss Wyverne, whose father dragged her off to Bath before she could collect them. He's trying to marry her off to Lord Samford, and I fear she is rather unwilling."

Cornelius sighed. "We have no authority to intervene, Primrose. None. He is her father… and unless I am misremembering things, Miss Wyverne has reached her majority and cannot be forced to marry."

"Men can always find a way to force women to do what they wish," Prim replied sharply. "In some ways, I think you are more naive about the world than I am."

Cornelius said nothing for the moment. In truth, he didn't even take offense to what she said. He couldn't, as it was undoubtedly true. He'd known of his father's debauchery but only secondhand. At no point had he been forced to witness it. And in all of his life, other than the gossip that had followed the events at Blackfield five years ago, he'd never been victimized by another. That was not true for Primrose or her siblings.

"I will make inquiries and see what can be done," he relented.

She let out a shuddering breath. "Thank you. I can't bear to think of some poor girl being forced to marry such a man!"

"Miss Wyverne is not an unattractive girl, but she is rather reserved and has a limp. While she has a great fortune, the family's connections are not so high as to entice a great deal of interest… given all of that and her predilection for preferring books to people, she has limited marital prospects. It could well be that our interference might not be welcomed. Her hesitance could have been nothing more than nerves or a lovers' spat, Primrose," he reminded her.

"But we can discover this and be sure? If she wishes to marry him, truly, I will say nothing more… but I would not see any woman forced to marry where she did not wish!"

"Like you are?" he asked. It should not have stung, and yet it did. She was being forced, albeit for far different reasons.

"That isn't what I meant," she said stiffly. "Not at all. I've given you my agreement and I've done so of my own free will!"

"Despite the circumstances?"

"Had those circumstances not occurred, it would never have been a question that would need to be asked," she said sharply. "And the man responsible for those circumstances could even now be forcing a girl to marry him against her will, just so that he can have her fortune for himself."

"Had I asked under any other circumstances, Primrose, would your answer have been the same? A very reluctant yes?"

Cornelius didn't know why it was so important to him to know that answer, but it was. He didn't want to be the villain in her story.

"I cannot say. I had never given it thought beforehand because it was such an absurd notion… why would you ever offer for a girl like me?"

A girl like her. Beautiful. Strong willed and independent. Fiercely intelligent and fiercely loyal to her family. Protective of all those she cared for and willing to sacrifice anything, including her own happiness, for their well-being. And yet he knew precisely what she meant. Despite every admirable quality he listed, her birth was not only low but scandalous. She had no connections, no fortune and, by most standards, would have been more suitable for a mistress than a wife.

"Because I can," he confessed. "Because rules, even those that society holds fast and dear, are meant to be broken. Because there is not a single thing I would alter about you."

She drew in a sharp breath and her lips, tempting as they were, remained parted afterward. He could think of nothing but that moment in Wolverton's garden when he'd given in to his desires and kissed her. Had they not been standing in the middle of a busy London street, he would have done so again right there. Kissing her seemed as necessary to him as breathing. So he did the only thing he could.

Moving quickly, Cornelius half-dragged her into a small alley between buildings. In the darkened recesses, hidden behind crates and barrels, he gave in to the need to taste her sweetness once more.

If there was one consolation, it was that she met his kiss eagerly. Her head tipped back and she lifted her face to his in anticipation. Whether she wished to be his wife or not, there was desire between them. It would have to be enough to sustain him. For Cornelius realized something about Primrose Collier. She had awakened him. All the passion and fire in his soul that had been under lock and key for so long had suddenly ignited, surging forward and demanding to be freed.

He accepted all that she offered and demanded more. When her lips parted on a sigh, he swept his tongue into the softness of her mouth. It was a blatantly carnal kiss, mimicking other more intimate acts that he found himself eager to complete. She never shied from him, never attempted to push him away. Her hands slid into his hair, tugging his head down, holding him in place. *As if he had any desire to be elsewhere.*

Even as their passion flared, as she pressed the softness and warmth of her body against him, he was aware of their surroundings. They could be discovered at any moment and that was not an indignity that he would ever visit upon her. Slowly disentangling himself from her, pressing dozens of small kisses against her lips, the soft curve of her cheek and the stubborn jut of her chin, he stepped back. Only the sound of ragged breaths broke the silence.

Staring at her, cheeks flushed, lips swollen from his kiss, she was even more beautiful than before, if such a thing were possible. And she would be his, no matter the cost.

All his life, he'd been determined to never be driven by anything other than his intellect and his conscience. But there was something in Primrose Collier, something from the very moment he'd first set eyes upon her, that demanded more of him than that. For the first time in ages, he felt. She sparked his desire, his anger, his admiration and his— Cornelius stopped that thought. It was a word. Only a word. And yet it represented something that he had never thought to feel in his life. Love. Did he love her?

Whether he did or whether he did not, it was not something she was ready to hear from him.

Chapter Twenty-Seven

THEY RETURNED HOME with two footmen laden with packages that were promptly taken up to Primrose's room and unpacked by the maid who had been assigned to her.

"Come into the study with me," he said. "There is something we need to discuss."

A frown marred her brow briefly. "Is something wrong?"

"No. But—I've made some arrangements for the children's future. Lila's and Rowan's. I'd like to review them with you and be certain that you approve. I suppose I should have done so beforehand, but I was uncertain how to proceed until speaking with my solicitor. Everything is preliminary and can be changed if you desire," Cornelius replied.

Prim fell into step behind him as he led her toward the study and the sheaf of papers that was likely waiting on his desk, hand delivered by his very eager to please man of affairs. While he'd left her in the capable hands of Madame Le Faye, he'd been attending to the promise he'd made her. No matter what happened to him, no matter what fate had in store for them in terms of their marriage, neither Primrose nor her siblings would ever be at the mercy of anyone else for their living ever again. She would be well provided for. They all would.

Once in his study, he closed the door firmly behind them. There was no need for nosy servants, particularly Headley, to be privy to what they were about to discuss. No doubt, the gossip would spread far and wide if he let it be known.

"What sort of arrangements are you speaking of, Cornelius?"

"Financial ones," he answered. "I've settled a sum on Lila, in trust for her for when she marries, with approval of course, or when she reaches her majority, that is equal to the settlement our father left to Nicholas. The portion I set aside for Rowan is a bit smaller, but not by much. My hope is that with proper investment, it will equal if not surpass that for Lila by the time he is of age to claim it. And then there is Hyacinth."

"Hyacinth?"

"Yes," he said. "Hyacinth. I suspect that your sister would adamantly refuse to accept any amount of money. But I do not think she would balk at accepting a house. So the cottage at Avondale is being deeded to her, along with a small annuity that should see to her needs and comforts for as long as she lives. Now, she need not reside there. I'm happy to have her stay with us for as long as she likes. But at some point, Hyacinth may wish to marry. If so, I wanted her to have a place of her own, something to put her on equal footing to whatever man she might become entangled with."

Prim stared at him, wide eyed and confused. "Why would you do this?"

"I promised you that I would see to them, Primrose. I keep my promises," he replied evenly. It was incredibly important to him that she know that. That she believe it. "And that is why I've created a trust for you, as well. Whatever happens to me, whether we have children or not, there is a sum of money that has been set aside and will be used to provide a home for you for the rest of your days. Avondale is not entailed. It will be yours. Always, with enough funds and revenue for you to maintain the lifestyle that I hope you will become accustomed to with me."

She accepted the sheaf of papers that he offered to her, reading through them one by one. With each one, her eyes grew wider. Her face paled. When at last she was done, she looked up at him. "You cannot be this wealthy. These numbers are staggering."

"Primrose, my father, for all his faults and all his extravagance, was an extremely gifted man. He invested well. Very well. And somehow, despite having been spared all his vices, I have been blessed with that same insight when it comes to discerning where to put my money, as it were. Why do I feel like that displeases you?"

IT DIDN'T DISPLEASE her. It terrified her. The man was richer than Croesus. Certainly, she'd known that he was wealthy. It was evident in everything he said and did, though he was never boastful or overly extravagant in his dress or purchases. Still, it had been apparent to her. But this was something else. Something she couldn't even quite fathom.

"The entire world will think me an opportunist," she said. "I didn't even know the extent of it and yet I now find myself wondering if an opportunist is not exactly what I am."

He laughed at that. "You've no notion of just how magnificent you are, Primrose. People will whisper. The gossips will monger and the jealous will bite. They always do. But I would sacrifice every shilling in the family coffers for you. Do you realize that?"

"You're mad."

"Perhaps," he admitted. "But not until the day I met you. From the first moment I saw you, I was struck dumb. At first by your beauty, but then by your spirit. By the strength and wit and will that made you who you are. You are the most beautiful woman I've ever seen in all of my life, Primrose, but I can be entirely honest when I say that your beauty, striking as it is, is the least compelling thing about you. If I'm mad, Primrose, it can be laid solely at your door. And I'm content enough with it not to wish it altered."

Prim gaped at him for a moment. She'd never had anyone say such things to her. "I cannot begin to understand you, Cornelius."

"But do you trust me, Primrose?"

"I do," she said. "More than you can possibly know. I've never known a man as honorable as you."

"Then that's a start, don't you think? I want us to be happy together. I'd never given thought to the marriage. But in facing the prospect now, I can state emphatically that I want it to be a happy one... for both of us. And I can think of no better footing to start on than trusting one another."

"There is love," she said.

"So there is," he said, and the warmth in his gaze as he uttered those words made her yearn to reach for him. She wanted to press her face against his shoulder and hide there.

"And with trust, perhaps we shall get there," he continued, "Perhaps we shall get there."

"One day?"

"One day," he agreed. "Now, you should go and ready yourself for dinner. I have to write to Nicholas and send him on errand for us, and for Miss Wyverne. With any luck I can get it out on the last mail coach of the day."

Chapter Twenty-Eight

D R. NICHOLAS WARNER found himself in the uncomfortable position of playing spy for his brother. It had been easy enough to determine where to gather more information about Miss Wyverne, per Cornelius' request. The dowdy spinster's name was suddenly on the tip of every tongue in Bath. Abducted from the street, whisked away in a hired carriage while out shopping with her friends, the girl had suddenly garnered all of the attention that had previously been denied her.

He didn't understand why Cornelius needed to know about the girl, other than the possibility that it might have something to do with Samford, his betrothed, and his new wards. Regardless, when the missive had been delivered asking him to look into it, he had not hesitated. Now, standing on the doorstep of the Villiers' townhouse in a respectable but not quite posh street, he questioned the wisdom of his ready cooperation.

Lifting the heavy knocker and letting it fall, Nicholas waited and silently cursed his brother. The butler answered and the dour face of the man did not make Nicholas reconsider his current irritation with his sibling.

"Dr. Nicholas Warner here to see Miss Judith Villiers."

"Miss Villiers already has a physician," the butler said firmly.

"I am not here in the capacity of my vocation, my good man. I am here because Miss Villiers and I have a common acquaintance… Miss Wyverne." To call the girl an acquaintance was more than a stretch. He'd seen her at the Pump Room and once at the Assembly Rooms when Viola had dragged him, rather begrudgingly, to a ball.

"Forgive me, sir. Please do come in. Terrible thing about poor Miss Wyverne," the butler said. "Miss Villiers is not really accepting callers but, under the circumstances, I think she'd be relieved to talk to someone else who knows Miss Wyverne."

Given what he'd learned from Miss Sally Carter, whom he had visited prior to making his way to the Villiers' house, Nicholas had his doubts about it. He wasn't all that thrilled to be there either as Miss Carter had said, rather dryly, that if he batted his eyes at Miss Villiers all would be confessed.

In the drawing room, he waited only a few moments before a girl entered. She was probably older than Viola, truth be told, but she was very much a girl. There was something childlike about her.

"Miss Villiers, I've come to discuss Miss Wyverne and the events that led to her abduction," he said preemptively.

"I don't know what you mean."

"I am Dr. Nicholas Warner. Lord Ambrose is my half-brother and he finds himself curiously invested in the welfare of Miss Wyverne, due to concerns that his fiancée has about the character of Lord Samford. I believe you are acquainted with him are you not?"

Miss Villiers stepped deeper into the room and sank heavily onto the settee. "I've done something terrible, Dr. Warner. But I didn't know it was terrible. I thought I was helping."

"Miss Wyverne or Lord Samford?"

"Well, both naturally. I just assumed that Kitty had gotten her pride wounded and that if he proceeded with the elopement, she would get over it," Miss Villiers said forlornly.

"To clarify, you helped a man you barely know, a man your friend professed to want nothing to do with, to abduct her for the sake of forcing her into marriage?"

"Well, yes. But he's very handsome and he's titled. And Kitty will never get a better offer!"

"Where was he taking her?"

"To Gretna Green. Where else would anyone elope to?" the girl asked. "You don't think me a terrible person, do you, Dr. Warner? I really only wanted to see her wed to someone who would elevate her station."

"Miss Villiers, you ought to have wanted what would have made your friend happy. With friends such as you, Miss Wyverne hardly needs enemies. Now, if you'll excuse me, I need to see what I can do about sparing your friend a fate that might very well be worse than death."

"What could be worse than death?"

Nicholas shook his head. "You are the silliest of girls. Your father ought to lock you up and never let you see the light of day again. Samford is a villain! A man whose family has long been involved in blackmail and abduction schemes! His sister attempted to murder Lady Wolverton after faking her own death and framing her husband for it! What on earth were you thinking?"

"He's not like them!"

It was like talking to a wall. The girl was absolutely daft. "Good day, Miss Villiers."

Nicholas left in a hurry, stalking out of the house and returning to the townhouse he and Viola had taken for the time being in the Royal Circus. He would dispatch a letter to Cornelius immediately. With luck, he could get it on the next mail coach. If not, he'd be riding ahead to Hungerford and intercepting it there. Time was of the essence for Miss Wyverne, after all. Traveling by private hired coach would be slow going. They might be able to catch them before Gretna Green, but it would be a near thing.

Cursing Cornelius, cursing Lord Samford, and hoping he did not wind up in the middle of some dashing rescue attempt that would lead them all on a merry chase through England, Nicholas quickened his pace as he made for home.

THE TOWNHOUSE ON Curzon Street exploded with sound. Hyacinth was there, attempting to curb the exuberant shouts of the children as Arabella constantly reminded them to mind their manners. Servants bustled to and fro, carrying bags up to various bedchambers.

Descending the stairs, wearing one of the simple day dresses that Madame Le Faye had completed and sent over early that morning, Prim listened to those familiar sounds with relish. She'd never been parted from her siblings for so long before. It raised questions for her though. Would she and Cornelius truly share their home with her entire family or after a time would he shuffle them off to cottages on the estate or to other estates altogether? He had said that he would not, and she believed him to be a man of his word. But at the same time, no man wanted his in-laws underfoot. And no woman wanted to be a third wheel living with a married couple.

Frowning, she didn't realize she had reached the bottom step until a warm, sturdy body hurtled into her, hugging her fiercely.

"I th-th-thought you was dead," Rowan said. "They said you w-w-w-wasn't but I was afraid, Prim!"

The slight stammer was more pronounced than usual, a clear indication of how upset the dear boy truly had been. Prim sat down on the last step and hugged him tightly to her. Her arm still pained her, but she had left off the hideous white bandage and was instead simply using one of the paisley shawls from Madame Le Faye as a sling. It was a vanity, but one she needed. Her pride wouldn't allow her to appear weak. "I'm not dead, obviously. I'm quite well, if perhaps a bit like a lame bird." For good measure, she jerked her head in the direction of her wounded shoulder. "It popped out like a wishbone, so I'm told."

He grinned. "It did not! Now, I know you're well. You only tell big 'uns when you're well!"

That grin was worth it, she thought. Turning to face her other siblings, she saw Lila's reservations and Hyacinth's fear. She'd tackle them one at a time, she decided. "Lila, why don't you and Rowan let Lady Arabella take you into the breakfast room and get a bite to eat? Poor Hyacinth looks like she's bursting to tell me what you all did in Bath without me."

"It was so much fun!" Rowan gushed.

"You'll tell me about your fun later… after Hyacinth tells me whether or not you behaved," Prim said with a slightly menacing tone.

Rowan rose immediately and went to take Arabella's hand. The older woman smiled. Poor Rowan, he was incapable of behaving, bless him.

When the children were out of earshot, Hyacinth rushed toward her. "You don't have to do this, Prim."

"I do actually… it's for the best, Hyacinth, for all of us."

"You said you never wanted to marry… that you would never let a man have such control in your life," her sister reminded her sharply.

Words spoken when they were much younger, when it was easier to be ruled by fear than by desire, than by the idea that, perhaps, she could have something more with Cornelius Garrett than she had ever imagined possible. To even say such a thing was the height of foolish romanticism and yet the thought was there, the belief that he truly was not like other men.

"Hy, I'm not being forced into this. The simple truth is, we should be grateful that he is the sort of man whose honor required him to offer. We are not the sort of women men are held accountable for ruining, especially when the ruination was merely circumstantial rather than factual," Prim said.

"And was it? Merely circumstantial? You've been alone with him for days!" Hyacinth's voice was little more than a scandalized whisper.

"Yes," Prim said. "It was circumstantial. I was injured, Hy. You know that. Do you really think he is the type of man who would take advantage of such a thing?"

"No. But it's the fact that you seem to have no suspicion of him that I find concerning, Prim! You are always suspicious of men. What spell has he cast that you are suddenly trusting and fair-minded when it comes to the opposite sex? That is the source of my concern. Any man who could sway your mind so easily could also sway your heart and I do not wish to see you hurt!"

Prim entered the drawing room just off the entryway and dragged

Hyacinth in with her. "If I don't marry him, I will be considered a fallen woman. Which would not be so terrible given our lowered circumstances before, Hyacinth, but if he means to provide a life for Lila as his recognized sister, she is already at a disadvantage for being the daughter of a woman who was a known—" She stopped, unable to utter the word.

"Prostitute," Hyacinth finished for her.

"Yes. That is bad enough. But for her elder sister to also be the subject of such controversy… and given that Lord Ambrose has his own infamy to contend with, can you not see that this is the only way to ensure her future and Rowan's? And yours, too! Whether you choose to marry or to seek employment or simply to remain with us, I don't want people to whisper about you or about the children!"

"And I don't want you to marry a man, and tie yourself to him forever, as a sacrifice," Hyacinth shot back.

"That isn't the only reason," Prim admitted. "I like him, Hyacinth. I might even more than like him, but I don't know. It was like that from the moment I met him and this just feels so…. inevitable. Like fate is driving me down this path. If I don't do it, I'm terribly afraid I will regret it for the rest of my life. And not out of some altruistic need to see to the welfare of my family. I think, ultimately, the way it will benefit everyone else is just an excuse, a way to give in to what I want without sacrificing my pride in the offing." The admission was freeing. The weight of that knowledge had been pressing on her and having now uttered it to her sister, all she felt was relief.

"You really want to marry him?" Hyacinth asked, her eyes wide and her voice filled with shock.

"Yes. I do. I can't explain it any more than that. I'm not in love with him. I don't think. But I recognize that I could be, that there is something in this connection between us that is so different from everything else I have known in my life. Don't worry for me, Hyacinth. I know what I'm doing and I will be fine. We all will be." It was a fiercely uttered promise. To punctuate, Prim took her sister's hand and held it tightly. "We will be fine."

"I think we might be, after all," Hyacinth replied softly. "I pray he does not break your heart. I do not want to hang for then breaking his head."

Prim laughed. "Then I shall endeavor to always be happy and spare you the hangman's noose. Let's go get breakfast before Rowan eats it all."

Chapter Twenty-Nine

THE LETTER FROM Nicholas slipped from his fingers and fell to the table as Cornelius let out a weary and heartfelt sigh. It had been a brief missive, but one that contained a wealth of information, as well as a clipping from the Bath news sheet that detailed the abduction. It had arrived early in the morning aboard one of the mail coaches traveling from Bath. Nicholas had done as he asked and looked into the whereabouts of Miss Wyverne. And once more, he had to concede that, perhaps, Primrose was correct and he was naive.

The very notion that Samford might have abducted Miss Wyverne would never have occurred to him. But Prim seemed to have some instinct about when men would behave badly. What had occurred in her life to give her such insight? Perhaps it was cowardly that he did not truly want to know.

The children shuffled in, their faces animated and excited. He'd known that they had arrived as they had come on the same coach as the letter from Nicholas. It was likely the only time in Arabella's life she'd ever ridden on a mail coach. But it had been necessary for them to reach London in time.

While Rowan and Lila fell on the heaping sideboard with ravenous appetites, Arabella came and sat beside him. "So you will marry her tomorrow?"

"I had thought to. But we may have to do it today."

"Surely one day will not make such a difference! Will it?" she asked.

Cornelius met his aunt's questioning gaze and spoke candidly.

"Arabella, I'm afraid that Samford has done something horrible. And if I do not leave for Scotland almost immediately, a young girl may find herself tied to him for the rest of her life."

"If she marries him, that won't be long," Arabella added. There were rumors about the death of his first wife. Rumors that they were all well aware of. "Brides and grooms who get tangled up with that family have a way of expiring most unexpectedly."

"True enough. That is even more reason to act swiftly. Pardon me, Aunt, I need to discuss this with my betrothed."

Cornelius rose and was poised to exit the breakfast room when the doors opened once more and Hyacinth and Prim entered arm in arm. He saw the happy smile on her face and the ease she had with her sister.

"Primrose, may we speak privately?"

Her lips pursed in a concerned line. "Is something wrong?"

Cornelius held the door open and they stepped together into the hallway. "You were right about Lord Samford... again. He's taken Miss Wyverne captive and is absconding with her to Scotland."

"Oh, dear," Prim said on a shuddering breath. "That is more than I had feared he was capable of. Are you entirely certain she is unwilling? Perhaps, he swayed her to elope."

"He did not. She was abducted by an unknown person on the street... she had refused him completely. Nicholas discovered that one of her companions aided Samford in the abduction despite Miss Wyverne's very firm assertion that she had no interest in him as a suitor at all."

"What will we do to help her?"

"We will go to the church at once. I have the license. We can be married this morning, and then I will leave for Scotland on horseback and attempt to intercept them before he can force her hand entirely."

"Only if I follow in a coach... she doesn't know you, Cornelius."

"She doesn't know you either," he pointed out.

Prim gazed at him as if he were some sort of dunderhead. "No, but I don't pose a threat to her. And yes, I know you do not pose a threat to her, but she doesn't. And right now, she has no reason to trust men."

"I don't think—"

"She's been taken from everything she knows by a man who doesn't even see her as a person. Just a means to an end. She will be traumatized. And you do not understand, Cornelius, what it feels like to be powerless. I'm going with you. I will not just abandon her to the fates."

Cornelius stared at her, at the stubborn jut of her chin and the fire flashing in her eyes. She was magnificent and he was well and truly sunk. He'd worried initially that it was only infatuation, that it would fade and, over time, they would grow discontented with one another. But that worry fled in the face of one startling realization. He was already in love with her. Hopelessly besotted and entranced by her wit and her will. But that was not something she was ready to hear from him. Not yet. So he would bide his time.

"If we take the mail coach as far north as possible from the city, we can then hire a carriage and perhaps even be ahead of them," he said. "But not without our vows being spoken first. We've flouted enough conventions already."

And he didn't want to wait. Not another day. The sooner she was his wife, the sooner she could be his in every way.

⚜

THEY HADN'T GONE to an inn, though that was just as well for Kitty's sake. The last thing she needed was someone recognizing her or Samford. Instead, he'd taken them to a hunting box outside of Cirencester that belonged to a friend. Given that it was littered with empty bottles, discarded playing cards and a few hair ribbons, she could only guess that hunting was hardly what it was used for. True to his word, he hadn't touched her. But he had locked her in the bedchamber she'd been given. She'd spent hours the night before using every hairpin she possessed to try and pick the lock, all to no avail. There would be no housebreaking for her. That was for certain.

The house had, eventually grown silent and she had realized that he was not about to ravish her in her bed. At that point, Kitty had slept. It was as much from exhaustion as preparation. She needed to be sharp, to have all her wits about her and use any opportunity for escape that presented itself.

Now, the following morning, Kitty was seated on the bed waiting for him to free her. When she heard the scrape of the key in the lock, she let out a shuddering breath. The door opened and he stood there, quite obviously still foxed from the night before. Clearly, there had been more to be had within the confines of their filthy abode than empty bottles. There certainly hadn't been any food and she was starving.

"Get up. We need to go," he sneered.

"I've been up. It's you who slept the morning away… sleeping off your excesses it would seem," she snapped back at him. Regardless of his threats, she'd made a decision not to be cowed him.

He sneered at her. "Not even married yet and already you have perfected the art of nagging. If you can get your crippled self down the stairs, we'll be off. I've an aching head a need for more brandy."

The quip had stung, far more than she wanted to admit. Even worse was the notion that she would have a lifetime of that to put up with. At some point, she would have an opportunity to escape him, she reminded herself. And he was clearly underestimating her based on her physical limitations. If he planned to spend the entire journey drinking, those chances would improve.

"Then let's be off. Perhaps the carriage will crash and we'll both be spared the misery of marriage to one another," she said bitterly and preceded him down the stairs.

They had neared the bottom when he grabbed her upper arm, spun her around and pinned her forcefully against the wall. "You listen to me, Kitty Wyverne! You are lucky, do you understand that?"

His grip on her arm was bruising and the abrupt movement had caused stabbing pains in her leg that reminded her sharply of the disadvantages she currently faced. "Lucky? To have been abducted and forced into marriage with a drunkard?"

His hand flew back, but the blow never fell. He caught himself before actually striking her. Kitty stared at him, wide eyed and afraid.

"I can't have my bride-to-be standing before the blacksmith in Gretna Green with bruises on her face, now can I? But I can hurt you, Kitty Wyverne, without leaving a mark. So don't test me further." With that, he dropped his hand from her arm and stepped back just a bit. As if he was seeing her for the first time, he reached out and took a lock of her hair between his fingers. "And drunkard or no, you'll not make a better match. We both know that... no other man would have you even before I sullied your precious reputation beyond repair."

With that, he strolled past her, down the few remaining steps and out the door to the waiting carriage. Kitty was left to follow. The implication was clear, of course. If she did not follow him, he would simply come back inside and retrieve her—by force if necessary.

Shaken, terrified by the violence and unpredictability of him, Kitty did as was expected of her. But as she made her way toward the door, she paused long enough to snatch up a knife from the table left over from the dinner he'd apparently enjoyed the night before. It was no longer simply a matter of escaping him. She realized that it might very well become a question of life or death.

Chapter Thirty

T HE INN YARD at the Swan Hotel on High Street in Birmingham was a bustling place, even after dark. The mail coach that had carried them thus far was changing horses, a speedy process that allotted only a few moments to disembark. Jumping down from the box where he'd ridden next to the driver, Cornelius hoped that Primrose had fared better inside than he had out. Half-frozen, his clothes damp from the misting rain that had fallen for a good part of their journey, he knew the inside of the stage was not much better. Traveling at such breakneck speeds, the wind would have howled through the vehicle nearly as strongly as it did atop it. And he, at least, had been blessed with the ability to move in his seat, to reposition himself at times for comfort.

Inside, crammed into the small confined space with more than half a dozen others, that would not have been so for her. Opening the door, he spied her sitting stiffly on the edge of the seat, clearly anxious to be free of it.

"Is this where we get off?" she asked.

"It is," he said, and held out his hand to her. Birmingham was far enough north that they should have gotten ahead of Samford and Miss Wyverne. It was near dawn, and they would not be stopping for long.

He watched as Primrose carefully extricated herself from the tangle of passengers, attempting to disrupt others as little as possible. There would be other passengers waiting to board presumably as there had been some changes at several of the stopping points along the way. With Birmingham being one of the more bustling posts along the way, it was a good bet.

Taking her hand, he helped her down just as the new team was fully fastened to the coach and a fresh driver was climbing atop the box, shouting for any passengers to board. The scene was chaos. Someone threw their bags down from the top of the carriage, slinging them into the dirt before them with such force that Prim jumped and Cornelius wondered how the cases did not simply split open. With a baleful stare at the overzealous worker, he picked up the bags, one tucked under his arm and the other in his hand.

"What are we doing now?" she asked.

"I'll rent a private carriage, get us some food from the inn and we'll be off," he said.

She nodded, though it was a weary gesture.

"This was too much for you... too much and too soon following your own accident," he said.

"It was my choice to come," she said, stretching her neck from side to side. "I'll not complain nor will I slow you down. Miss Wyverne does not have the luxury of waiting for me to feel better."

"I'm going to procure a room for us for an hour or so. That way, you may wait somewhere privately while I make the arrangements for the carriage." He would not have her waiting alone in a public room at a busy inn. Even covered by her cloak and with the hood pulled up, he didn't feel she would be safe.

"That's unnecessary. I'll stay with you," she said.

"Primrose, I have to go the stables and procure a driver and a coach. At this time of night, there could very well be a very unsavory element about. I don't want to risk it."

"And if you don't return?"

Cornelius paused, considered his options and then decided that, once more, telling her the truth was best. Opening his great coat, he revealed the sword strapped to his thigh, the pistol tucked into the inner pocket and another blade hanging from a belt at his waist. "I did not come unprepared."

She blinked up at him. "I should say you did not. Were you so heavily armed even during our wedding?"

He had been. They had left immediately following the ceremony, not even bothering to have a wedding breakfast as was the custom. Instead, they had left the church, taken a hackney to Ludgate Hill and caught the next departing mail coach. "I'll get a room for you where you can rest for a bit and refresh yourself. I'll return for you before the sun is fully risen," he promised.

"Please be careful."

"I will not leave you here penniless. There will be a way for you to get back to London and to your sister if something should happen to me!"

Her jaw dropped, lips parting in what appeared to be shock, before drawing tight in a firm line of disapproval. "Do you honestly think my concern for your welfare is because I'm afraid of being stuck here?"

"I hope it is not," he admitted. It was wrong of him to want her to worry for him, but that she might gave him hope. "I would like to believe that you have a care for me, at least a little. But now is not the time to discuss such things. Right now, Primrose, I need you to promise me that if I do not return to fetch you within an hour, you will get back to London and abandon any efforts on Miss Wyverne's behalf. You are no match for Samford and I would not have you be so bold and reckless alone."

"I do care for you... and I would see you come back safely regardless of what happens with our efforts to save Miss Wyverne."

Cornelius became aware of two men leaning against the building watching them. He was only too well aware of how men reacted to her beauty. Reaching for her, he drew the cloak tighter about her and pulled the hood up so that it concealed her face. "We have drawn attention to ourselves here... unwisely. Let us get inside."

Ushering her into the hotel, he quickly arranged for a room. Key in hand, they went up the stairs and located their chamber. It was large and comfortably furnished.

"Rest while you can," he said. "I'll be back as quickly as possible. Do not open this door to anyone but me. There were some unsavory characters outside and I do not feel good about this."

He'd turned to go, his hand on the door handle when she called out, "Cornelius!"

"Yes?"

She moved toward him in a rush and wrapped her arms about him. "Please be careful. I can't help feeling that something awful might happen and I am so afraid for you!"

"I'll be well and cautious," he vowed. Of their own accord, his lips found hers. It wasn't a kiss intended to incite passion, but rather to seal the promise he'd just made her. But like all good intentions, it failed in the face of such temptation. Holding her close, feeling the softness of her full lips crushed against his own, it would have taken a stronger man than he was to deny his urges.

>ᴇ

THE KISS SWEPT her away. Her exhaustion, the pain from being bounced and jostled in the mail coach, all of it fled at his touch. Everything else seemed to vanish and only the points of contact between them were real and tangible. The hard press of his chest against her, the way his lips moved over hers, the thrill as his tongue teased her own, the crush of his arms around her, holding her tightly—those were the only things that existed for her in that moment.

It was both terrifying and sublime. In so many ways, he was everything she'd ever feared—a man so compelling and so irresistible to her that she might lose herself. But she was coming to realize that she feared losing him more. Somehow, he brought out her true self. His very presence forced her to acknowledge her fears, to face them.

Clinging to him, her arms about his neck, Prim slid her hands over the breadth of his shoulders, then down his back. He made a sound of pleasure, a low growl in his throat that raised gooseflesh on her skin and made her shiver.

He broke the kiss. "We cannot do this, Primrose. I would not have our marriage consummated in a hurried encounter in a bustling inn."

"Where would you have it consummated then?" she asked. "We are alone and we are married."

"And you wanted to wait," he pointed out.

She had said that. Because she feared all the things he made her feel, because she feared the awareness of him that had settled upon her like a cloak. "I'm tired of being afraid of who I am, Cornelius, of who I might become. Do you understand that?"

"Better than you realize… but you are not your mother and I am not my father. When we have real privacy and not just the illusion of it in a place such as this, when we have the time for me to make love to you, Primrose—because that is what I mean to do—then we will indulge our desires. But I won't see you cheated by some hurried coupling in a rented room. And I won't cheat myself that way either," he insisted.

"Maybe I am my mother, after all," she said.

"Because you feel desire?"

Prim's hands clenched together in front of her as the shameful admission tumbled from her lips. "No. Because I'm willing to forgo everything else to see that desire fulfilled. Because it was my idea to come haring off to Scotland and rescue a girl we don't even really know, and now, I could wish her to the devil just to be alone with you."

He smiled at that. "But you won't. And I won't. Because without you insisting this was the right thing to do, I would have already abandoned Miss Wyverne to her fate. If nothing else, this should prove to you that we are better together than apart."

"Hurry back. And be safe. I still feel… dread, for lack of a better word. I worry that we've been foolish in this."

"It'll be fine. I promise."

He left the room and Prim locked the door behind him. She felt bereft without him. Not in the needy way that her mother had pined over every man to ever abandon her, but rather as if she'd sent him out to face his doom. It had been her idea to rouse a rescue for Miss Wyverne, but it was Cornelius who was facing all the danger while she remained locked away inside the safety of their temporary lodgings. But she'd told him she'd remain there and much as it pained her to do so, she would.

Worried, her own thoughts tormenting her and a dozen scenarios playing out in her mind, all of them seeing her new husband coming to a very bad end, Primrose began to pace the room. There would be no rest for her. Not until she knew he was safe.

Chapter Thirty-One

"**I** CAN CARRY you and your missus to Carlisle, but no further. But I know a fellow that can take you from there on to Gretna Green if need be."

Cornelius nodded at the driver in agreement to the terms. "My hope is not to have to travel beyond Carlisle. Can you tell me if another gentleman has come through here to change horses? It would have been in the wee hours at the very earliest. Dark-haired man? He would have had a young woman with him who walks with a slight limp."

"No. Not seen anyone like that, m'lord. Sorry to say. I take it he's a bad man?"

"He's done a bad thing to be sure," Cornelius agreed. "This young woman is an heiress and he has determined that he should marry her regardless of whether she consents to the match or not. Is it possible that you could get word out to the other stables in town to be on the lookout for him?"

"I can, m'lord. What's his name?"

"Lord Samford."

The stable master's face shifted into an expression of pure disgust. "I know him well, m'lord. Everyone in town knows him. He left this town owing a lot of money to a lot of people, m'self included. And ruined several of my horses in the process. He won't be stopping in Birmingham, nor in Walsall for that matter. Likely he'll head on to Stoke-on-Trent. He'll find no welcome in between to be sure."

"We'll stop and check there then. Thank you for the information."

"I hope you catch up to him, m'lord. He's a bounder through and through."

Cornelius left the stables, still mulling over the information just imparted to him. He'd secured a carriage, quality horseflesh and a driver. All that was left was to gather some provisions for the trip from the hotel's kitchen. It would be an hour or so until they departed and he hoped that Primrose was taking advantage of that time to sleep.

As he rounded the corner to head back to the hotel, he stopped abruptly. He spied two men there, the same two he'd seen eyeing Primrose in the yard when they'd disembarked from the mail coach.

"I say, that was a mighty fine looking girl you was with, sir."

"My lord. You may address me as my lord," Cornelius said.

"Lords don't ride the stage, now do they?" the first man asked.

"They do if they are in a hurry," Cornelius replied. "And I am still in a hurry, gentlemen, so I'll ask you nicely to remove yourselves from my path."

The second man chortled but it was not a sound of cheer. Menacing and ugly, it showed only too clearly that they were spoiling for a fight. "Well ain't you high and mighty? I think I'll help myself to that coat you've got on and start calling myself a lord, too."

"You're welcome to try," Cornelius replied.

The first man laughed loudly. "You're a game one, that's for sure. I'm more interested in that bird you had with you. Only ever seen faces like that in paintings at the church... not that I go all that often."

"I'm more interested in what she was hiding under that cloak," the second man said. "She's got a fine arse, don't she?"

"You'll not speak of my wife that way."

"Wife! I don't think so. Men like you don't marry women like that... she's as baseborn as the pair of us. And lord or no, you're still a toff," the first one added.

"It ain't nice to lie... who is she? And how much for a few minutes alone with her? We'll be gentle like," the second man added, a chilling smile spreading over his cracked lips.

Despite the anger that suffused him at such a suggestion, Cornelius kept his composure. With one quick movement, he withdrew the pistol from inside his coat with one hand and the blade that had been strapped to his thigh with the other. "There is no inducement that would be effective. Now step aside."

"There's no call to be like that now! We're just a bit of fun, ain't we, Harry?" the first man said.

"Aye. Fun," the second man agreed. Neither made any effort to move and clear his path.

Cornelius continued, "Regardless of your disbelief in my claims, I am a lord... Lord Ambrose as a matter of fact. You will not be the first men I have killed. But you will be the killings that cause me the least inconvenience. I have but to claim attempted robbery and wash my hands of the entire mess. I would not even have a trial. Do you really want to test it?"

As if realizing they had chosen a mark that would not be as easy or compliant as they had imagined, the two men mumbled and turned away, heading away from the hotel. Regardless of their seemingly easy capitulation, Cornelius remained wary as he crossed the remaining distance to the hotel. They might have left, but that didn't mean they would forget about him. It most certainly didn't mean that they'd forget about Prim.

Entering the hotel, he climbed the stairs to their small room and hoped that she had done as he suggested and taken advantage of that time to rest. It hadn't escaped him that their room looked out over the yard and would have provided her a perfect view of the exchange he'd just had with the two would-be brigands.

As he neared their chamber door, it became quite apparent that she had, in fact, seen everything. The door opened as soon as his feet halted in front of it. Primrose was wide eyed and frantic.

"Are you hurt? What did they want?"

"I imagine they wanted whatever coin I had on my person," he replied. There was no need to tell her what they had suggested about her. Such things were unfit for her ears and he did not wish to bring up ugly doubts or memories for her.

"That's all? You talked to them for that long when they wanted to rob you?"

He shook his head. "They didn't demand money immediately. They used that short conversation to take my measure and determine whether or not I would be an easy target. Clearly, I would not, and so they left. But we will not push our luck. They may have friends or, more accurately, accomplices waiting to join them. The driver will be here in just under an hour. We'll go below, get something to eat, have something prepared for the journey ahead and be off. I don't want to linger here any longer than necessary."

It was very possible that those men would return and with reinforcements. His simple armaments would hardly deter them in greater numbers.

Taking Prim's arm, they descended to the hotel's public rooms to break their fast and start the second leg of their journey.

⟩⌇⟨

KITTY WAS PRESSED against the squabs of the carriage as it barreled down the road. They were going at a reckless pace and the horses hadn't been changed for the last two hours. There was no way they could continue at such a pace.

"We have to stop," she said.

"I don't recall asking for your opinion," Samford said, his hand draped over his eyes as he suffered through the worst of the aftereffects of his drinking from the night before.

"Exhausted horses cause accidents. Perhaps your own life holds no value for you, but I certainly value mine!" Kitty snapped.

"We'll change horses at Stoke-on-Trent and not before."

"Walsall is but a mile or so ahead," she said. "It's a bustling town and no one will pay attention to two people passing through!"

"Run to Gretna Green many times, have you?"

Her grandmother had summered at an estate near Carlisle. She'd traveled that road often, but felt no need to share such information with him. He had no interest in it anyway, or in her for that matter. Recalling the rumors of his first wife's death, Kitty had to wonder if a similar fate would befall her.

"We need to stop soon. Or it will not go well for either of us," she said simply.

"Stoke-on-Trent. No sooner," he reiterated, clearly at the end of his patience. "I've burned too many bridges in Walsall, and Birmingham for that matter. Had a bit of bad luck in a card game there and I'm in deep to the cent percenters."

Of course, she thought. It would be something like that. Clasping her hands in her lap, Kitty touched the hilt of the knife tucked into the sleeve of her spencer. It wasn't that she was bloodthirsty or felt inspired to violence, but she wouldn't be a weak and easy victim for him either. If an opportunity came, she would use it.

"I find that not surprising at all," she said. "Burning bridges seems to be something you are quite adept at, Lord Samford."

"Can you not just cower quietly in the corner?" he asked. His irritation with her was obvious. "Do I actually have to strike you to get you to be quiet?"

Arching an eyebrow imperiously, she suggested, "You could set me out here if I am too much of a burden... find some other women to marry who is too blinded by your charms to see the hideousness underneath."

"Shut up. If I set you down here, I'll wring your blasted neck before I do it and you'll be nothing but a bloated corpse on the roadside for someone to stumble over."

Kitty turned her head to look out the window and ignore her captor. Her nerves were more rattled by his threats than she wanted to admit, certainly more so than she was willing to show to him. Any hint of weakness would be exploited by him. That was a certainty. The only other certainty she had at that moment was that no one was coming to rescue her. Her father would have happily sold her to him without a qualm of doubt just to be rid of her.

If she was going to escape him, it would have to be on her own. And it would have to be in Stoke-on-Trent, if they managed to arrive there in one piece.

Chapter Thirty-Two

ANOTHER EIGHT HOURS on the road, this time in a private carriage as opposed to the stage, and they had reached Stoke-on-Trent and their destination of The Old Crown Inn. They stopped at the stables and their driver made discreet inquiries for them as to whether or not Samford and Miss Wyverne had arrived.

Prim was waiting in the carriage while Cornelius conversed with them. She was curious to know what he'd discovered. As he turned to walk back to her, his expression was dark.

"Have they passed already?" Prim asked.

"No. They have not yet arrived, unless perhaps they've taken an alternate route. As our paths have not yet crossed and we've seen a limited number of likely vehicles on the road, I'm beginning to wonder if that is not the case. If, by chance, he took her from Bath to the coast and they sailed to Scotland… she is already lost."

"He didn't. He wouldn't have taken the chance of either the captain or a crew member intervening on her behalf," Prim said. "He'd need privacy if she is an unwilling bride. And a lack of witnesses."

Cornelius nodded. "Let us hope that is the case. I think for now, we need to wait them out. If they are taking this route to Gretna Green, they should pass through here this morning. I've made arrangements with the lads at this stable and they will pass the word to the others in town to notify us if they should arrive."

"So we simply wait?"

"Yes," he said. "But not in the open. We'll sequester ourselves inside the inn, well out of sight. We won't take a room upstairs so that we can move quickly if need be. But we'll get a private dining room where we will have full view of the street and the stables."

"Will you be able to recognize Miss Wyverne?" Prim asked. She knew Lord Samford's face, though they had only met the one time. But Miss Wyverne was unknown to her.

"I know her well enough to recognize her. She has dark hair and has a mild but distinctive limp and uses a walking stick. I suspect it was that infirmity that prompted Samford to begin courting her. Given the rumors that surrounded his wife's passing and the other scandals that have swirled around his family, he was likely looking for someone he thought would be grateful for the attention."

Prim frowned. "Do you really think she should have been grateful?"

"Not I. On the occasions where I met Miss Wyverne, she was pleasant and attractive, but I was not drawn to her. I strongly suspect that she was equally unmoved by me. Samford needs money, and she possesses it in abundance. He's also quite convinced of his own importance, Prim. The man is puffed up like no one else and, whether it's true or not, would have viewed her as being beneath him. Not because it's true but because that's who he is."

Mollified by that explanation, she walked side by side with him as they moved toward the inn. It was smaller than the George Hotel had been in Walsall, but it was also older and not nearly as well maintained. Still, they were ushered into a small private room that faced the street and gave them a clear view of the stables.

One of the serving girls followed them in and then went scurrying off to get the tea and food he requested. She returned momentarily with a laden tray and deposited it before him. Prim watched as Cornelius handed the servant a coin that was likely equal to several months' pay for the girl.

"We shall be here for some time, but it's imperative that news of our presence here is handled with the utmost discretion," he said.

"Mr. Findley, the innkeeper, is gone to Manchester for the day and won't return until tomorrow. There's no one to know that you're here, my lord," she said.

"If we can keep it that way, there'll be another sovereign for you," Cornelius told her.

The girl bobbed a curtsy and then disappeared. When she was gone, Prim said, "You do realize that is a fortune to a girl like her." *And a girl like me*, she thought.

"It is an easy enough thing to be generous," he said.

"It really means nothing to you does it? Money has no worth to you," she mused. Would she ever grow used to living a life of abundance rather than penury?

"I am not immune to its influence, Prim. I carefully consider every investment I make and try to ensure that they will be as profitable as possible. It's because I take care with those investments that I can afford to be generous. Does it really bother you that much?"

Bothered wasn't the word. It made her uncomfortable to be in the presence of such largesse, especially since only weeks earlier she would have been scrambling to earn a sovereign that would mean the difference between having meat for the week to feed her family and coal to keep them warm or going without. He had changed everything about their lives and he was continuing to change hers. Day by day, hour by hour and minute by minute, she was altering slightly. But not negatively. Instead, she was releasing the fears that her life to that point had hammered into her. Because she felt safe with him, she realized. Even when his very presence pushed her boundaries and made her reevaluate everything she thought she'd known, she felt freer than before, able to let herself fall. But first, Miss Wyverne had to be saved and Samford had to be stopped.

As if her thoughts had summoned him, Prim's eye was drawn to a movement outside. Samford was crossing the street, dragging a young woman by the hand in his wake. It was clear that she was struggling to keep up.

"Cornelius!"

He turned to look, as well. But no sooner than they had both laid eyes upon them than a bell rang out signaling that the charity line at the church should begin to queue. People began to emerge from alleyways and buildings, making a beeline for the church where a hot meal would be served.

Miss Wyverne and Samford drifted in and out of sight as the charity seekers blocked their view. But then the crowd parted to reveal Miss Wyverne raising her walking stick high. She struck out with it, bringing it down over Samford's temple with significant force. With a violent movement, she pulled free from his grasping hands and fled.

Cornelius rose from the table and hurried outside and Prim was left to scurry after him. By the time they reached the street, Samford was gone, pursuing Miss Wyverne as she fled into a throng of workers who were just leaving the shops. They disappeared down a warren of narrow streets lined with warehouses and workshops.

"Where did they go?" Prim asked, her gaze scanning the faces in the crowded street.

"I don't know," Cornelius admitted. "Go back to the inn and wait for me. I'll look for them."

"How?"

"I'll ask people if they've seen them."

"I can help."

"It's dangerous, Prim. He's dangerous. Please!"

"I'm going with you," she said. "You may not realize it, Cornelius, but I have more in common with these people milling about than you do. Of the two of us, whose questions would be more likely to be answered?"

SHE HAD A point. He didn't much care for it, but he couldn't deny the accuracy of it. "I don't like it."

"I don't like it either. He'll be angry. And if he senses we are in pursuit, he'll be dangerous to her," she replied.

Cornelius turned to head toward the line of people waiting outside the church. Prim was right. The only thing in their favor at that moment was that Samford remained ignorant of their presence. He was chasing Miss Wyverne while they, in turn, chased him.

They approached a young woman holding a small child in her arms. Prim spoke first. "There was a young woman who ran through here moments ago, with a limp... and there would have been a man chasing her. We need to help this woman. Can you tell us which way they went?"

"Why should I? No one helps me, do they?" the woman replied.

"We'll help you."

"A few pence, a shilling? It'll just be taken from me."

"What of a job?" Cornelius asked. "What if I offered to take you on at my estate as a housemaid and offered a place for you and your child there."

"No toff employs a housemaid with a child."

"I will," he promised. "I have a very unconventional household. Growing more unconventional on a daily basis."

Prim could have laughed at that. It was true. And he didn't seem to mind in the least. "He does. He married me and I'm as common as they come. Let us help you and help us to help this poor girl."

"He went down that alley yon. I never saw her, but I did see him," the girl said. "Now, where's this estate?"

"For now, you will go to my house in London. 217 Curzon Street. You will speak to my aunt, Lady Arabella, and she will get you settled into your new duties," Cornelius said. Discreetly, he passed the woman a sovereign. It would be enough to pay passage for her and her child to London and to buy food for them for the journey. "Tell her you assisted us in our search for Miss Wyverne. That will assure her of our agreement."

"Miss Wyverne," the girl repeated. "I will. Thank you, my lord."

They ducked down the alley the girl had indicated, but it was deserted save for stray cats. It appeared closed at the end but, as they neared it, it became apparent that it simply doglegged around the back of one building before opening up onto the mews of those buildings. With a half-dozen ways in and out, wagons, carts and carriages here and there, not to mentions stables and back entrances to businesses, the possibilities were endless.

"They could be anywhere," Prim said.

"So they could," Cornelius said, as he dropped to his haunches and touched a damp spot on the dark flagstone that marked the entrance to one of the buildings. His fingers came away red. "Apparently, Miss Wyverne drew first blood."

Realizing that Samford had left a trail for them to follow changed the nature of their search. It was no longer a question of randomly knocking on doors or asking passersby. They simply followed the blood.

THE AWAKENING OF LORD AMBROSE

Primrose. I don't think it unreasonable to imagine that her father will not go to any great lengths to do so. But at this point, we've lost all sight of her. We were following Samford all along, assuming he was hot on her trail... but now we must assume that he's run afoul of someone else."

"Where can she have gone? Will she hear that he has been killed and seek assistance? Or will she just continue running in fear and do more harm to herself than good?"

His lips firmed. "We can knock on every door and ask every passerby we meet. We may still turn up empty-handed, Primrose."

Prim's head dropped, her chin resting against her chest for a moment. "She must be terrified."

"No doubt. And we will continue to do whatever we can to see to her safety. But our active part in searching for her is done. Can you live with that?"

Was there any other choice in the matter?

Chapter Thirty-Four

DISHEARTENED, FILLED WITH doubts and fears for what might happen to a young woman alone, Prim walked numbly beside Cornelius as he led her back out of the alley, through the narrow and dangerous streets back to The Old Crown Inn. There was no dashing rescue, no sense of victory. Samford was dead, Miss Wyverne was missing and they were miles and miles from home with nothing to show for their journey except their own exhaustion and the undeniable feeling of failure.

At the inn, Prim took up residence once more in the small room they had claimed for their base of activity earlier in the day. The same serving girl brought in a fresh pot of tea and plate of small sandwiches. Prim had no appetite for them but ate them anyway, mechanically and without thought. She wasn't so immune to the idea of scarcity of food that she would simply ignore it when placed in front of her.

It was flurry of activity. Magistrates were called, arrangements were made for the body to be claimed by the undertakers and prepared for its journey home. In all, it was hours of talking, of an endless stream of people in and out of their little corner. Prim continued to look out the window the whole while, hoping for some sign of Miss Wyverne who she might now at least recognize. But there was nothing. Outside that window, everything looked normal as people went to and from their jobs and children played.

In all, it was anticlimactic for her. The rush to find the young woman and save her had ended with no prize at all. The villain was defeated, not by their hands or hers, but by some unseen person. And all they were left with was so many unanswered questions.

"Are you all right?" Cornelius asked, finally sitting down across from her.

"I think I'm very tired. I don't think I realized how tired until just now," she admitted. "What will happen now?"

"The magistrate sees no need for an inquest since we both stumbled upon him together. As I only had one pistol with me and it had not been discharged, he is not questioning my innocence, at least. That is something. Perhaps he is unfamiliar with my reputation?"

Her lips quirked at his attempt at self-deprecating humor. "You shot one man, Cornelius. That hardly makes you the villain of the century."

He shrugged. The gesture was deceptively casual but from the dark shadows beneath his eyes, it was obvious that he was as exhausted as she was. It had been more than a day since either one of them had slept or had a decent meal.

"One is all it takes," he stated simply. "The magistrate has taken a description of Miss Wyverne and will have a group of men scouring the streets for any sign of her. I think, most likely, she has fled and is trying to make her way back home. Descriptions will be provided to the drivers of any public coaches in the off chance that she is attempting to get home by way of the stage. We've done all we can, Primrose. Samford was our only lead and, terrible yet unintended pun it may be, he was a dead end."

Prim asked the one question that kept circling back around in her mind. "You don't think she killed him, do you? Even if she had, he'd abducted her... but it makes no sense."

"The magistrate said it himself, and had I been thinking clearly, I would have reached the same conclusion. If Miss Wyverne had been in possession of a firearm, then Samford would never have gotten her out of Bath, much less all the way to Stoke-on-Trent. They were three days in a carriage together. The horses pulling that rented carriage and the driver who is long gone now are done for. He drove them into the ground. I doubt they stopped many places at all, and I doubt that she would have been given enough freedom at any of them to obtain and secret away a weapon."

There was more than was being said, but Prim's exhaustion kept her from being able to hit upon it fully. But then, it was as if a veil lifted, and the horrifying realization came crashing in on her. "The man who shot him might well have Miss Wyverne now. It may very well be that she never escaped from him fully, at all. She simply traded one captor for another."

"We do not know that."

Prim's eyebrows shot up. "I didn't realize how honest you have been with me from the start until just now. You're a terrible liar, Cornelius."

He sighed heavily and then steepled his hands on the table in front of him. "We don't know it. It's highly suspected by everyone at hand though. Miss Wyverne, given her limp, the fact that her walking stick was shattered in the street there when she struck Samford, would likely not have been able to get away so cleanly. Not unless she was taken up in a carriage or cart by someone else."

"It's all for naught," she said.

"No it isn't. Had we not been here, had we not known that Samford had taken her in the first place, no one would even know that Miss Wyverne had even been here, much less that she is in danger. Our role in her story is not to be her saviors, Primrose, but the cryer sounding her disappearance," he explained. "And for now, we must content ourselves with that."

"And now what do we do?"

"We rest. I've procured a room for the night. Our bags are still with the carriage but the driver will bring them over. We will recuperate here and tie up any loose ends tomorrow. And then we shall go on an adventure together... one that is not quite so fraught with worry."

A smile curved her lips. "An adventure?"

"Did you know that I own a castle in Scotland and I've never set eyes upon it?"

"I did not know that," she admitted. "But I am not surprised by it. A castle?"

He leaned forward. "We'll go there for a week or two, enjoy the Highlands together. And if you'd like, perhaps we can send for your siblings and bring them to Scotland in time for Christmas."

"I've never been to Scotland. I imagine it's a wild enough place to keep Rowan entertained and offers enough vistas for watercolors that Lila would be thrilled."

He took her hand in his, holding it gently, his thumb stroking over the lines that crisscrossed her palm. "You don't have your heart set on spending the holiday in London, then?"

"I think that I have my heart set on spending the holiday with you, wherever that may be. This holiday, and every one thereafter. How did you do this to me, Cornelius? How, with little more than a glance and a few stolen kisses, did you sway me so easily that I cannot bear to be parted from you now?"

"Well, I'm handsome. Wealthy. Titled. And I think I was infatuated with you the first moment I laid eyes on you... but I knew I loved you when you demanded that we go haring off on a wild chase to save a girl you didn't even know."

Prim's breath caught. "What did you just say?"

"That I love you. Does that really surprise you?"

"Yes," she admitted. "It does."

"Why? Do you think me incapable or do you think yourself unlovable?"

It was a hard question to answer, but Prim tried to answer it honestly. "I loved my mother. I love my sisters and my brother. But I never believed in romantic love. I always thought it was just something silly young girls convinced themselves of and that men used to get what they wanted. That sounds very cynical, doesn't it?"

"It does, but you aren't entirely wrong. It is those things frequently... but not always."

"I know that. But I also thought that if love happened between a man and a woman it was a gradual thing. Attraction, understanding, and then one day you've been with this person for so long and you just think they're part of your family now, part of the little corner of the world you've dug out for yourself. I didn't know then that a person could simply walk into your life one day and instantly be important, instantly be a part of you. But I think you were." It was a hard thing for her to say, to admit that kind of vulnerability, but she wanted to be honest with him. She wanted him to know that his feelings were returned and she needed him to understand that she wasn't simply saying it because he had, that she meant it with all of her heart. "I was afraid of you from the first. Not because I thought you were a bad man or because I believed you to be dishonest. I was scared of you, Cornelius, because from the very first moment when you stepped into that little cottage where I'd been so safe and so isolated—"

Primrose stopped. She needed to gather her wits.

"What is it, Primrose? There's nothing you can't tell me."

She nodded. "That day, you walked in and I knew that it was different. Not that you were, but that when you were present, *I was different*. I don't want to be that girl anymore, Cornelius. I don't want to be afraid of who I am and I don't want to lock myself away behind cynicism and disdain. I think I loved you before I even knew you. I almost feel like I'd spent my whole life waiting for you to appear, only I didn't know it until it happened."

Chapter Thirty-Five

THOSE WORDS, UTTERED so hesitantly but with such feeling, were a balm to both his heart and his ego. He'd almost settled himself with the idea that he would love her and she would only ever tolerate him. It had hurt more than he could say, but the thought of not having her at all was simply not something he would entertain. One-sided love was better than no love at all.

"Come upstairs with me," he said.

"I know you must be exhausted," she offered.

"I am tired, Prim. But not so tired that I am ready to pass up this opportunity. I want to make you my wife in every way. No more doubts, no more delays. Only the two of us starting our life together now."

He didn't ask for an answer, but held out his hand. When he felt her small hand settle in his, a breath he hadn't even known he was holding rushed out of him. As discreetly as possible, he led her from the public areas of the inn and up the stairs to the room he'd procured for them. The serving girl had stated it was the finest room in the establishment, but by inn standards that hardly meant much. Still, it was warm, a fire burning in the hearth. The curtains were drawn to keep out the chill and the large bed in the center of the room was freshly made with clean linens. It wasn't luxurious, but it was private and, for the moment, that was all that mattered.

The door closed, the soft snick of the lock clicking into place was the only sound in the room. Cornelius turned to face her. Not for the first time. Even exhausted beyond measure, disheartened and disappointed by the outcome of their journey, she was still the most beautiful woman he had ever seen.

Closing the distance between them, he simply took her in his arms and kissed her. He claimed her lips and plundered the sweetness there with one intent—to wipe away any lingering doubts and to banish any painful memories. He wanted her to be so focused on what was occurring between them, that nothing from her past would have an opportunity to intrude.

She sank against him, soft, pliant and more tempting than any woman he'd ever known. And she kissed him back, her lips moving beneath his in the sweetest supplication. The tentative touch of her hands at his shoulders, along the back of his neck, then her small fingers threading through his hair felt like a victory that should be shouted from the rooftops.

But he wasn't content to just taste her lips. He kissed her neck, the soft curve of her jaw, the delicate shell of her ear, and that perfect curve where her neck and shoulder met. When he felt her hands pressing against his chest, pushing him back, he didn't resist, but his disappointment was short-lived. With an arm's length between them now, Cornelius watched in utter wonderment as she loosened the front of her gown, and then carefully pushed it down to where the flare of her hips briefly halted its progress. With the dark blue fabric pooled at her feet, the white lawn of her petticoat soon followed. Then she stood before him clad only in her chemise and stays.

He wanted to touch her, to feel the indentation of her waist beneath his palms as it gave way to the lush curve of her hips. But when he approached her, she stopped him once more.

"I think it's only fair that you should be as undressed as I am," she insisted.

A grin curved his lips. "Never let it be said that I am not a fair man." Quickly, he stripped off his boots and his jacket. His waistcoat followed and then he stood before her in only his breeches and shirt. "Is this enough?"

"For now," she said.

He'd thought she would be fearful, but he should have known better. Primrose, despite everything she had endured in her life, was no meek and timid woman.

Lifting her in his arms, he carried her to the bed and placed her in the center of it. As she knelt there, he reached for the laces of her stays and tugged them free. A blush stained her cheeks, but she made no move to pull away or hide herself from him. When the task was done and one less of her garments remained between them, he waited for her to return the favor. He was not disappointed. Her delicate hands reached for his shirt, tugging it free from his breeches and then pulling it up and over his head until it, too, could be tossed aside.

Cornelius paused for a moment to look at her. The linen of her chemise was so fine it was nearly transparent. He could see the curves of her breasts, the dusky pink-tipped peaks beckoning him. He wanted to see all of her, to commit every perfect inch of her to memory. As if she'd sensed that thought, she reached up and released the ties of her chemise, the neck gaping wide. The garment slithered over her skin, finally pooling at her knees on the bed and baring every lush and beautiful part of her in between.

Had there ever existed a more beautiful woman?

NAKED BEFORE HIM, Prim had thought she would feel vulnerable, exposed, embarrassed perhaps. But as his gaze roamed over her, and she could see the wonder and appreciation in his gaze, she didn't feel any of those things. She felt powerful, seductive, beautiful. For perhaps the first time in her life, she was thankful that she had inherited that unusual combination of features that made her so appealing to others. It was, in that moment, more of a blessing than a burden.

But just as he was taking that moment to appreciate her, she was also surveying him. Broad shoulders and a wide, heavily-muscled chest lightly covered with crisp dark hair, all tapering to a lean waist. The line of hair that bisected the ridges of his abdomen and arrowed downward until it disappeared behind the fall of his breeches entranced her and piqued her curiosity.

Reaching out, she allowed her fingertips to trail over the skin of his stomach, marveling at how firm he was beneath satiny flesh and how warm he was. But he caught her wrist, effectively halting her explorations.

"You don't like it when I touch you?" she asked.

"I like it too much, and I don't want to rush this," he replied, his voice deeper and rougher than before. It raised goosebumps on her skin and made her shiver.

But then he was there, bearing her back onto the bed, his large body atop hers. Heat and sinewy muscle pressing against her, chasing away the chill and leaving only the warmth of desire in its wake.

His mouth was on hers, crushing her lips as he teased her with his tongue, his teeth nipping at her lower lip in a way that left her gasping. The kiss gave way to caresses, and his hands were at her breasts, touching her where no one ever had, and making her feel things that were alien, overwhelming and yet so intoxicating that the idea of asking him to stop never entered her mind.

Each touch swept her further away, clouded her senses and left her gasping. She clutched at his shoulders, holding on to him as the entire world seemed to shrink until it consisted only of the two of them and the narrow bed they occupied.

Then his mouth was moving lower, scattering kisses along her collarbone, the swells of her breasts and then lower still, until he claimed one turgid nipple with his lips. Prim let out a soft moan, unable to hold back the sound, as her head fell back and she arched into that touch, eager for more. And he gave it. He teased that tender flesh with lips, teeth and tongue, driving her to a point of near madness before turning his attention to her other breast.

When his hand left her hip and coasted gently over her stomach to slip between her thighs, she was so mindless with pleasure and need, she never thought to protest or make any attempt to halt his progress. Instead, she welcomed him eagerly, parting her thighs. Another soft moan escaped her as he touched her intimately. It quickly became a gasp and then a broken sob as he found the very center of her pleasure. She hadn't known she was capable of feeling such a thing. Every touch drew that pleasure out, intensified it, and at the same time, built a sense of anticipation, as if there was something hovering just out of her reach.

His touches grew more insistent. His mouth returned to her breast and those intense sensations in tandem left her gasping and shuddering with the onslaught. It happened suddenly. Her thighs began to tremble and the muscles of her stomach drew taut, quivering, and then pleasure simply engulfed her. She trembled and quaked when it crested within her.

Gasping, clinging to him desperately, she was given no reprieve. He moved between her parted thighs even as he freed the buttons of his breeches. Eagerly, Prim reached for him, wanting to touch him, to give him some of the pleasure he had just shown her. But he gripped her hands once more, halting her.

"I am clinging to my control by the merest thread," he muttered, softening the words with a kiss.

"I want to touch you," she insisted.

"You may touch me all you want... later and at your leisure, but not now. Not yet."

Prim relented and placed her arms around him, pulling him even closer as her hands skimmed over the smooth skin of his back, savoring the feeling of sinewy strength in him. She knew what was to come next. The mechanics of it were known to her, but the feeling of it was not.

She could feel his arousal pressing against her. But there was no fear or hesitation—only eagerness. When he pressed inside her, parting her flesh with his own, she closed her eyes. There was a small amount of discomfort, a single flash of pain, and then it was gone. He went utterly still, waiting, holding himself back and denying his own urges.

He was waiting for her, Prim realized, waiting for some signal that she was ready to continue. Without words, she moved her hips. It was more than just pleasure. More than just the physical sensations of their bodies touching. There was an intimacy, a closeness with him in that moment. It wasn't about surrendering her body to him, it was about the two of them surrendering themselves to one another.

As he began to move within her, that same tension she now recognized began to build anew. But it was more powerful than before, and more eagerly anticipated, because she would be sharing it with him.

Their movements became more frantic, her cries more insistent. Sweat slicked his skin and his muscles tensed and bunched as they strained against one another. But it was too much. The spiraling pleasure simply took her and as she cried out with it, she felt him shudder against her, felt the flood of warmth as he, too, gave himself up to it.

In the aftermath, held tightly against him, their breathing ragged, a kind of peace and contentment she had never known settled over her. Prim felt safe and whole with him. Perhaps, she thought, that was truly what love was. It filled in all the missing chinks in her, the things that her fractured childhood had taken from her.

Chapter Thirty-Six

KITTY HUNKERED IN the back of the cart, hidden behind a stack of barrels that she prayed fervently would not collapse atop her. With every rut in the road, she feared that fate more and more. She had thought the cart a Godsend when first she saw it. Now, as it took her further and further from Stoke-on-Trent, she wondered if she had not been hasty. But as she recalled her last glimpse of Lord Samford entering that narrow alley, the echoing report of a pistol and the emergence of a dark-haired man with a scarred face, she knew that she'd had no other choice. If, by some miracle, Samford had been spared death in that alley, her fate with him would have been sealed. Had they known of her presence in that alley when that pistol ball had ended him, she would likely have met a similar fate. Very few murderers would willingly leave a witness alive to tell the tale.

They were heading northwest. She could tell by the setting of the sun behind them. Likely, they would be heading to a port city. The barrels would be loaded on a ship and taken to heaven only knew where. She had no money, but she did have her locket and a ring that she might sell. It might be enough to book a passage for her back to Bristol and on to Bath. Or it might be better to take the stage to Carlisle, to get to her grandmother's house, empty though it currently was save for a few aging pensioners. There, she could write to her father and have the necessary arrangements made for safe passage home.

They hit another rut and the barrels, jarred for miles on end, shifted once more. This time one of them struck her with enough force that it knocked the wind out of her. She let out a loud "oomph." And then panic struck. Had they heard it?

The cart slowed, the rhythm of the horses' hooves striking the road changed. And then the wheels stopped moving altogether. Everything lurched. Kitty wanted to run, but after hours cramped in the same position, lying on her side with her body curved under the backboard and around the barrels, she couldn't move.

"Who's in there? Show yourself!"

The command was uttered gruffly. But it was not accompanied by the barrel of a pistol pointing at her or a sword to poke at her. Feeling, if not optimistic, then at least less terrified, Kitty slowly managed to drag herself up into a sitting position and then to her feet. Her legs were numb and she had to lean against the barrel to remain upright. As she lifted her head, she found herself staring into the face of a man with dark hair and a long scar that ran the length of his cheek, from the corner of his eye to his jawline. Half of it disappeared into the dark beard that covered much of his face, but she could still see it plain enough. It wasn't jagged, but a clean slice. Made with a knife or sword, she thought.

He tipped his hat back and gazed at her levelly. "Who are you and what are you doing in this cart?"

"I'm trying to get to the nearest port," she said. "I was eloping and I changed my mind. He refused to return me home and I have no money for the stage."

"So you were going to stow away on board my ship then?"

"You have a ship?" she asked. He was also a murderer or at the very least the companion of murderers, but then the person he'd been party to murdering was Samford and Samford had rather needed killing, so that wasn't necessarily a point against him. So long as he remained unaware that she could name him or Samford's killer, she would be fine.

He laughed. "You really expect me to believe you didn't know?"

"Why would I know? You were in a landlocked city!"

"I'm famous, love," he said.

"Famous for what?" she demanded, hoping to just brazen it out.

He moved around the edge of the cart, close enough that his fingertips brushed the skirt of her dress when he leaned against the boards. "Piracy."

Oh. It was not good. It had gone from bad to worse and she was still stuck in the middle of it.

"You could ransom me back to my father," she said. "He's very wealthy. It would get you paid and get me home. I'll cause you no trouble."

He looked up at her thoughtfully. "Any woman who says she's no trouble will be nothing but trouble... that's a fact if ever there was one. And I don't do kidnapping or ransom. I like my jobs to be tidy. But I'll get you to Ellesmere Port and help you sell that bauble on your finger for a good enough price to get you home. But you have to do something for me."

Kitty swallowed convulsively, praying it wouldn't be something utterly depraved. "What's that?"

"How good are you at flirting?"

"I'm not. Not at all."

He eyed her up and down, his gaze moving over her in a way that expressed both interest and appraisal. "No, I didn't think you would be. Flirty women are never so buttoned up. But you've got enough curves hiding under that plain gown that if we dress you right, it won't even matter. Come on down from there and ride up on the box lest you injure yourself permanently and I go from pirate to murderer."

"I thought pirates were murderers," she retorted, still keeping the damning knowledge she held to herself.

He grinned at her then, but his gaze was hard. "Only when we have to be."

Kitty blinked in surprise, but said nothing. He offered his hand to help her down, a gesture that bespoke manners and a better raising than she would have expected in one who was a self-proclaimed pirate. She stood there for the longest time, staring at his hand as if she didn't know what to do with it.

"Do you want my help or not?" he demanded.

"I do. You'll really help me get home?"

"I'll make sure they don't cheat you at the pawnbroker," he said, "And I'll make sure the ship you're on is one manned by men that can be trusted. As far as men can be, that is."

Feeling very much as if she were making a deal with the devil, Kitty placed her hand in his. He helped her climb over the seat and onto the box and then climbed up beside her.

"What's your name, love?" he asked.

"It isn't love. It's Kitty," she said, mustering as much disdain as possible. It helped to conceal her terror.

He grinned at that and picked up the reins. He said nothing else until the horses were once more at full cantor. "Now, tell me, Kitty, where exactly was this cart when you climbed up and concealed yourself in the back of it?"

"I don't know what you mean."

"Well," he replied, "What I mean is that this cart was only unattended twice. Once when I loaded it, and once more when I parked it near an alleyway and took care of some business. Either way, you'd have been in the back of it at that time and heard the business I was taking care of. Which was it?"

She'd been had. He knew all along that she knew about Samford. So Kitty said the one thing that might save her life. "I don't care if you killed him. He was a terrible man. He deserved to die and, frankly, by doing so, you've spared me the horrible fate of being married to him. So you needn't worry that I'll be telling anyone about your *business*."

He smiled again. "Maybe I was wrong about you, Kitty. Maybe when you said you'd be no trouble at all you meant it. Let's hope for both our sakes that you're right. Because any trouble you make for me, I'll give right back. You understand?"

"I understand," she agreed.

"Then we have a deal... for the moment."

Epilogue

"KEEP YOUR BACK straight, knees tight," Cornelius said, his voice loud enough to carry the distance but his tone congenial.

"Oh, I can't look. He's going to fall off and break his neck," Hyacinth muttered.

"He'll be fine," Prim insisted. "Cornelius would never have put Rowan on that horse if he thought it would be dangerous for him. He's wild for the boy."

"I do think it breaks his heart a bit that Lila would rather draw a horse than ride one," Hyacinth offered.

Prim smiled at that. It was true. While he and Lila got on well, and it was clear that he was over the moon to have his sister with him, he and Rowan were developing a special bond. Cornelius claimed it was because they were the only men in the house and had to stick together. At which point, Rowan would puff out his little chest and strut around like a peacock at being called a man. He was becoming unbearable with it.

The idea of having children had never really been there for her. With Lila and Rowan, she'd never been without children, even though they'd been her siblings rather than her own. But with Cornelius, she wanted that. She wanted to give him a son, not just because he required an heir, but because she knew it was what he longed for. She could see the need to surround himself with family so strongly in him.

"You really love him, don't you?"

"What?" Prim asked, coming back from her mental wandering. "Well, yes, of course I do."

"No. I don't mean in that he's my husband and duty requires it sort of way," Hyacinth corrected her. "I mean you love him all the way to your soul. And you're happy in a way that I never dreamed was possible for any of us."

"I am happy. And I do love him, with my heart, with my soul... with every fiber of my being, I love him," Prim admitted. "I want that for you. I want you to find a man who makes you feel safe and whole, and who gives you the thing we lived without for so long!"

"Money?"

"Hope," Prim said with a laugh. "Money helps. But no. I meant hope."

Hyacinth turned once more to look at the small paddock where Rowan was taking to his riding lessons like a duck to water. Prim followed her gaze, but let it drift past her younger brother to the man who was calling out encouragement and direction. His patience with Rowan and with Lila was remarkable. They had only been married for one month, and yet that time seemed more real to her than all that had come before it. Her past, the scrounging and worrying, the constant fear, those were becoming distant memories.

"I want it," Hyacinth admitted softly. "That kind of love. Mother searched her whole life for it and never found it."

"Because she didn't really know what it was," Prim said. "Desperation and need were all mixed in her mind with love. A man paid her a compliment and she'd have them married off in her head, only to find out he already had a wife. She thought desire and love were the same, but they're not."

"I'm not so innocent that I don't know what those long and lingering looks between you and your husband represent, Primrose," Hyacinth said. "You need both in life to be happy, I think. Love and desire. I'm glad you've found it."

"You will, too," Prim said.

Cornelius called out and Rowan halted the pony. He dismounted with aplomb, like he'd been born to the saddle. The horse was turned over to the stable master and the two of them crossed the paddock to the small bench where she and Hyacinth had been watching them.

"Let me take Rowan inside and get him warmed up with a nice cup of chocolate," Hyacinth said, rising from the bench, and taking the boy's hand. "Then I'll check in on Lila and see how many sketches of the loch she's made this morning."

They were only a few yards away when Cornelius said, "The two of you were deep in conversation."

"We were. Sharing sisterly secrets," she said teasingly.

"That sounds ominous… for me, at least," he offered with a grin as he took the seat recently vacated.

"It isn't. But I think Hyacinth is lonely."

"How can she be lonely when Rowan and Lila are all but glued to her side?" he asked.

"Not that kind of lonely! I think she's a little envious… not in a mean way."

"Envious?"

"Of us. Of what we've found together," Prim replied, resting her head against his shoulder. "I think she's longing for romance and love."

"How do you think we should rectify that?" he asked.

"Do you have any friends?"

"Yes, and they're all married," he said dryly. "After Christmas, we'll go back to Bath. Or London if you prefer. I suppose I can brave the gossips and dray myself out into society for the sake of my pretty sister-in-law. We'll be hard pressed to find a man good enough for her, though."

Prim smiled. "Thank you."

"For being willing to jump back into the fray?" he asked.

"For many things, that amongst them. Mostly, thank you for being you and for loving me."

His lips curved in a slight smile as he leaned down to kiss her. "You say that as if I ever had a choice. I think I was born loving you. I just had wait for fate to throw us together."

"We could sneak into our bedchamber while Hyacinth has the children occupied and you could show me how much you love me."

She didn't need to ask twice.

The End

This is not the end of the Lost Lords Series. Look for a very special novella featuring Mr. Branson Middlethorpe and Lady Sarah Middlethorpe, his widowed sister-in-law, in *A Night of Angels: A Magical Christmas Collection* from Dragonblade Publishing. Miss Wyverne will also be getting her own novella in the very near feature in another series. I love all of these characters and this world so much that I'm not quite ready to say goodbye to it yet.

Author's Note

Thank you so much for joining me on the journey of the *Lost Lords Series*. Writing this series has been such a blessing and a joy for me and I hope that you've gotten even a fraction of the pleasure from reading these books that I received from writing them.

Like with any good thing, it's sometimes hard to see it come to an end. There could be future novels or novellas from the *Lost Lords Series*. If you're interested in seeing this series continue, please email me or find me on social media to let me know. The links are all listed below and I'd love to hear from you.

I will be continuing to work with Dragonblade Publishing on a new series, *The Hellion Club*. I hope you'll join me on that wild ride, as well.

Thank you so much,
Chasity Bowlin

About the Author

Addicted to caffeine, chocolate and internet cats, Chasity Bowlin lives in central Kentucky with her husband and a menagerie of animals that make every day a challenge. It's usually a worthwhile challenge. Usually.

Growing up in Tennessee, spending as much time as possible with her doting grandparents, soap operas were a part of her daily existence, followed by back to back episodes of Scooby Doo. Her path to becoming a romance novelist was set when, rather than simply have her Barbie dolls cruise around in a pink convertible, they time traveled, hosted lavish dinner parties and one even had an evil twin locked in the attic.

49840791R00140

Made in the USA
Columbia, SC
28 January 2019